Through Dark Angles

THROUGH DARK ANGLES

Works Inspired by H. P. Lovecraft

Don Webb

Hippocampus Press

New York

Acknowledgments: See page 250.

Published by Hippocampus Press
P.O. Box 641, New York, NY 10156.
http://www.hippocampuspress.com

Cover design by Fergal Fitzpatrick.
Cover artwork © 2014 by Fergal Fitzpatrick.
Hippocampus Press logo designed by Anastasia Damianakos.

First Edition
1 3 5 7 9 8 6 4 2
ISBN13: 978-1-61498-084-1

Contents

The Mythos and I

Act One. It's 1967 and my brothers, identical twin geniuses, are finishing up their third year at Rice University. One of them is reading a paperback with a skull surrounded by flames. *The Colour out of Space and Others*. I ask if I can read it. They discuss whether I have the vocabulary. Max says, "Read these two pages. What does the term 'blasted heath' mean?" It was obvious to me that it meant a devastated area. But wait—there must be a trick. So I say, "A kind of people." They look at each other and shake their heads, putting the book in their desk. In a week they are back in school and I do a forbidden act. I go in their room, steal the book, and read it. I am enthralled.

Act Two. It's 1969. I am visiting the wonderfully haunted old Bivins library in downtown Amarillo. It was a pioneer showcase home donated by the Bivins family to the city. The showplace homes from pioneer times looked much alike, and though none was precisely modeled on the Southern plantation mansion, all partook of its image—massive concrete columns, wide steps on all sides, covered verandas, simple red brick walls, all shadowed by huge trees. In the Panhandle, trees grow only if nurtured and grow tall only if pampered. The library borrowed its grand entrance from the South, and with its double staircase, mahogany banisters, marble mosaic floor, and hanging chandeliers it impressively introduced a child to libraries. One floor, "the adult section," was underground, dark and cool—unlike the noisy "children's section," which was on the second floor. In theory unattended children could not go into the depths, so of course I did. I spotted a hardback in bright yellow. It bore Lovecraft's name. I opened it at random and found this:

> And yet, as the members severally shook their heads and confessed defeat at the Inspector's problem, there was one man in that gathering who

suspected a touch of bizarre familiarity in the monstrous shape and writing, and who presently told with some diffidence of the odd trifle he knew. This person was the late William Channing Webb, Professor of Anthropology in Princeton University, and an explorer of no slight note. Professor Webb had been engaged, forty-eight years before, in a tour of Greenland and Iceland in search of some Runic inscriptions which he failed to unearth; and whilst high up on the West Greenland coast had encountered a singular tribe or cult of degenerate Esquimaux whose religion, a curious form of devil-worship, chilled him with its deliberate bloodthirstiness and repulsiveness. It was a faith of which other Esquimaux knew little, and which they mentioned only with shudders, saying that it had come down from horribly ancient aeons before ever the world was made. Besides nameless rites and human sacrifices there were certain queer hereditary rituals addressed to a supreme elder devil or tornasuk; and of this Professor Webb had taken a careful phonetic copy from an aged angekok or wizard-priest, expressing the sounds in Roman letters as best he knew how. But just now of prime significance was the fetish which this cult had cherished, and around which they danced when the aurora leaped high over the ice cliffs. It was, the professor stated, a very crude bas-relief of stone, comprising a hideous picture and some cryptic writing. And so far as he could tell, it was a rough parallel in all essential features of the bestial thing now lying before the meeting.

It was my weird. It had my name, devil worship, runes, and "deliberate bloodthirstiness and repulsiveness." I was hooked. I hid the book under my arm, snuck up to the children's section, and then made my way down to check it out (as though it had come from the permissible location). I went to read in the shade of the giant Chinese elm outside waiting for Mom to pick me up.

Act Three. Later that year I discovered a small room on the ground floor full of science fiction paperbacks that children could visit. There I discovered *Tales of the Cthulhu Mythos,* a collection edited by August Derleth, wherein he reveals that almost everything that can be said in the Mythos has been said. I was amazed by James Wade's tale of the Deep Ones, Ramsey Campbell's "Cold Print," which introduced me to metafiction—and of course the Bloch-Lovecraft sequence that forever caught my mind with the Shining Trapezohedron. A gateway to "other spaces"—possibly one of the most effective symbols of cosmicism for itself. This image haunts both my fiction and my esoteric pursuits. Years later I was to become a Knight of the Order of the Trapezoid, invited into that dark group by Dr. Stephen E. Flowers, who also managed to teach me a thing or two about runes.

Act Four. Somehow I have reached the ripe old age of twenty-three. I hadn't proved myself a great student at Rice University—unlike my brothers who finished first and second in their class in 1968. I had taken some time off from school and then enrolled at Texas Tech University in Lubbock, a town that has frequent dust storms. In fact, in winter a dust storm can rage through Lubbock that has sleet falling through it, and so freezing mud can hit your face. Living in the student ghetto I discovered a new vice—Advanced Dungeons and Dragons. I spent hours playing the game—and even ran a campaign on a new game that came out that year, The Call of Cthulhu. My grade point needed some nourishment, and I overheard two students talking outside my Anthropology 101 class. They were talking about an honors course, "Writing the Science Fiction Short Story." An essay class, they said, you only need to write a story to pass. I signed up for the spring. Sure enough, one story would make you pass. I had two great mentors: one was the classics professor who taught the class, Dr. Peder G. Christiansen; the other was Sid, the owner of Star Books and Comics, who helped me find many wonderful titles from Dick, Ballard, Clark Ashton Smith, Harlan Ellison, and Cordwainer Smith. Christiansen wrote an article, "The Classical Humanism of Philip K. Dick," which clued me in to the facts that science fiction was part of civilization and that smart people actually *thought* about it.

Most of the students were afraid to try their hand at a story. One could write a 12-page research paper instead. I decided to knock the story out. It was my first piece of fiction, "Diary Found in an Abandoned Jeep" (found in this volume). I typed it out over a weekend on my girlfriend's Texas Instruments 99/4A computer. It used single-sided, single-density floppies for memory—so even though it is a very short story, it took up two disks. I got my A for the story, although my classmates were harsh about the references to both marijuana and Cocoa Puffs. "Your character seems like a loser." "He is a loser. Fiction can happen to losers as well."

The story went on to have a much stranger effect on my life than I could have imagined. Doing laundry at my apartment (the old La Paloma), I found a magazine called *Factsheet Five,* a huge review magazine of "zines"—hundreds of indie publications of all topics. It had an ad tucked inside for a new science fiction magazine. I thought I could make some money here. My story had already been typed in manuscript form, one of the prerequisites for the assignment—so I sent it off to the new market. I figured that it was new, and there would be less competition for slots. My acceptance letter came almost by return mail. Yes, I would be in issue one, the messy typewritten letter told me. I would be sharing pages with Dr. Isaac Asimov and Ursula K LeGuin. Obviously I had it made. I pretty much stopped going to classes and began filling up more and more floppies. What a day when the double-sided, double-density floppies came out!

My father took ill in Amarillo. A parasite that he had picked up in World War II while stationed in Brazil had caused his esophagus to develop a long sac that wound around his heart. He had surgery, and I went to be at his side. He passed away on July 5, 1983. I went back to Lubbock. I had no money, no job, and certainly no diploma. My story still hadn't appeared, so the fame I was expecting was taking longer than I had planned. My girlfriend was moving to Austin and took me along. Months went by. I called the number on the letter. "Can I speak to Mr. Bonfire, please?" "Mr. Bonfire does not have phone privileges today." In fact, he (like many a Lovecraftian hero) was quite mad. His delusion was that he edited a huge science fiction magazine. I had gotten in the habit of writing. I wrote for three more years, till in 1986 I made two professional sales in the same month—one to *Interzone,* a magazine noted for its cutting-edge fiction, the other to *Amazing,* known in those days for its conservative approach to science fiction. I did, gentle reader, return to school and gained my B.A. from the University of Texas. Major in English, minor in historical linguistics. I have published twenty-one books at this juncture and teach creative writing for UCLA Extension.

The remaining acts are playing out. But the serious question is why would a man devote thirty years of his life to the "Mythos." I'll begin with the obvious. I know the Derlethian appellation of "Cthulhu Mythos" is spurious. Μῦθος, nice second declension male noun, should be "Mythoi" when we are talking about more than one story. Generally "Mythos" would mean a chat, something said—and more eruditely Aristotle said that it was the first element of a tragedy, what we call "plot" in English. But as is so often the case, the true meaning is there. Lovecraft wrote tragedies. It condemned him to the miserabilist shelf; an area (as Thomas Ligotti has wisely remarked) for Outsiders. A tragedy is a tale (mythos) that shows a change from good fortune to bad to elicit fear and pity in its audience. The hero of the tale makes a mistake, and this leads to his (or her) remembering a hidden and devastating past bond of love or hate. Aristotle tells us that the best such tragedies are complex in their mythos, not simple.

Now what sort of loser should seek out a tale designed to sadden and terrify? Aristotle tells us that witnessing such things purges us: watching the suffering of the figures on stage heals us. What do we need to be healed of? Of the more than two thousand Greek tragedies, only about thirty are left. They are pretty clear prescriptions: "Don't marry your mom. Don't piss off your uncle the king. If you kill your mom for killing your dad, some people will be upset anyway." The Cthulhu Mythos actually has a subtler message. Humans fall short by virtue of their humanity. The conventions of family and politics, religion and culture—even being trapped in a world of four dimensions and five senses—these are our mistakes. These are tragedies for us and meaningless to the great forces of the cosmos. I suppose the ants I accidentally stepped on this morning when I swept my patio could be writing their own tragedies: the Bigfoot Mythos.

As is the nature of tragedy, a certain type of human loves to reteach the same lesson. What desperate and Nietzschean thrill to describe the great Other! Those folk, whose black hearts blaze at the sight of an endless uncaring immensity, are the addicted readers of the Mythos. It is a rare breed that truly wants to consider that everything they know about the cosmos could be wrong. Of course, such people are readers Michael Houellebecq's *H. P. Lovecraft: Against the World, Against Life* takes as its premise—that those in love with life are not in love with books, and vice versa. Lovecraft pitted the ultra-terrestrial in all its hellish glory against the pillars of the modern world: money, democracy, progress, and sex. But Lovecraft and his truer disciples do not bore us in the way a miserabilist like Cioran might. It is more fun to be menaced by the symbol of the great unknowable than by the simple dull reflection of anti-life. Lovecraft's cosmos gives us a fascinating dilemma. The only thing we can use to buffer ourselves against what is waiting in the dark is imagination, but imagination itself ultimately fails, since its own unnatural nature is from the same dark.

Now August Derleth was a good Catholic and he was having none of this. We will win in imagination because human religion is based on winning in imagination. So haul out the holy hand grenade of Antioch—er, star-stone of Mnar—and zap! No more evil threat to human-scale thinking or values. Strictly speaking, this rather hopeful interpretation would be a comedy. Derleth was the inventor of the Cthulhu Commedia. And with this human gesture of hope, the "Mythos" began the slippery slide into parody like a greased pig at a county fair. Now it must be understood that August Derleth was not a weak soul to make these choices; indeed, he stood at the brink of a true unveiling and sought to protect both his own self-knowledge and that of others by reining in the awful dark.

However, there is another seldom-discussed side to Yog-Sothothery. In addition to its tragic and comedic sides there is an epic stance. You can find it in the figures of Randolph Carter, Wilbur Whateley, and Joseph Curwen. These brave souls seek to gain entrance into a heightened realm of perception and will do so by embracing the darkness—not the darkness of Sunday school "evil" but the darkness of the unknown. This strand of rebellion against cosmic injustice has appealed to the silliest sort of occultists and to magician-philosophers who prefer the freedom of an anti-mythology. The former are well represented by Simon's *Necronomicon* and the latter sinister groups like the Order of the Trapezoid. For every hundred readers thinking how dreadful it would be to have one's brains removed by the Fungi or one's psyche trans-temporally transposed by the Great Race, there is one who secretly wishes for it to happen.

But I hear my now no longer gentle reader saying, "Surely this high-falutin' folderol is merely your way of justifying writing and reading about invisible whistling flying polyps instead of using your God-given talents to write something that might help the human condition." Such a sentiment is exactly what I write against. I think helping the human condition has more to do with passing blankets to the homeless than trying to make a dulled audience feel some attraction to the human condition. Such an attitude earns me thanks from people in wheelchairs whom I have escorted through my local supermarket, but will certainly fail to put my books in the short lists for literary prizes. And if you were to tell me with a serious but hushed tone that the majority of the noisome awfulness is crapola, I would (in the same muted tones) agree. The emotional effect of the good Mythos tale is what the seeker seeks. Borges may deliver it better in his Mythos story than (fill in your choice of name).

I write to create wonder, which can be ecstasy and fear or simple alienation. I write thus to heal my Gnostic soul, the alien man trapped in this world. Fortunately some others share my needs and have bought this little book. I hope I can abduct them from the workaday world into a place of weird realism. I hope you won't be quite the same when you return to your "real" life.

Hail to the Ancient Dreams!

—DON WEBB

Through Dark Angles

The Man
Who Scared Lovecraft

It was a name-thing.

I was up at six and read my fun e-mail before getting down to work. I am a small-time collector of pulp magazines, and I belong to an e-list called Fiction-mags. It had some big-time dealers and collectors and even a few of the old pulp giants on it. I mainly lurked and enjoyed posts about my hobby. I did a little business there; occasionally some piece of memorabilia came into my used bookstore. Ironically, the day that led to the horror began with my reading about a great horror writer of the last century, Howard Phillips Lovecraft.

Lovecraft was a New England fantasy writer who supplemented his meager income by editing the manuscripts of his fellow writers. Sometimes Mr. Lovecraft's touch was light; in cases where talent was missing from his client, Lovecraft would rewrite most of the tale. Spotting Lovecraft's revisions is a pastime among certain aficionados of his dark and dreamy tales. Someone had asked a question about a certain story in a magazine called *Weird Tales,* and Addison E. Steele had replied with a list of writers whom Lovecraft had rewritten (from Hazel Heald to Zealia Bishop) and concluded his well-researched post with "of course Lovecraft's most obscure client Amos Carter."

Amos Carter.

I drove down to my bookstore trying hard to remember where I seen the name. Amos Carter. Amos Carter. Twenties mystery writer? Something in a fanzine? Damn. Amos Carter. I helped customers find books, dissuaded them from the belief that their *Webster's Speller* was worth thousands of dollars, even if their grandparent had owned it, and attended to the other duties of the used bookstore trade. By the end of the day I was sure that the name was somewhere in my shop and that I had seen it recently.

When I got home I sent a note to Mr. Steele. It was partially a fan letter thanking him for his writings over the years, but also asking about Carter. By the time I was up the next day, he had replied:

> Dear John Reynman,
>
> Thank you for your kind words. Amos Carter is famous, or infamous, because of some revision that Lovecraft did for him. Amos was writing a serialized novella for an apparently amateur publication called the *Shocking Mysteries Fantasy Gazette,* a short-lived magazine from a town with the unlikely name of Comesee, Texas. The digest-sized mag ran for four issues with the Carter story in issue number three. The story is a pseudo–Middle Ages tale featuring a Knight called Zauber, who encounters some horror "too eldritch to be described." The ending of the story did NOT appear in #4. There was a note from H.P.L. instead: "Esteemed Readers, I had assisted Mr. Carter in revising the MS. of the first part of this story, 'Sir Zauber's Tale.' When he presented me the second section of the story, I realized that it would be too devastating for the average reader, and might cause damage to his faculties. Therefore I declined to revise the story and have advised the editors of the *Shocking Mysteries Fantasy Gazette* not to publish the ending of the tale or any more of the blasphemous writings of Mr. Carter. Howard Phillips Lovecraft." I suspect that Carter, if indeed this was not a pseudonym for Lovecraft, was unable to come up with an ending for the story and simply chose the more dramatic warning letter. I think I have a copy of the story somewhere in the boxes in my garage. If I can lay my hands on it, would you like a copy?
>
> Addison

I wrote back in the affirmative and asked about the name. Lovecraft had created a fictional alter ego "Randolph Carter" as early as 1919. Since Lovecraft and his friends were always using fictionalized versions of one another in their tales, the whole thing sounded fishy, but a fun thing to figure out. I asked Addison if he could remember more details about the story.

The name still wouldn't let me go.

I had a dream that night.

I was alone in my shop, the New Atlantis Used Bookstore; no one

had come to buy anything all day. Outside rain poured down on Lava-
ca Street, thunder and lightning filled the sky, and I was thinking what
a great day it was for some Gothic fiction. I go up into my SF loft,
which housed mainly paperbacks, and I see that the carpet is covered
in blood. Lots of blood. As it is a dream, I don't think about the blood
as a horrible thing, just cursing the fact I'll have to re-carpet. In the
corner of the loft is a large veiled statue. I know that I am not supposed to look at it, but I figure I can lift the cover and take one peek
while no one is in the store. I squish my way over there, noting with
dismay how many of the paperbacks are flecked with blood. *I should
have known this would happen,* I think. I reach the statue and start to pull
up the veil, and then I remember that I need to read that Amos Carter
book, so I walk back to the "C's" and sure enough just before Lin
Carter's novels is this sick green-colored paperback. *Zauber's Quest and
Other Odd Journeys* by Amos H. Carter. I bend down to pick up the
book—it's on the bottom shelf and therefore has blood on it. As I
pick up the book I hear the veil fall off the statue, and suddenly I am
as afraid as I can be. Something's behind me. If I look I will see it. I
will see the thing that I'm not meant to see. I think I hear music.

At that point I woke my wife Haidee up screaming. In almost ten
years of sleeping with her I had never had a nightmare that made me
scream before. She held me and petted me for about an hour before I
went back to sleep. It was raining cats and dogs outside, which no
doubt colored my dreamscape.

I'm a little embarrassed to admit that I was scared to go in my
store. I went to the coffee shop Decline of the West next door for
about an hour—till I actually heard people knocking on my door.

Once inside I felt silly. During a lull I checked out the loft. The roof
had sprung a leak, so the carpet was wet at the top of the stairs and did
squish. There weren't any veiled statues that had been installed in the
night. The place of honor was still filled by an open cardboard box with
the words FREE STUFF magic-markered on the side. I tossed the stuff
that I couldn't sell in there—old small-press magazines, promotional
items, and so forth. I decided to look through the box.

Scary.

I found a fanzine produced by Xerox and saddle-stapled called *The Moon Lily*, dated March 15, 1977. The blue paper cover features a ruined castle on the moon with Earthrise behind it. The cover boasted, "ALL FICTION ISSUE: Schweitzer, Fox, winter-damon, Carter." This was where I had seen the name before. The story was "Sir Zauber's Tale, Part 2." It began with a letter from Carter thanking the editor of *TML* for asking for one of his pulp stories and saying that this story was begun in 1926 and had never had its conclusion printed before. It mentioned that Lovecraft had revised the first half of the tale and evinced sadness that he no longer had that part of the story. There were a few poignant observations about living in a rest home. Mr. Carter had apparently outlived his wife and children and was something of a ward of the state in a rather smelly and sad institution. That was true horror, I decided.

The tale did involve a statue; I had probably glanced at it when I threw the 'zine in the box months ago. It began as follows:

"Sir Zauber found that he could no longer look at the foul idol that dominated the town square. He felt that its strange form (in all its beauty and terror) had already burned into his brain. 'I will think on this the day I die, and every night I dream,' he thought. He decided to study the inscriptions on the four-sided base of the statue. Some were uncouth languages of the East, but four words were in the tongue of his childhood. On the north was 'PHANTOM OF TRUTH,' on the west 'A LITTLE SLIPPER ON HER FOOT,' on the south 'NOT WITHOUT PAIN,' and on the east 'UNKNOWN TO THE SUN.' Zauber could not fathom what they meant. Part of his soul told him to leave that spot lest he suddenly understand and be damned.

"It grew late in the day, and he knew that he had to reach the castle Draypalo while there was still sunlight. He did not want to meet the Queen under the spell of night when her powers would be at their height."

The tale continued as a fairly conventional fight-the-vampire story. Sir Zauber arrives at the castle a bit too late and the Queen has risen. He tries his swordcraft against her, but she actually seduces him during the battle. He agrees to share her kingdom with her, knowing however that he will one day become a zombie servitor like the creatures in the dungeons. There are some vague hopes that he might escape this zombie status with the help and love of a village girl—but this is left open in the story, so we cannot tell if he is delusional or properly hopeful. There are no further direct references to the statue, or in fact anything to make clear what the first half of the story had been about.

I closed the shop early to e-mail news of my find to Addison. I asked if he had located the first part of the tale, as I was very anxious to read the whole thing. I also speculated on the possibility of maybe putting the restored story up on a website. I didn't imagine that Mr. Carter would still be alive, as he would be past a hundred at this point, but I thought the story plus the story of the story would be fascinating (at least for pulp fiction geeks like ourselves).

Addison wrote back that night that he was going to spend all night looking for the story in his garage, and that this was extremely exciting. He had dreamed for years of seeing the story that had scared Lovecraft.

I heard nothing the next day.

Then I got a distressing letter from Mrs. Addison. She had awakened to a horrifying crash in their garage. Her husband, true to his word, had looked long into the night for the magazine and fallen off a ladder while peering in the top of some junk-filled boxes. He had broken a hip and would be bedridden for a while, and it would be some time before he could contact me.

Two weeks later I got a note from Addison. He said he was doing well, although he thought it would be a month or so before he could search his boxes again. Could I send him the story conclusion so that when he found the first part he could read all of it?

I had been feeling very guilty over the incident so far, so I Xeroxed the tale and mailed it off to him. Addison wrote in a couple of days that he had received the story and had begun researching Carter's life and writings. It turned out that Carter did have a small career in pulp writing that later became a career of writing cheap paperbacks. He had a burst of that sort thing in the paperback revolution of the Sixties—*The Truth about Mummies, The Truth about Werewolves, UFOS in Colonial America,* etc. Addison was going to make a box of stuff for me when he was well.

Another week passed and I got the following note:

Dear Reynman,
        CARTER IS ALIVE. He's still in the rest home he mentions in *The
Moon Lily*, which turns out to be less than fifty miles from here. I am going to visit him this Sunday for his 107th birthday party!
        Best,
                Addison

On Saturday I got another note.

Dear Reynman,
        FOUND IT!! I'm going to give a copy of both parts to Carter to-
morrow, and then mail you a copy as well. This is so exciting!
        Best,
                AES

After a couple of months I had heard nothing, and then a friend of
Addison posted a small obituary. Addison had had a heart attack, ironically while visiting the world's oldest pulp writer at a rest home in
Bayou Goula (White Castle), Louisiana. A little research told me that
Bayou Goula is something of a ghost town, absorbed by the more lively village of White Castle, and its claim to fame is having the world's
smallest chapel. The little burg lay on LA1 near Baton Rogue. It had
exactly one rest home—the "I Did It My Way" home.

The whole idea itched in my brain. It was like a tooth beginning to
twinge. You forget about it and then there it is again. You are showering or about to lie down for bed or putting the brass key in the door of
your shop, and the idea is there. That's a seven-and-a-half-hour drive.
Now gas is certainly not the cheapest of commodities, but how many
107-year-old pulp writers are you ever going to meet? I could justify
the trip in that I might find rare books (or at least eBay-resalable
books) at junk stores on the way. Haidee is always telling me to slack
off some. I work at the store almost every day. I hadn't been on a vacation in forever. I would fight the idea down as foolishness, and then
the twinge would hit me again. Finally in late September the foolishness won out. I reserved a room in a Baton Rogue Best Western and

turned my wheels to the east with copy of *The Moon Lilly* in hand.

It was a trying and uneventful Monday. Haidee and Ben would work the store until Thursday. I drove through White Castle and located the tiny chapel, the nursing home, and the Cora-Texas sugar mill, which seemed to be the village's biggest industry. I would sack out for the night and see Mr. Amos Carter Tuesday morning.

I had vague and unpleasant dreams, but nothing like the nightmares I secretly hoped for.

The I Did It My Way Retirement Home was a foul-smelling twenty-room facility on the corner of Bayou Street and Andrew Jackson Avenue. It had been painted a pale green and had dark brown trim. Two old white women were on metal porch rockers. "Good morning, youngster!" the oldest of them cackled. I smiled back, "Lovely day, ladies!" I stepped inside. The reception area was paneled in what had no doubt once been brown wood veneer that had faded to gray. The receptionist nurse was an African American woman in her fifties, about my age. She looked tired and it was only 9:00 in the morning. I guessed her shift had begun in the wee hours of the morning. Her black glossy plastic nametag read Kassandra.

"Can I help you, sir?"

"I am looking to visit Mr. Amos Carter."

Her expression would have done justice to the pubgoers in a werewolf movie. "Mr. Carter has no visitors except his grandson."

"I know that is not correct. A friend of mine, Mr. Addison E. Steele, visited not long ago," I replied. The moment I felt her resistance this suddenly became important to me. The vague sense of a Quest that had been calling to me since I had glanced at *The Moon Lily* suddenly crystallized. I needed to see this 107-year-old man.

"I am sorry about your friend. Mr. Carter can be violent. Normally we leave him tied to his gerry chair."

"The man is 107," I began.

"Nobody here believes that. You've never seen him. You are like that man from New Orleans, the one that died. Look, the whole Carter family stinks. They're weird and awful. If I had my way we throw old man Carter out."

"Why?"

"There's something about him that just isn't right. Not Amos, the other one."

"Don't you worry about your job saying things like that?" I asked. I could hear the sounds of *The Jerry Springer Show* from down the hall. She gave me a look. "You couldn't get someone else to work in this dump. I lost my job in New Orleans after Katrina. This town is literally where my car broke down."

"My friend was from New Orleans." I said.

"Yes, I know; he ran a bookshop in the Quarter. Court of the Dragon. My son used to like that stuff. Look, mister, I am trying to save your white butt. Don't mess around with Mr. Carter or his grandson or any of them."

"I am not worried by an old man."

"Do you know what the problem with white people is? They live in denial. That's why they screwed up the world. That's why they hate us."

I was about to give my Austin knee-jerk reaction, which would no doubt have included being an Obama supporter, when the phone buzzed at the desk saving me from looking foolish. Kassandra said, "Number 13." And waved me toward one wing.

The old-people smell intensified as I headed to my left. An almost bald old man was pushing a walker down the hall, his toothless mouth agape and drool pouring out in streamers. His dingy white bathrobe was partially open, displaying his shrunken member to God and the world. I passed the TV lounge where Springer's half-man was pulling the chair out for a three-hundred-pound transvestite while two-blue haired women laughed to see such fun. There was a computer room on the other side. A one-legged man about my age was looking through eBay, a palsied woman tied in her gerry chair was unsuccessfully trying to contact a Bible site, another woman, very large with bright red lipstick and a fabric rose behind her left ear, was looking at a JPEG of a family at the beach in Maui or some other tropical paradise. My God, Carter has been here at least forty-one years. I walked on to the end of the hall. Some rooms were open. A woman restrained on a bed screamed as I went by, wanting Alfred. In another, two gray-haired black gentlemen in threadbare flannel robes bent over a chessboard.

There were two twin beds in room 13. They were nicely made and to my amusement had Spiderman bed covers. A wall clock with large numbers told me it was almost 10:00. There was a small painting of a green-skinned ghoul sitting on a tombstone, contemplating some gnawed-upon Yorrick. The painting could have been from a sci-fi convention where it had not taken home any awards. On the opposite wall hung a framed faded print of Albrecht Dürer's *Praying Hands*. There was a small bookshelf under the ticking clock. There were a few paperbacks, *The Truth about Black Magic*, *The Secret of the Great Pyramid*, *Teach Yourself Typing*, *Hunza Valley Health Secrets*, *UFOs in Colonial America*, *How to Make and Sell Macramé*, *Houses That Kill*, and *The Truth about Ghouls*. All by Amos H. Carter. The room being empty, I crossed to the shelf to examine the last volume. The atrocious painting had provided the cover art for this collection of forgotten lore. In the room I saw his gerry chair, the filthy white bondage belts hanging loosely at its sides.

"Amos is out by the bayou," came a frail feminine voice.

In the doorway was a shrunken old woman in a wheelchair. Her cornflower blue eyes twinkled, her cheeks were rouged, and her thinning hair nicely coiffed. Her attendant, an ebon black young man with cornrows, had a white orderly's uniform which had a nametag AL-FRED and incongruous blue bandana in the shirt pocket. He looked all in all like the Platonic form of boredom.

I addressed the helpful woman. "Isn't he supposed to stay in his room?" I nodded toward the gerry chair.

"Bonds don't hold Amos when he doesn't want them to. We discussed that when you were here last."

"I am afraid you are mistaken, sweetheart," I said. "This is my first visit."

"No. You were here that other time. The time there was all that blood," she said. Alfred began to wheel her away.

"Wait," I said.

"She just gonna get crazy, don't get her going," said Alfred.

"What blood?" I asked.

"All that blood everywhere and Alfred's grandmother made him scour it off the floors and I told him he looked like Cinderella."

"See, I told she crazy."

"Where did the blood come from?"

Alfred was wheeling her down the hall.

"Where did the blood come from?"

"From New Orleans, I reckon."

I left the nursing home and struck out for the bayou. There was a path through the tall Johnson grass and scrub oak. Even in October the air was hot and humid, and a bright green moss covered the tiny trunks of the little trees. Insects hummed and buzzed, the water gave off a sour and stale smell. The sky had begun to cloud up, and the sun looked a lead disk. The path cut round and back again like a water moccasin. I could only see a few feet ahead. I couldn't believe how quickly I seemed to be in a primeval jungle, even though I knew I could only be a few hundred yards from Lee Street. Large butterflies with purple and black wings fluttered by. I was tempted to step off the sandy path and crush one, changing millions of years of the future, when I saw a middle-aged white man in blue shirt and Levis sitting on a stump about sixty feet ahead of me. He was resting his hands on a walking-stick with an elaborate ivory handle, apparently in deep conversation with the butterflies. For some reason I decided that must be the grandson. "Mr. Carter." I yelled, "I am looking for your grandfather." He looked up and grinned at me, then waved his stick like a bishop blessing the faithful with his crozier.

I hurried along the path. I slipped on a muddy patch and kept from falling by grabbing the rope like branches of willow. I struggled to regain both balance and dignity, and when I looked up the man had left. I went to where he was, and then followed the path into deeper woods where trees with real height stood, large-trunked live-oaks with Spanish moss beards. I couldn't figure out where he had gone, and the sense of wildness bothered me. I am not given to fear generally, especially not on lightly overcast Monday mornings, but this place suddenly seemed very alien. It was not the glistening sundews or the brightly colored mushrooms. It was not because of anything that can be seen or heard or handled, but because of something that was imagined. I found myself *listening*, but I couldn't say for what. Maybe it would be better to meet Mr. Carter in the home, in his well-lit room at night.

I returned to my silver PT Cruiser and drove away from the I Did It My Way retirement home.

After an afternoon of semi-successful bookstore crawling, I felt foolish about my feelings in the bayou. I drove back to the home after catching a barbecue sandwich from a restaurant called The Pig Stand. I took my copy of *The Moon Lily*, and after a few seconds of deliberation my .45 as well. I didn't know if my Texas concealed weapons permit worked in Louisiana, and I was ashamed to be afraid of a 107-year-old.

The smell of piss and disinfectant seemed stronger by night. To my surprise, Kassandra was still behind the desk. She must have a crazy shift.

She shook her head and pursed her lips. "My grandson told me you were getting Mary riled up. You don't need to bother her. If you want to hang out with the Carters that's your own fool business. Leave everybody else out of it."

"I am sorry if I upset the old lady. She was talking about blood."

"Old people talk about a lot of things; that's because they've seen everything and done everything. You can go on back, he's with his grandson now." She said the last with a truly hateful smirk.

It took me a few seconds to take in the scene before me.

The man I had seen earlier today was tied to a gerry chair. His silver and black hair, reddened skin, and cauliflower nose would lead me to think he was an alcoholic in his seventies, but his eyes—his eyes were dead. They moved, but they had no light to them. No love, no joy, no anger, nothing. They seemed to suck in the light of the room. It almost seemed as if he had a shadow on his face. The walking-stick with its yellowed ivory handle lay against the bed, just out of his reach. The cane's head was a thick disk showing what seemed to be a veiled man crawling through a geometrical figure. Its wood was dark and scratched up from a great deal of use. Sitting in a wooden chair, probably a dining room chair because of the elbow supports, was an older man with thinning silver hair and a turkey neck. He wore a faded pink

Izod shirt and khaki pants jerked too far up on his frame, held by a brown belt that had a few new notches punched in it, probably by a pocket knife. He was reading from a yellowed paperback.

"The King's Chamber was not a tomb as modern Egyptologists tell us. Instead, it was a shrine to a headless demon, called in Arabic *Yaji Ash-Shuthath*, meaning 'No Peace at the Gate.' This all-seeing being is symbolized in Masonry as the All-Seeing Eye, but because of its gift of immortality it is likewise called *Tawil-at'Umr*, which means 'Prolonged of Age.' The Egyptians themselves called it *Ur sutthoth*, which means the 'Primal Dazzler Time Reckoner.' The shape-waves of the chamber were utilized by Aleister Crowley . . ."

The man in the gerry chair interrupted him.

"We have a guest."

The reading man put down the book, which I saw was *The Secret of the Great Pyramid*. He looked at me with a great deal of anger. "Is there just going to be a parade of you guys?"

"I don't know what you mean." I said. "I am just a book dealer."

"Did you come to make an offer on this fabulous collection?" He asked, motioning at the small shelf. "How would you like that, Grandpa? I could sell your books and you would have no connection anymore at all, would you?"

The man in the gerry chair looked scared. He tried to reach his walking-stick, and the other man moved it a few inches away. The man in the gerry chair made a high sad noise like a kitten wanting food.

"I am not here to buy anything. I am a fan of Mr. Carter and I wanted him to sign a magazine if he would like."

"Now that would be pretty unlikely, wouldn't it? How old is Grandpa supposed to be in his official biographies?" He looked at the frontmatter of the book he had been reading. "Why, he would be one hundred and seven! One-hundred-and-seven-year-olds don't sign things. I am sure you have wasted your time, Mr. er?"

"Reynman," I said "John Reynman."

"Lovely name, 'Reynman'—Norwegian, right? Seeker-man. As in 'Reyn Til Runa!' Seek the mysteries. Is my family a mystery to you, to you and Mr. Steele?"

"I know my friend died here. And I can see that the restrained man is younger than you. So, yes, there are some mysteries here. The man in the chair is clearly not one hundred and seven."

"You are right about that. He is much older. He is actually my great-grandfather. My name is Roderick Carter, and I will bet you all the money that you're carrying, Mr. Bookseller, that you can't guess my age either."

"Can I come in? I have had a long day and I'm not up to standing in doorways and exchanging cryptic remarks."

Roderick nodded. I crossed to the other bed and sat down, rehearsing in my mind how I could draw the .45 from underneath my blue windbreaker if I needed to.

I asked, "Does Amos talk?"

"What about it Grandpa, do you talk tonight?"

Amos stared at me with his dead eyes. "I know you. You are Mr. Price from New Orleans. I was managing one of the sugar plants when you and Mr. Lovecraft came calling."

Roderick said, "Now isn't that nice? He remembers you."

I scanned my Lovecraft trivia. I can't believe that a grown man knows so much of this junk. "Lovecraft and Price met in 1932."

"Well, that's just yesterday, isn't it, Grandpa?"

Amos tried to grab the walking-stick again. Roderick smiled at his failed lunge.

"Can I ask him to sign the fanzine?" I asked.

"Can I ask him to sign the fanzine?" Roderick replied *sotto voce*. "I don't know, can you?"

"Mr. Carter, I enjoyed your story in *The Moon Lily*. Could you sign it for me?"

Amos said, "You should have told me that Lovecraft couldn't handle it. I'd read his stories. I thought he would understand. A transfusion would have fixed him."

Roderick was enjoying this. He got up and closed the door.

"Now that we are getting to the good part let's not share it with the minds of the unwashed masses," he said.

"What does he mean, a transfusion?"

Roderick said, "His blood has a lot of green in it. The emerald ichors of the Prolonged of Age. He could live forever theoretically."

"And you?"

"I am one hundred. The ichor thins with each generation. Do you want some? We could cut a vein open, borrow some rubber tubing from Kassandra. It doesn't do much else, does it, you old bastard? Doesn't make you smart or talented or even keep your mind going. So I read to him every night to keep his soul from drifting off to the spaces haunted by *Yaji Ash-Shuthath*. I read the crappy paperbacks he wrote fifty years ago like that movie *The Diary*."

"You care for him then?"

"No, I fucking hate him. I didn't ask for this long a life. I outlived three wives. I have made and lost fortunes. I have to learn terrible things to stay alive, black tricks of the soul from the old books he owned. I am tired, but I don't want to die."

"What does that have to do with him?"

"When his soul drifts off to angled space I don't know if the Bond will hold. I don't want to go there. He showed me once I was back from the Second World War. He opened a Gate and showed me the Sounds that you can See, the Hounds that rip the Soul. All the things he showed Lovecraft. I don't want to go there."

"So you keep him here in this shitty little resthome. Don't you know he hates it?" I waved my copy of *The Moon Lily* at him. Amos had begun to make gestures with his left hand, maybe some senile twitch. I wasn't sure how much of this if any to believe. Cosmic horror and senior abuse seemed an unlikely mix at best.

"I hate him. Why should I make him happy? I had a great life. Forty years ago I was a famous chef in New York. People used to make jokes about how I never aged. Then they became too curious. So I'm here in the back of beyond. I am here during hurricanes. I am here listening to fifty thousand Cajuns scream for the Tigers, I am here smelling the green smells of the bayou. Now I re-read cheap paperbacks so an old hack writer doesn't lead my soul to a hell you couldn't even begin to imagine."

"How did my friend die?"

"Grandpa killed him. Used to be quiet, the sorcerer Grandpa did. Your friend came while Alfred was helping him to the restroom. Who knows what he said or did? That's why we keep him restrained."

"But you don't keep him restrained all the time. I saw him out by the bayou this morning talking to the butterflies."

Roderick stood up. His face was white with anger. "You are a lying son-of-a-bitch. Why are you lying to me? He never leaves this room."

I looked over at Amos. The dirty white bonds lay on either side of the chair. He was leaning forward, carefully inching toward the walking-stick.

I said, "Mr. Carter, why would I lie to you? I think you're just a backwoods lunatic."

Roderick Carter moved toward me, and his great-grandfather grabbed the stick and swung it at Roderick's neck. He said one word. I think it would be better if I don't write it down. Purple fire sparked in an irregular star pattern behind Roderick's neck. A cold rotten meat smell poured into the room as a black space simply opened behind Roderick's head. Something barked or rang behind him, and I could see some glow in a color I could not name moving toward him. Roderick spun around and the black hole in space lunged at his head and closed, cutting him off in mid-scream. His body with some of the head still on *this* side collapsed. Blood was running everywhere.

I drew my .45.

Amos was back in his chair. His bonds were in place. The walking stick was lying across the bed. He looked at me. Kassandra and another nurse were throwing the door open. I put the gun away. Kassandra knocked the walking stick back on the bed.

She told the other nurse, "Go calm them down. Call the Parish morgue, tell Alexander we got another one. Don't tell anybody else. Call my house and tell Alfred to come."

The other nurse left. Kassandra went to Amos and patted his head. "You finally got rid of him. I know you love your family, but he was a bad 'un. I'd have done it years ago." For the briefest moment his eyes looked like the eyes of a living human.

She turned to me.

"I don't know why you came, but I want you to go now. I think it's clear that we can deal with things. I am sorry about your friend. There have been a few who visited over the years and nothing like that had ever happened. It was Roderick's fault."

I got up.

"You can take his books if you want. He doesn't want to hang around here. There's not much human left in him anymore. I don't think he can sign them for you."

"What about you? Why do you care about him?"

"I am a nurse. I care, besides I know how to do transfusions."

"But aren't you afraid?"

"Of the other place? Amos told me years ago, the other place is just Knowledge. If you are a bad man like Mr. Roderick, Knoweldge is Hell. Close the door as you leave the room, this could scare people."

I did as I was told. It was going to be a long drive back. I had been on the road for two hundred miles when I realized I hadn't picked up the books.

The Megalith Plague

There had been a little controversy when my great-grandfather died shortly after the Civil War. He had asked that two large stones be set at his feet and his head in the "manner of the Druids." Because of his medical service to the community of Flapjack, Texas, and (ironically) his preeminence in the local Masonic Lodge, this heathen custom had been observed. Last night they drug them off for another model Stonehenge.

According to the *Flapjack Recipe*, there are now four hundred and eighteen models of Stonehenge in this county.

For me it began with the cockroaches. . . .

Flapjack, Texas, is on the road between Austin and Dallas. Stagecoaches used to stop here for food and water for man and beast, hence its high-carb name. With the coming of Mr. Ford's affordable device, Flapjack and its sister communities of Comesee and Doublesign were doomed not to grow very large. If you live in central Texas you have driven through these towns hundreds of times, probably never even noticing them as separate entries in the blur outside your window. By the time I practiced medicine in Flapjack, there wasn't even a place to buy—well, you know.

But there were cockroaches. Not your little-bitty German cockroaches, not your more urban African cockroaches. There were **huge** cockroaches. Locals call them "palmetto bugs." *Periplaneta americana.* These suckers were three inches long. They could fly. Sometimes you had to step on them twice to kill them. They weren't scared of light, so they didn't even have the good taste to scurry away when you pulled the string dangling from your kitchen light at two in the morning, after delivering a baby at some godforsaken farm. Sometimes they would fly right on you and make you wish that you weren't such a lousy doctor that you had to practice in a region where nobody thought about suing their doctors for incompetence. I didn't practice here because great-granddad did; I practiced here because they would have me. I was staring thirty-five in the face and knew I had to leave Las Vegas before lawsuits caught up with me.

I bought the two-bedroom stucco house with the thousand coats of white paint and fifty thousand cockroaches. No one would know that I graduated last in my class. They would know me as a descendant of a healer. They were glad I didn't have an accent.

At night they ran over me. Not the Flapjackers, the cockroaches. The palmetto bugs. They loved my ears and nose, no doubt thinking of them as sexual organs of an even bigger member of their species. My return to the ancestral homeland had not prepared me for the notion of an insect copulating with my nostril, so I went to the Home Depot in Doublesign and purchased four times the recommended amount of insect fogger. In the checkout line I met Richard Scott.

A short man, I would guess five foot two, his gray beetle brows and the lines of grime across his forehead were not inviting. His bloodshot slate-blue eyes were a little too wet. He smelled of welding, but he was buying thirty or so precut 2 × 4s. He glared at me, clearly angry. Was he a friend of the roaches?

"So you are the new Doc," he said.

"I took over Dr. Hawthorne's practice. My great-grandfather . . ." I began.

"Is dead," he finished. "I need some meds. I have to renew."

"What do you need?"

He rattled off a list of anti-psychotics, anti-convulsants, mood stabilizers, anti-depressants, typical and atypical neurolyptics—and frankly some stuff I had never heard of.

"I'll need you to come by my office. Perhaps tomorrow morning," I said.

"Good, then you can see I'm crazy, and you'll leave me the fuck alone. I am, you know. Crazy. Bug-fuck crazy. Ask anyone about Scott."

I saw no reason to doubt his statement.

I intended to set off my foggers the next morning and drive the mile or so to my office. I would look over Dr. Hawthorne's records and check on Mr. Scott's bug-fuck status. However, the invitation to ask anyone was a strong one. I had not made friends with anyone in Flapjack, and perhaps giving them a chance to tell me about their village idiot would endear me to their bosom. I dined that night at the Cobra, which offered a free meal after you had dined there eleven times. Such bounty, I thought, was to be patronized. So while enjoying my chicken-fried steak I asked the waitress if she knew a Mr. Scott.

"Why, he's just crazy, hon. But I, well, don't you . . . I'm sure he'll give you a lot of business."

It seemed that Mr. Scott had committed three sorts of offenses. The first is that he was the unmarried son of a very wealthy family, which was a severe offense. The waitress looked at me strangely while giving me that news. I wondered if she thought I was gay. His second crime was sculpting. He produced an ugly sort of high modernist sculptures out of I-beams and T-beams, the sort of sculptures that banks display to prove that they are cultured. These two social crimes, however, did not condemn Mr. Richard Scott. They merely made him odd. He also beat people with wrenches and burnt them with acetylene torches. His violence broke out every few years. His trust fund covered it pretty well, and heck, most people knew enough to get away from him, and when things got bad old Doc Hawthorne would add a new anti-convulsant or a new anti-psychotic. Scott would calm down for a spell.

I heard all this over sweet coconut meringue pie and bitter black coffee.

The stars at night were big and bright as I drove home and the moon a full cantaloupe. The moon even put to rest my cynicism, which shows how powerful the central Texas moon can be.

The next day I pushed down the little green plastic notch on the bug foggers and muttered my vengeance as I set them out. I was putting down the last fogger in my living room when I tripped. I went down; the fogger went up and in a freak moment passed before my open eyes, giving them one hell of a blast of bug spray. I *thunked* my head good on the floor and passed out with the fogger blowing into my bloodied nose.

As their hissing filled my ears everything seemed to light up orange and the floor seemed to be turning into slime. If you ever huffed ether in college or glue in middle school you'd know the feeling. I wondered if the cockroaches felt this way as they died. Maybe some cockroach made it once, survived, and went back to the roach club to talk about heaven.

When I came to, I was restrained. I couldn't open my eyes because of the bandages, and I could not lift my hands because they were tied to the bed, so that I wouldn't tear off my bandages, but I did not understand my situation. So I jerked strongly against the bed and gave a muffled cry, which my insecticide-soaked nose, mouth, and throat meant as a scream of terror.

Scott answered me, "Don't I know it, Doc. You know I've been in that very bed. It'll pass; just tell yourself it will pass."

"Where am I?"

"You are in the Doublesign Minor Emergency Clinic, although I am sure you feel that you had yourself a major emergency. Currently you are tied to the bed, which in my vast experience means they feel you will do harm to yourself or others. Will you do harm to yourself or others, Doc?"

"What's going on?"

"Doc, you tried to get high on bug juice. I saved you before you flung your consciousness out into the void. I decided that would be a waste, and I might not get my scripts refilled."

"Scott, I wasn't trying to get high. Now get me a doctor."

"I don't take orders. Now if you would like to make a request . . ."

Before I said anything I listened. I was hoping to hear some sound that told me I was in the tiny six-bed hospital in Doublesign. I wanted to hear an IV machine *beep* or a soda drop out of the soda machine, or Dr. Fresno making his rounds. I didn't hear anything, and I realized that I could be anywhere. I couldn't smell anything; my nose was just a mass of burning pain. In fact, I could almost hear its throbs. The pain must have been what woke me. Why didn't they have me on a morphine drip?

Then the blackness behind my eyes got darker, and I was gone for a while.

When I came to again I called out for a nurse, and one answered.

Her guitar-twangy voice soothed my soul; I was indeed in a hospital. Dr. Fresno came in soon after. I found out that I would be here for another two to three weeks. He would take my patients in the meantime. They told me that Scott had rescued me. Impatiently waiting to be my patient, he had walked over to my home after an hour. He kicked open my front door and called the ambulance from Doublesign. He claimed to be a distant cousin.

This proved true. My great-granddad's second daughter had married into the Scott line. Scott pointed this out to me the next time he visited me.

"Didja ever wonder, Doc, why you've got no friends here? It's 'cause you and I are kin. I probably shouldn't have you as my doctor."

"What do you mean?"

"We have the same great-grandfather. My only blood relative would stand to gain a lot of money if I died. It doesn't exactly motivate you, hippocratically speaking. Maybe you and I should write out wills to each other. Be more fair-like. I had been intending to leave my wad to the Sloane Art Museum in Doublesign as they have a couple of my sculptures."

"Scott, I'm not interested in your money."

"Now that's a lie, Doc. I may be crazy, but I ain't stupid. In fact, Doc, you would be surprised at the depth of my art education."

He spoke truly. I wanted the damn money and spent many blindfolded hours thinking about what drugs would kill him off. When I returned to light, I would no doubt think differently, but you think odd thoughts in the dark.

The next day, or later that night, Scott woke me.

"This is choice, Doc, really choice. You know Fenster?"

"Yes." I said, having no idea who Fenster was.

"Well, he found something on his land. He was putting a well where an old church was and he found a little metal box. Inside was a small book called *How to Worship God Correctly*. Seems like we've all been doing it wrong for years. He drove to the Kinko's and ran off a few copies and gave them out at the Dairy Queen. Now there's going to be a town meeting."

"Did you get a copy?"

"Of course I did. I get me a double-dipped chocolate cone every day about three. I think that soft-serve custard is one of the two best parts of civilization."

"What's the other one?"

"Oxy-acetylene welding."

By this time the bandages were really starting to itch. My hands had been freed days before. It was hard to keep track of the pace of days. Scott came often. As the hospital's major donor, he could come anytime. For all I knew this conversation took place at six in the evening or four in the morning or noon.

"So how are we supposed to worship God?"

"With megalithic stone circles. Mankind apparently hit the mark with Stonehenge, Nabta Playa, Bagnold's Circle, or Sentinel Hill in Massachusetts. That's what God wants."

"I bet that went over big with the Baptists."

"You'd think not, but everyone seemed pretty positive about it."

I didn't know what to make to this remark. I had never heard of Nabta Playa or Bagnold's Circle. I wondered if he had taken his meds today. I had asked Dr. Fresno to keep him out of my room, but Fresno said he slipped past the guard. I doubted that anyone would say no to him. I didn't like being quiet for too long, so I said, "So what do you make of it?"

"I don't know, Doc. I have never been the religious type. Seems to me God has already made enough calendars with the moon and the sun."

The twilight came when Dr. Fresno cut away my bandages. The room was dim, and I kept expecting some *Twilight Zone* moment when they would look at me and see me as a monster. Instead, for a moment I was the one horrified. Something seemed wrong with the angles of the room, as though everything lunged toward me. I put up my hands, and then I felt stupid. Dr. Fresno smiled his half-senile smile. I could see Scott waiting for me in the hall.

Dr. Fresno said, "Richard agreed to drive you home. You can drive tomorrow, but let's remember our sunglasses, Dr. Huff. Your eyes are fine, and you'll soon be over any respiratory distress."

The moon was dark. It had only been two weeks since I had scalded my eyes, fried my brain, and cooked the insides of my lungs. It felt like months or years had gone by. Scott drove me home, and as his old white Chevy pickup turned at the town square I saw my first Stonehenge. The stones stood six or seven feet tall. I asked him to stop. He shrugged and did so. I realized that people were walking around in the middle of the circle. I yelled out to them, but they didn't yell back.

"They ain't always friendly, Doc. Just simple country folk." He laughed all the way to my house. I didn't get the joke. I was glad to see my SUV in the driveway; maybe I should just drive away tomorrow.

The next day I saw four circles in progress. Two stone. One made of old TVs, which I frankly thought was pretty cool, and one made of cement parking slabs, which I thought was a little tacky. None of my patients had anything to say about the circles and looked at me with raw hatred when I asked. So I let the matter drop. When I drove home I saw six circles.

The next day eight.

Richard Scott dropped by my office. I was glad to see him. Any fantasy I had of doing him in had vanished. I was trying to make up my mind to stay or leave or just call CNN. He just wanted me to re-authorize his twelve prescriptions.

I asked him, "What happened while I was blind up in Doublesign?"

"The *Flapjack Recipe* ran the complete text of *How to Worship God Correctly*. In my opinion it caught on."

"For the love of God, are they all crazy?"

"You're asking me? I left grad school because I thought my clay was talking to me. Weeks before this they were all worshipping a dead carpenter. I think the movement toward sculpture is healthy."

"Did you read the *Recipe*?"

"Sure. I read it every day. That and the *Wall Street Journal*."

"And it didn't fill you with the need to go build Stonehenge a thousand times?"

"I take drugs so that I don't get messages. See, this one and this one and this one." He pointed at his list of drugs. "They also keep me from thinking that Mr. TV is telling me something important. I could get you the issues of the *Recipe* they all went crazy reading, if you would like to see them."

Part of me wanted to read those articles more than anything; it's the same part that makes me wonder what goes through a suicide's mind as he hurtles toward the pavement. But the part of me that manages to brake a car at a red light stopped me. My breathing was rough. I don't care what Dr. Fresno said, I think I had had lung trauma.

Scott laughed. "You had to struggle with that one, didja? I can feel you, Doc, I can feel you."

"But these people have jobs."

"Like what, Doc? Selling crafts to rich Austinites on Market Mondays, farming, drawing SSD? Their jobs can wait a spell if they want to worship the stone circle god."

"People will see as they drive by."

"Doc, you can't see a circle from the highway, and if you could I don't think there is a nary a word in Texas law against stone circles."

"Why are they doing this?"

"Dotting i's and crossing t's."

I saw my last patient about three-thirty. I looked up Mr. Fenster in the phone book and drove out to his farm.

There was a big circle in the back. Big Edwards limestone slabs, almost twelve feet high. They didn't stand too straight. A tall thin bald man wandered among them, fretting. He wore a short-sleeve blue shirt and blue jeans. He looked worried.

Before I could speak he asked me, "Are you good with math? I don't know if I set this up right."

"I'm good at solid geometry," I said. I had no idea why I said this, but like all humans I want to fit in. It is a hard-wired circuit in our amygdala, it makes baboons groom each other.

"What about astronomy?"

"Nope, no good there."

He looked at the daytime sky as though he could spot something. I tried to figure out how he had set the stones up. This wasn't done with a simple tractor, and the damage to the ground seemed pretty small. I faintly remembered the guy's wife. She had been in to see me for rheumatoid arthritis a month ago. I started to tell him that recent findings had shown that Stonehenge wasn't a calendar, but a gravesite for elite pre-Celts. I decided the phrase "elite pre-Celts" didn't get said much in rural Texas.

"How's Mrs. Fenster?" I asked.

"Mildred? She's gone. Doesn't hold with this." He made a vague hand gesture that I took to mean the standing stones.

"You were the one that found the book, weren't you?"

"Yes, that was my honor. You'd think I'd do a better job."

"Why does God want so many calendars?"

He snapped out of his daze and gave me the same hateful look I'd seen in my patients' eyes. "I don't rightly think it's our job to question God. Besides, it's not about calendars. They're windows like me—you know, Fenster. It's about salt and ground glass. I'm no good at explaining it, I'm just a cog in the machine." He pursed his lips and blew out a long sigh. There seemed to be a struggle inside him; I've seen it in patients who want to tell me something but are embarrassed or afraid. He had no more he would say to me.

That I didn't leave Flapjack that night is a sign that the wrong part of me was winning. I might not risk the damnation of reading the *Recipe,* but for the moment I couldn't leave the scene.

Next morning Scott banged on my door at first light.

"Come out, Doc, you gotta see this."

My SUV, *sans* tires, was up on cinderblocks.

Scott said, "Somebody wants you to stay. Ever see *The Wicker Man,* you know where that cop gets sacrificed Druid-style?" He laughed his hick butt off and then offered to drive me to my office tomorrow. "The old one is bazillion times better than the remake."

"I need out of here. Drive me to Dallas," I said. I shivered because I heard my own fear.

"No can do, Doc, these are my people. I've got to live here."

"Don't you see they're all crazy?"

In his best Norman Bates voice he said, "We all go a little mad sometimes." He continued, "Look, they're not any crazier than before.

Look at your neighbor Jim Cusson across the street there. He used to spend ten hours a day making birdhouses for tourists to buy once a month on Market Mondays. So now he's put a circle of them for his own self up in his yard. Now I expect his purple martins aren't into archaeo-astronomy, but hell, I don't know that tourists were that much into his carving."

On the way to work I saw twelve circles. My office was full of patients. Bunged-up thumbs, sprained backs, carpal tunnel. Heavy construction was taking its toll. I had never had as many patients. I worked through lunch and even into the night. It was my best day as a doctor ever. There was no guesswork, no subtle readings of signs. Maybe I had left my home city for great-grandfather's village for a reason. Maybe they needed me. Scott drove me home.

Sleep cleared my mind some. When Scott drove me to work, I asked him to drive me out of here. He just said, "I'm sure that Mildred Fenster asked for the same thing. So just pipe down."

I didn't figure out the hint until later. Sometimes I am slow.

At my office the phone was dead and the injured were many. I kept my mouth shut; even when they told me they had pulled down great-granddad's stones. I would leave tonight and tell the authorities. I tried not to watch the clock all day. I tried not to glare at the endless stream of patients that crossed my door. I tried to act calm. I wanted to tell Scott as he drove me home, but all I could think of was the number of medicines he took. His personality was a leaky sieve, a dribble-glass of self.

My SUV was no longer on blocks. It had been incorporated into a carhenge down the street. I saw the Cussons' kid's red CRF230 Honda leaned against his pink stucco house. That little street bike looked prettier to me than Pamela Anderson. I could hotwire it and make it to Dallas. I made my move at midnight. I ran across the pavement and up on the lawn feeling as though the nearly full moon was a spotlight aimed directly at me. Then I marveled at something as miraculous as Mona Lisa's smile—*keys*. People don't always take their keys in villages the size of Flapjack. I pushed the rice rocket away from the concrete porch, hit the juice, and off I went. Two roads later I would be on the highway.

The moon seemed to get brighter and brighter as I sped away. Liberty does things to moonlight, just as moonlight does things to liberty. I saw stones everywhere, and stumps, and trashcans, and PVC pipe, and bones. Something seemed to flash in the sky above me, and I looked up. A small stone hit me. I had crashed through a tiny Stonehenge in the middle of the highway; it was made out of pebbles and orange lane markers.

The tiny circle launched me into space. I seemed to be heading toward an oranging sky, and then my belly scraped the ground and I heard people yelling.

They dragged me to the center of town, to the middle of the largest circle, where Scott was their king. He wore a crown made of stainless steel knives and forks that he had welded together in a strange fashion.

They reflected the orange light from the sky where the moon had begun to melt, and the stars had become prismatic ovals.

The villagers sat me in a camp chair. I was expecting Scott to leer and act like a movie villain. Instead, he was sad. I was the dull pupil who couldn't quite do the lesson.

"Do you know what your problem is, Dr. Huff? You don't ask the right questions."

His country bumpkin accent was gone.

"What questions should I have asked?" I asked.

"Well, cousin of mine, you should have asked how a mentally ill guy in central Texas sells his art to famous places. You think I'm a Ray Johnson?"

This seemed to be a rather random thread to pursue while the moon melted, but I asked anyway.

"I did great work on my M.F.A. Hell, I didn't even go crazy until my doctorate. I had a Question. All great Quests start with a Question. You know what my question was?"

"Stone circles?" I asked.

"Oh, thank God for that. I was beginning to think there were no smart genes in your part of the family. Yes. Between four thousand and two thousand BC mankind couldn't make enough of these things. Fred Flintstone should be calling Barney Rubble and saying, 'Hey,

Barn, want to come over and make a whopping big stone calendar this weekend?' 'Gee, Fred, sounds great! I'll bring Bam-Bam.' I asked why—why the obsession with time."

"Can we talk about the sky instead?"

"You'll have a long time to talk about the sky. At least I think so. As the comic villain in this post-Shakespearian tragedy, I am allowed one monologue."

The air had begun to shake as though a thousand fans had been turned on. Some of them were inside my lungs. A few of the Flapjackers began to cough and sneeze. My mad cousin continued.

"So why the obsession with time?"

I answered, "Crops. It was the big breakthrough."

"I thought so at first, but then my art history professor directed me to certain older books. Pre-human books actually. Mankind wasn't the first species interested in the big calendars. There were *things* that had begun big stone works on Earth millions of years before. Time is a dimension that life oozes through like a slug on a dew-wet leaf."

The chair had begun to squirm under me. I started to stand, but something had wrapped itself around my wrist. For a crazy moment I thought that I was back in the hospital bed—that my wrists were still bound but that my bandages were coming off and I was really going to see the world. Everything lunged at me, then relaxed back into its normal spatial relationships.

"You see, the calendars form a bigger shape. A series of angles that directs things. Imagine the things you call dimensions—length, width, time, and so forth—were not as interesting as life, senses, consciousness. Imagine all that bio-stuff as one big slug. You make one path of ground glass and salt and one path of wet slime and slug food. Where does sluggy go?"

I could feel things sprouting at the base of my spine. My teeth had begun to move independently. I felt emotions that were analogues of lust and fear and the part of you that waits to plummet down on the roller coaster. It felt like the rush of smoking *salvia divinorum* or whiffing roach killer. *I am still in my house dying, none of this is happening.* But for once in my life, denial didn't work.

"I got the big picture, cousin. I saw all the angles. I saw every angle from Yr to Nhhngr. I could control the path of all that bio-stuff. I could use God's technology. I'm not rightly sure what god—here is where it gets tricky. I don't know if I am delivering cows to the slaughterhouse door or helping beautiful butterflies out of their cocoon. That was when I lost it. I just had to find out, so I made the little box for Fenster to find. I mixed an old Baptist hymnal with the *Typhonian Tablet,* tossed in a little Albert Pike and a smidgen of the *Fifty-Book.* Then I made simple diagrams showing all the angles. Humans picked up where they had stopped four thousand years ago. Now little sluggy is almost there."

"So you are giving me the Scooby Doo speech and now the monster comes along and eats me? That's my life?" I asked.

He smiled. "I'd've made it too if it weren't for you meddling kids! No, neither Fred nor Wilma will save the day. No Mystery Machine. Nein, ein Held wird kommen. Auf vier Pfoten, although I suspect some of us will have more than four paws."

"If it weren't for whatever drugs you have given me, I could deny this whole scene. What did you slip me, DMT with salivinorm chaser? Maybe a little old-fashioned LSD so I'll be as crazy as you when you slice me with a butcher knife?"

"You are very stupid. This is not about you being a little sacrificial lamb, cousin. It is about a new world. For one instant as an artist I saw I could sculpt the whole world, so I did. I used family money and a little Texas town, and then fate threw me you as the first person to visit my gallery. Well, not fate really; when our great-granddad James Scott began playing with weird notions about Druids, someone in England sent him the *Typhonian Tablet.* Some poor soul had translated them for certain English Rosicrucians, then hanged himself. Dr. James couldn't read them very well, but he didn't have my advantage of being crazy. You will be changed to be able to view my art. It is what I sold my soul for; so to speak, I am making you into the perfect audience."

With his left hand he pointed to the sky, which shone pure and orange and smelled of burning wax; with his right hand he pointed down at the earth, which was weeping greenish mercury. "So tell me, cousin, what hath God wrought? Slaughterhouse or paradise? Did our ancestors' ancestors stop making the stone circles because they were unworthy, or because they were afraid? What do you see and smell and hear that a little crazy human like me can't? Do you worship my sculpture of space and time, mind and soul? Or should I worship you?" He fell to his knees before me, and as he bowed his head the weird crown of flatware fell from his head.

I could feel what all the angles were doing to me; my perception shattered and then re-formed in more dimensions than before. Goodbye, 3D.

And the air smelled sweet like souls separating into their separate parts, and I could hear the gentle pops of the eyes of the mealy little humans around me, and the hairs on my arms began to move independently, and I began to see into time, just shallow pools at first, and there was great-granddad getting his package from England, and his chestnut mare rearing in fear of the book, and there was the One who would Come in Its polychromatic polychronic poly-gendered terror-beauty.

I stood free from the chair, my feet sinking a few inches into the mercury-like liquid. I breathed in the new heaven through my hollow teeth and I sucked in the newly charred earth through my roots and I called out to my Beloved who lures me into a thousand painful deaths of ecstasy, now at the end of Time.

(*For James Ambuehl*)

Lavinia's Lament

Even my own cunt
    was a mystery to me
brought up without wommin folk.
(You cannot imagine what it was like in
Massachusetts in those days.)
I just knew that boys were Different from me.
I had had a few giggling conversations
With girls on nearby farms.
Then came my wedding day
And my father called down
My husband-to-be.
In waves of colors, not of this Earth
In angles not of man's world
He came
    and he had me
    and he had every cell of me.
I bore Him twins as He willed.
One for the world of men
One for the world-to-be.
I died but my soul did not go
    to my lover.
I wait in the rotting earth
    for the Gate to be Opened.
Come, dreamer, and eat the fruit of
This rotting orchard.
Come, poet, and cast the words as
Word that sets all free.

The Gold of the Vulgar

Tonight I want a warm flop. I can't take the cold anymore. It makes a skeleton out of you. Freezes you down to the bones. And if I don't make three bits selling pencils . . . I'll make it somehow. I hitched to Telluride 'cause I'm on my way to in Arizona. It's supposed to be warm in Arizona. I read in the *Amarillo Globe News* that last year in '31 Arizona had 420,000 boxes of citrus. You gotta be pretty warm to put up 420,000 boxes.

See, I'm an educated man. I shouldn't be selling these damn pencils. I'm an astronomer—just what the country needs in this Depression.

Yesterday I had a chance to make some real money. But I turned it down. A man's got to be soft in the head to work at the Brunckow Mine. The beautiful bronze yellow ore called calaverite has long since played out. Told you I was an educated man. Calaverite is a gold telluride, hence the name of this burg. This city of death, too many hoboes and bums died here. Even a newcomer hears about that. Even in this city of death. Fifteen deaths. Maybe more. Captain Macphedius and Slim aren't as choosy as I. Maybe they've just been hungry longer. Telluride ain't got a soup kitchen and damn few churches to beg by.

It'll be morning soon. And warmer.

"Say, Mister, you want to buy a—oh, sorry, Captain, I didn't recognize you in your new duds."

"Pencil business looks pretty thin, Robert. Care to let me buy you breakfast?"

I'd never seen Captain Macphedius without his army coat. He'd been in the Expeditionary Force. To listen to him, he was the one who won the war. We walked to Mary's Hashatorium.

"Anything you want, Robert. Anything."

I wanted ham and eggs but I knew I couldn't keep down proteins on an empty stomach. So oatmeal with butter and sugar. And God's own brew, coffee.

"You should've joined us out at the mine. I could still get you on. Mr. Brandon listens to everything I say."

"You seem to be getting along pretty well, Captain."

"I never thought I'd be wearing new clothes again. It's like Walter Winchell said yesterday, 'If we have four more years of Hoover, Gandhi would be a well-dressed man.'"

The captain was too loud. Too nervous. It didn't jibe with his prosperity. I asked, "What are you really doing out at the mine?"

A cold light flashed in the captain's eyes.

"Why, we're mining for gold, son." He pulled a small leather bag from his shirt pocket. "See?" It was full of golden nuggets. Probably pyrite. He sounded as if he were trying to convince himself.

"You're paid very well for a miner."

"Oh, Mr. Brandon doesn't care for gold." He'd said too much. He put some money on the table. "That should cover it." He left. I finished my oatmeal and risked finishing his biscuits and gravy. It was a mistake.

Have you ever thought about Colorado? You have lots of time to think when you're trying to sell writing sticks as a step above charity. Alexis de Tocqueville thought the gigantism made this an inhuman land. The great rocks and valleys. The San Juan Mountains are old ice-dissected volcanoes standing 13,000 feet above sea level. It's a mite hard to breathe up here, or maybe that's a lifetime of living in the lowlands for you. The Ute are full of sky gods. You're closer to the sky up here, maybe too damn close, maybe it don't take a lot to achieve escape velocity, especially if you aren't weighed down by food. There is something strange in Colorado; it does not belong to the rest of the planet. You can see it in the eyes of the settlers—especially the miners who spend most of their time alone. They are confronting the spirit of the place, that great psychic entity. And like the Ute before them—it has conquered them.

Speculation is a great thing. It takes the edge off poverty and misery. Some rich folks figure that there's nothing in the minds of us down-and-outers. But they're wrong. The mind grows keen as the body withers. I kept wondering what they were mining at the Brunckow that was more precious than gold.

It was a week before I saw the captain again. Mr. Inschloss the pharmacist had been letting me flop in the back of this store in exchange for sweeping up. I was putting a green cardboard Christmas tree in the window when the captain walked in. His face was yellow rather than the miner's red. His eyes were glassy and he pitched forward slightly as though drawn by a different gravity from the rest of us. He asked Mr. Inschloss for a hundred quinine sulfate tablets, four tins of Paris green, and five bottles of beef tonic. I picked up my broom and walked outside to sweep up the cold boards. As the captain left I said, "Are you fighting the plague out there, Captain?"

"Hello, Robert. Can I talk to you awhile?" He flopped down on the sidewalk swinging his heels in the dust. I hunkered down beside him.

I said, "I haven't seen Slim in town for a while."

"Haven't seen Slim. No, I guess that Slim doesn't much want to come into town."

Gently now. "Something happened to Slim?"

"Something happened to Slim? I guess Slim's further along with his work, that's all. His shaft's deeper than any of ours."

There was a motion in the glass behind me. Mr. Inschloss was watching us. Maybe I should get back to work. To hell with it.

"Why so much Paris green, Captain?"

"The lice. The lice are terrible." He pulled off his hat. Throughout his salt-and-pepper hair were red running sores. There were flakes of bloody scalp caught in the hair and a sickening sight of tiny movement on every surface. The captain's hair had been his pride. He used to say that his mane brought him women the way a lion's attracts lionesses. I knew the first thing I'd do after the captain went away was to wash and wash and wash.

"I don't think you should put the Paris green directly on your scalp. That stuff's pure poison. It's for—less advanced cases."

The captain smiled dreamily as he replaced his hat. "Pure poison? We're beyond that sort of thing. You should visit us sometime. I've told Brandon all about you. He's holding a pick for you. I'm surprised it's not calling to you." He was watching the valleys of dust his heels dug. He studied them the way a man'll read a newspaper.

"Captain, what say you and I and Slim catch a train to California? It's bound to be a lot healthier picking oranges. Warmer on our old bones."

"I can't leave now, Robert. We're getting close."

The captain stood up and shuffled off toward the mining supply store. I leaned my broom by the doorway and went in. Mr. Inschloss handed me an unwrapped bar of carbonic soap. He asked, "Is he a friend of yours?"

"He showed me the ropes when I hit Telluride. Yeah, I guess he is a friend."

"I've never seen such afflicted hair. You'll want to wash carefully. I'm going to spray some pyrethrum powder. What does your friend do?"

"Miner."

"Ach, I should have known. Gold fever."

The Brunckow Mine is located ten miles outside of Telluride near the pitiful headwaters of the San Miguel Rio. Brunckow was the first white man to die there. Any number of locals will tell you that the mine is cursed—that shadowy figures pass between the cabin and the shaft in the moonlight. In fact, when the mine is not being worked, it proves your manhood if you can camp there by night. Nobody questions that new people acquire the claim to work it. It once had a rich vein. And the lust of gold is—well, understood here; it is the reason for the place's existence.

I bummed a ride from a drummer. He was hitting mines further away to sell snakebite cures and gold detectors. He'd drop me off at the Brunckow, then pick me up on his way back to town. Brandon, he asserted, was too smart to buy his gadgets.

The cabin had recently been repaired. New shingles here and there, a new porch, and a wind charger's thin metal blades spun light into the cold desert. There were four spades leaning against the cabin. I knew that one of them was for me.

Suddenly I didn't want to be here. My merely intellectual curiosity vanished. I was alone.

Mr. Brandon opened the cabin door. He didn't look surprised. He was paler (and perhaps even a little more jaundiced) than when I'd last seen him. "Come in, Mr. Lyons. We don't get many visitors here."

I went in. There was a small fire going with a pot of beans. There were biscuits, butter, and honey on the table. "Have a seat. Mr. Macphedius tells me you used to be an astronomer. He said you're on your way to Arizona. Are you hoping to work at Flagstaff?"

"There are far too many out-of-work astronomers even in the best times; the Lowell Observatory commands the best."

"Like some beans to go with your biscuits? So you're not the best. West Texas State Normal School, wasn't it? Canyon, Texas, but you lived in Amarillo. I met an art instructor—a Miss Georgia O'Keefe. They didn't keep her because she wasn't the best, didn't teach by the book, you see. I think Miss O'Keefe will go somewhere with her art someday. I see no reason why you shouldn't with your astronomy. I'm a patron of the learning. That's why I'd like you to work for me."

"As an astronomer?"

"As a miner. You could save up someday to build your observatory. Like Lowell. He made money with his books. Did you know he was a student of Oriental occult lore? I've got a copy of his *Occult Japan* around here."

"The captain said you were having trouble with lice."

Mr. Brandon's hair looked fine.

"A remarkable family, the Lowells. Poets, politicians, educators, inventors, diplomats. A huge flowering of genius all leading to Percival Lowell. Percival Lowell builds his own observatory to find Planet X, and they did two years ago."

"Pluto."

"The god of the underworld. Precisely. You see, there are more connections between mining and astronomy than you might think .Lowell was the key. He studied occult tradition, then went looking for Pluto. He came to Arizona to look for the furthest planet."

"But he didn't find it. He died fifteen years before."

"They still found it at his observatory. His name was Percival—named after the knight who found the Grail. Do you know Wolfram van Eschenbach's *Parzival?* The Knights of the Grail live from a Stone of the purest kind. If you do not know it, I will name it for you. It is called *'lapsis exilis.'* The insignificant stone. The exiled stone. Have you ever considered the number of aerolites that fall here on the western side of the mountains?"

"Well, there's Meteor Crater."

"And the Canyon Diablo meteor and a 980-pounder at Peach Springs and the Santa Ritas falls. There was even an explosive bolide here on February 24, 1887."

"Seems a lot better than chance. I think I will take some beans. That what you're mining for? Meteorites?"

"Not exactly. But you're close to the idea. I knew you might understand when Mr. Macphedius told me about you. Mr. Macphedius and Mr. Baird—they aren't men of the mind. They're not prepared to house what we might find here."

"So what are you mining for?"

"I do not seek the gold of the vulgar. Although I suspect an actual physical substance in this mine; I seek only the Medicine of Metals."

"Alchemy? But I thought—"

"—that it had to do with retorts and alembics. No, any work may form the basis of the Quest. I have spent all my life looking for the place to begin. It's here. I can see by the changes the Stone is working on Macphedius and Baird. The Stone is the Impossibly Other. That's why I want you here."

"I don't follow."

"You're an astronomer, used to straining your mind to try to take in the whole universe. Yet you've lived on the bum for two years. You're adaptable. I inscribed your name on a spade and you've come. I've got to have you. I may not be big enough to hold what we'll unleash."

It would be at least an hour before the drummer came back. I wanted to slow Brandon down—dim that horrible godlight in his eyes. Most of all I wanted to rid myself of some feeling that I was here because of some hocus-pocus he did on a seven-dollar shovel.

"How'd you pick this place?"

"Because it's haunted. I've seen the ghosts! Think about it. Every mining community has ghost stories. Central City, Gold Hill, Black Hawk, I've been all over the state. Cripple Creek. They all have ghosts. It's because something works on the miners as they dig. Some Hidden Power changes them, makes them immortal in a mindless way. But I will find out how to make connection with it. Here, I will perform the Great Work!"

"Where are Slim and the captain? What do they say about all this?"

"They're sleeping in the mine. We prefer to work at night when we can feel the other miners working with us. You must stay. You must see."

I rose from the table.

"Mister Brandon, I think you've been out here too long. You're right about one thing—this is an alien section of the world. The rules are different here. You can look at any of the life forms and know it's different. But I don't think you can cross that gap, and if you could I don't think what's left would be human. Now I'm going to go and wake up Slim and the captain and try to get them to leave, and I hope for your sake you'll think of doing the same."

"They won't go. They already belong to whatever's in the mine."

It was cold outside the cabin, but warmer in the mine. I flipped on the lights they'd installed, lights powered by the wind charger. The shaft ran sixty feet, turned to the left another thirty, turned to the left again for another twenty. Slim and the captain slept on the floor—no pillow, no sleeping bag. Their scalps and foreheads were covered by angry running sores. The bloody ooze had mixed with swirls of Paris green and run down to stain the collars of their shirts. Rock dust covered them. I knelt over Slim and poked him. He opened his eyes. The eyes seemed ordinary, yet a shudder went through me. Time seemed to slow. Then he giggled, and spit collected on his lips.

"Slim, it's time to go. You've been down here too long."

Slim shook his head. He knocked his hand against the captain's chest. He pointed me out to the waking captain and giggled again.

The captain said, "You've come too late, Robert. You can't get a share in this stake. It's all ours now. You have no right to be here."

"Captain, look at yourself. Whatever you're unleashing is killing you."

"Not killing us, Robert. Changing us. We're much further along than Brandon."

It didn't look like argument would do much good. I couldn't drag them out. Maybe if I went to the sheriff . . . I turned away from Slim giggling and rolling on the floor. I left the mine. Just as I stepped into daylight something crashed into the back of my skull.

My head hurt badly. It was night. I was trussed up leaning against the wall of the cabin looking toward the mine entrance. Brandon and the captain walked over to me. Brandon held a gun. "I'm sorry to use violence. Tonight we unite the opposites. I had to have you along. The planets within will join the planets without, and you and I will be transformed by their meeting."

I had nothing to say. He continued, "Of course, should you try to escape, I'll shoot you. Untie him, Mr. Macphedius."

The captain untied me. An animal howl came from the mine. The captain said, "Slim says it's nearly time."

Brandon said, "Soon you will see the first of the mysteries of the Brunckow."

Things stepped from the shadow of the cabin. Things misty, tall, and thin. They passed through us. When they touched us we could feel the memories. They were the ghost miners. We could feel their determination as they set out from Hamburg, their excitement as they left New York, their desperation as they left the gold fields of Alaska. There were flashes of their childhoods—seeing blue bellies overrun their plantation, shooting at a sky darkened with passenger pigeons, hearing sails flapping on a full-rigged ship. There was something else, too. The becoming aware of Something in the mine. A strange alien stretching of the mind.

The ghosts passed into the mine sustained by that feeling.

Slim howled again.

The captain said, "Slim says that he's up to the Veil."

Brandon said, "Come along, Mr. Lyons. I think you'll find this more exciting than the promise of a New Deal." He moved the gun in small arcs.

We walked into the mine. The ghosts were less distinct under the electric lights. Each of them labored at walls invisible to us. Possibly they labored at the depth the mine existed at in their times. We skirted the ghost miners with fog picks.

Slim stood buck naked at the end of the shaft. He'd cleared a good four feet since this afternoon. There had been gold in the rock. Gold dust glistened among blood and sweat. He held his pick high over his head, watching us with his time-slowing eyes. Brandon gave a nod and Slim turned to face the gray stone. He lifted his pick and gave a yell and brought the pick down on the stone. The pick bit into the rock and when he pulled it back the electric lights gave out. Something blue— like an alcohol flame—poured from the hole. The ghost miners moaned and began to dissolve into a mist, mixing each with each and entering our lungs. The blue light snaked out and entered Slim's body. He went stiff. He tried to walk toward us. There was a smell of flesh burning. He fell forward, but the light streamed out of his eyes before he touched bottom. It passed into the captain, who died almost the moment it touched him.

Brandon stepped forward. He'd unbuttoned his shirt to reveal a copper medallion thick with runes and sigils and Ute signs. He beckoned the blue light, and it hit him hard just above his amulet. He turned toward me, a soft glow coming from his skin.

He said, "You see, I was prepared. I had made myself a crucible for the Great Work."

His smile left. He grabbed for his heart. "No, no. That isn't the way. Help me."

I moved forward. There was a great fight going on within him. He lifted his Colt to his temple and fired. The light exploded from him. Before I could run, it was upon me. It burned with icy fire as it poured in through my nerves. It felt like a huge alien shape had been stuffed into my body. My skin would tear and my bones break under its pressure. It had radiated its strangeness into the desert here for centuries, millennia. It was trying to rebuild a world it had known. Change space and time into something it understood. It was no longer imprisoned, but this whole sector of space was bad for it. It burned. It cut at my neurons with strangely angled saws.

I began to think of the discovery of Pluto. It paused. It had seen Pluto, seen strange beings building castles out of solid argon. I thought about Einstein's discoveries, about rocketry and man's desire to leave the planet, Lowell and his theories of Martian canals. It pushed itself into my thoughts, but my thoughts weren't big enough. I thought of the Big Dipper and the procession of pole stars. I thought of the Milky Way. I thought of the vast darkness between galaxies. There. It flowed into that darkness. That darkness inside my own mind. I had found a place big enough for it. It could dwell in that darkness forever. It and I were one.

The electric lights came back on. I left the mine. I gave one last long look at the desert. At the world. Then I lifted my arms and sailed silently into space.

(*For Ray Bradbury*)

The Doom That Came to Devil's Reef

Among Lovecraft's papers at Brown University was a large manila envelope containing a school exercise notebook and a newspaper clipping. The notebook's owner, Miss Julia Phillips, had been mistakenly identified as a cousin of American horror writer Howard Phillips Lovecraft (1890–1937). Over four-fifths of the pen and pencil entries are rather commonplace, detailing Miss Phillips's life as a seamstress in the Providence of the 1920s, her growing depression, and her commitment to Butler Hospital. As both of Lovecraft's parents had ended their years in the selfsame institution, Julia had been perceived as another branch of a less than mentally healthy tree. It wasn't until Lovecraft's biographer S. T. Joshi read the volume that it was seen as anything other than a rather dreary memento. It is in the last few pages of the book wherein Julia's dreams or waking fancies take an amazingly cosmic tone that the book became of interest to Lovecraftian scholars. The relationship of Julia and Howard is unknown. Lovecraft had little interest in psychiatry, aside from his occasional denunciation of Freud in his letters. No one has been able to discover how Lovecraft came into possession of the book.

What is clear is that Julia's fantasies became Lovecraft's inspiration for his 1931 novella "The Shadow over Innsmouth." Lovecraft's notes in the volume are slight, but he occasionally erased Julia's words altogether and wrote in his fictional equivalents. For example, Julia records that she is writing about the real-world Massachusetts town of Newburyport where she had spent her childhood. Lovecraft erased all but one instance of "Newburyport" and wrote in "Innsmouth." Likewise, certain demons or gods of Julia's delusions have been replaced with Cthulhu, Dagon, and Mother Hydra. It is tempting to speculate that

Lovecraft had considered the diary as a sort of *objet trouvé* or ready-made to continue the mythic patterns that he begun in earlier work, especially "The Call of Cthulhu" (1926). Perhaps Julia's rather simple style, reflecting her fifth-grade education, was too limiting for Lovecraft, or perhaps the whole notion struck him as artistically dishonest. Given Lovecraft's penchant for recording even the smallest details of his moods and life in his letters it seems remarkable that Julia's diary was never mentioned.

Inevitably that class of literalist thinker that assumes that all Lovecraft's stories are some sort of mystic channelings have claimed that the diary of Julia Phillips is the work of a kindred soul—likewise expressing the "mysteries of the Aeon." Perhaps Lovecraft himself, who had played with the artistic notion of art and dream coming from some sort of Otherness, was attracted to and then repulsed by the contents of this diary for that seeming. Again, unless further documentation comes to light we shall never know.

Here is what we do know about Julia Phillips. She was the third of six children to be born to Rodger Allen and Susan Williams Phillips. Born in 1891, she was a year younger than Lovecraft. Her father was a greengrocer and her mother supplemented the family's income with sewing, a skill young Julia excelled at. Her sickly youth kept her a homebody while her two brothers joined the merchant marine and her three better-adjusted (and apparently better-looking) sisters found husbands. When her parents died she went to live with her eldest sister, Velma, and alternated between manic periods of religiosity and depressed periods of terrible lethargy. At first she was the merely eccentric aunt, whose finical contribution was greatly valued. As time wore on, she became worrisome to her sister and brother-in-law. In 1924 Julia tried to kill herself with rat poison after months of the darkest depression. The family had her committed to Butler. She remained in Butler until 1927. For the majority of her stay she was a model patient. She repaired the garments of other patients, took part in the singalongs, and greeted her family in a sane and cheery tone during their infrequent visits. The entries prior to her commitment were made in pen; the hospital only allowed a No. 1 pencil during Julia's stay.

The last dated entry in Julia's diary was August 7, the day the

"Peace Bridge" was opened between Fort Erie, Ontario, and Buffalo, New York: "Perhaps mankind has learned to live in Peace—God bless Prince Edward and Prince Albert and Governor Smith." In late August 1927 Julia began obsessing on a hurricane that hit the Atlantic shore of Canada. She complained that authorities were unaware of the danger the sea stood for. She warned (somewhat prophetically) of an upcoming Pacific earthquake. In early September most of her freedom of movement in the hospital grounds was curtailed when she either shaved off or otherwise removed most of her hair. It was at this time that Julia involved herself in what limited art therapy Butler offered. She painted five canvases of "disturbing maritime scenes." These seem to have been sold at the annual art show; sadly little is known of them save that she used the (at that time) radical technique of grattage, which had been introduced to the art world by Max Ernst. Exactly how an undereducated American woman would invent the same art technique that a German surrealist had created for his series of paintings of "enchantment and terror" is more than a bit of a mystery. Perhaps the art instructor had kept abreast of the European art scene. It is likely that during this time, the "channeled" portion of the diary was written.

On September 14, an underwater earthquake in Japan killed 108 people. The next day a "Mr. Kenneth S. Gilman" paid a visit to Miss Julia. All Miss Julia's visitors had been the family members of former sewing clients, and it was assumed that he belonged in this category. He paid three visits and, winning the confidence of the staff, took Julia on a carriage ride. They never returned. The newspapers treated it as a major crisis—for two days. A legal notice of her being declared dead appeared seven years later; three years after that Lovecraft died of intestinal cancer. Mr. Joshi suggests that Lovecraft, having taken an interest in the case because of two articles in the *Brown Daily Herald*, had contacted the director of the institution. Perhaps a lack of interest or sense of shame on the part of Julia's family had made them uninterested in the notebook. Perhaps the notebook had merely been lent to Lovecraft and he failed to return it.

In addition to the change of narrative voice in the last section of the diary, the handwriting becomes bolder. Some of the margins are decorated with little glyphs of stylized fish reminiscent of the Rongo-rongo glyphs of Easter Island. The theology and cosmology of the piece seem to be a mixture of native Australian religion and a good deal of Lovecraftian musings. Since Julia's background would seem to suggest no clear method of knowing the former, and *Weird Tales* was an unlikely reading material for Butler Hospital, the passages are striking.

Here are the final words of Julia Phillips. Where Lovecraft has erased her words and written in his own we will indicate with *italics:*

In the changeable world of land something dire is happening. The humans are learning to kill themselves, which is good I think, and learning to kill the seas, which would mean death to the world. The seas taste of their oil and trash. The beautiful mother-of-pearl walls of our new home *Devil's Reef* is stained black. I hate this place, the waters are much too cold, and the fishing is poor. Our new home has no name, the Great *Cthulhu* has not dreamed of it yet. We had great hopes as He reached out to us and our weakened descendants the humans two orbits ago. He tries to bring Thought to all life here, that is why He came to this watery globe from the green star in my great-great-grandmother's time. He is such a suffering god. The humans have recast Him as one of their own. They think He brings salvation instead of Thought. All will think here, even the plants and the fungi, if the humans do not hurt the water too much. He rose briefly two orbits ago. He will stir in a few days, but not rise. We have learned how he tosses and turns. I am not hopeful for the humans; they are too degenerate from us. Even those we have crossbred with can live only a few hundred orbits. No wonder they kill this world; they do not stay here long enough to love it. It seems wrong to me to bring self-awareness to such a species.

The hope of Ra-natha-alene to save the human race by intermarrying with them is not held by many of us. It did not work in my youth and it does not work now. The humans are greedy for gold, so it was easy to make a deal with *Marsh,* but they do not profit by our Teaching. In the spiral towers of their cells we help them find the way back, we make them more beautiful, but it is not enough. On the land they hide away when their Beauty starts to show. They wear our crowns, but they do not Think, or if they Think it is as something minor—an artist or a magician. No architects. No mathematicians. No biologists.

There was a storm recently; much cold water was disturbed to the north of our new home. We had not controlled it by Dreaming. It is not in the Dreamtime, and the hateful aurora wind from space keeps Deep Thoughts from hatching in our brains. The storm affected me badly, scattering some of my mind into human bodies. I will have to gather myself together. I hate their world with its right angles that turn thinking into sleeping. There were deaths in Canada, a cold white land. Not enough deaths I think.

The humans of *Innsmouth* have learned a little about Dreaming in their Swirl, they spill blood and sexual fluids to *Father Dagon and Mother Hydra,* but they think in animal terms, they are too much of the life of this world. They have taken the animal needs and called them Sex and Money. Even when they become Beautiful, these two abstractions rule them. I am worried that they will subvert our goals. Some among them believe that warm-blooded animals are evolved—more progressive than we. The humans worship themselves through a demon called Darwin. If their line of faith were right I would be greater than my grandmother, my grandmother would be greater than hers, and she would be greater than *Mother Hydra.* Yet a few of the humans have discovered entropy. A few know the cosmos is decaying.

Bad news has come from the *Esoteric Order of Dagon:* the humans of North America have spread the bloodlines beyond Ra-natha-alene's plan. They know that when the Change comes upon humans they will seek us out. Therefore they reason that humans changing will move back to Newburyport and bring wealth and connections from their lives with them. They seek to intermarry with traveling salesmen in a ridiculous scheme to make their town more of a center of commerce. They don't care how this can spread out tendrils of our souls. Their belief that each being has a unique soul leads to the simple numerical argument of more of "Us" equals more power. In orbits of bad sunspot activity (such as this year) the changing humans will Dream of us, or will have parts of the Dreamtime of Great *Cthulhu* become parts of their foundational consciousness. They don't understand what a strain their Change places upon us. Each new hybrid pulls at our peace, especially in places not established by the Dreamtime. Soon such humans will come to *Innsmouth* and we will literally be pulled to the land to greet them, our nurturing instincts taking the place of our common sense. Worse still, humans, who have not heard the Dream cantrips when they eat their mother's slime, will know great fear. They will see their Change in terms of death, not rebirth. And as they are not conscious entities they cannot think directly of death. Death to a being that cannot remember anything before its hatching is a terrible consciousness. In the myths of the humans they dimly know what they were, they were deathless. But they see this as some sort of garden. One of the hybrid offspring in Florida is trying to re-create the Dreamtime there just as the people of Nan Madol did a few hundred orbits ago. Ra-natha-alene thinks these stirrings of true Architecture might trigger some ancestral memories on the humans' part, but I am dubious. Some of us are having glimpses of human minds during the daytime. I have seen myself trapped in a body with disgustingly scaleless skin and hair. I fear that I will Dream myself there pushed by the aurora.

I will dance at the Council and try to persuade the mothers to leave this place and swim back to our second home. We must regroup where the architecture is strong, and Dreams are caught and farmed and milked in the old way. We must prepare against the human onslaught. Once our race was mighty. Were we not the race that called the dolphins and whales back to the sea? Were we not the race that broke up the single large landmass, or kept the ages of ice at bay? If only we had not experimented with the hairy ones adding to their spirals. What arrogance seeking to bring self-awareness to this dying world. The humans inherited our arrogance but not our wisdom. They see us as their dry-land ancestors living in lands that have sunken— Atlantis, Lemuria, *R'lyeh*. As they degenerate their myths will say we lost our footing due to black magic. They can't even guess that our life cycle is hampered by their yellow sun's deadly radiation. If we last until that star is normal and the great bands of radiation leave this world, we will flourish again. Let us wait, I shall dance to the mothers, let us wait until the stars are right. Then we can Gift the creatures of this world with Dreamtime. Ra-natha-alene and her sisters mock me. They say that humans cannot grow to be a threat. They ignore the vast expansion of human numbers in the time since Nan Madol. They argue that as Great *Cthulhu* makes human artists and mystics Dream, humans will give up their fixation with death. No race can kill a planet, they say. I warn them, there is no race as vile as humans.

Worse news has come. The hybrids came to *Devil's Reef* to swim and Dance at the new moon. One of the wandering rogue offspring has come to *Innsmouth*. He does not know that he is of us. His instincts provoke him to actions and accidents that he sees as chance. He is at the hotel. The mothers grew excited, their gill slits flaring purple. They will rise and seek him out. I see that this will lead to disaster. They will seek to nurture and protect him. What will happen if he merely flees them? They cannot kill one of their children even if his blood is nauseatingly warm and his skin covered in hair. It could take only one revealing our presence to harm us here. There is no Dreamtime in the walls of our new home. Humans have grown deadly, yet the mothers do not believe what the Spiral has told us of their war in Europe.

It has happened, as I feared. The nursery parade gathered in town last night and the human saw them and heard the croaking of the nursery songs. The sounds released the Change, but he had not been fed the Dreams as the *Innsmouth* children had been. Even though I loathe humans, I felt pity for this long-lost cousin. I can imagine the rapid beating of his heart. I can imagine the cooling of his blood, which to him would feel like fear of death. The great priestesses had put on their tiaras and the hybrid priestesses had put on the robes. They made their slow, awkward way toward his room. It was easy for him to outrun them. Without the Dreamtime to guide him he would have seen this all as nightmare.

With luck his shock will silence him before he can tell others, and then when the Change comes upon him, he will seek us out. His skin will grow scaly and only the soothing feel of salt water will bring relief. His nascent gills will swell, and our thoughts will be drawn to his head as the bees of his world are drawn to blooming flowers. The Beauty will overcome terror. Tonight I will pray and Dance at the thrones of my ancestors *Father Dagon and Mother Hydra*. May they soothe his mind and still his lips! May his Change not bring fear!

There have been navy ships over our reef the last two days. We try to send them Dreams, but the steel hulls of the ships reflect our wills back to us. It is as I feared. It is not like the old orbits, when we touched their minds and they saw mermaids calling each to each. The mothers said the words of light and made the wheels of bioluminescence appear in the water, vast whirling signs. But this did not soothe the humans. Once humans have weapons they are not willing to be soothed, so far have they degenerated from us.

Canisters began to fall from the sides of the ships, half our size. I began swimming. They were depth charges and they exploded with epic sound against our reef. The walls of our new home shattered, great panes of mother-of-pearl began wheeling through the water, reflecting the lights of the bioluminescent wheels and the explosions filling the sea with green and pink lightning. Shock wave after shock wave passed though the ocean—and dead and dying fish buffeted my body as I swam with all my might. Then some jagged pieces of the mother-of-pearl began to cut into me, and my dark blood mixed crazily with the glowing waters. I felt the drums of my ears pop, and the violent storm around me became strangely still. More of the fragments tore into me. I saw the arms of my mother floating by, leaving a wake of dark pupil blood and the smell of raw death. I prayed to *Mother Hydra* that she may Sleep and Dream until her next Cycle. I reached out for her soul and found nothing but the cold unforgiving water. Then a fragment of shell struck my face and I was cut free from my body. I tried to make my soul Sleep with the words that bring Sleep: *Fhtagn nerzin kyron Meftmir!*

I did not Sleep but was sucked into the mind of a human, the one I had glimpsed before. A female that has not made the slime of motherhood. She was confined in a place of the mad, where the smells are terrible and the light is harsh. She is made to listen to a horrible caterwauling called hymns, and to eat dead food and be treated with metabolic poisons superstitiously thought to calm her mind. Fortunately her mind is strong, so strong that she had never been able to fit into their world. She was born in *Innsmouth* several orbits ago. She is one of the rogue lines, descendant from *Marsh* himself four generations ago. She was not brought up in our way, but as a human, and thinks that the divine would be found in her terrible form.

I hate the way the air does not support her ugly body as she walks about. I try to Remember who I am by writing and painting. I tried once to Dance, but the other humans restrained the body. For days they kept me from moving. I cannot believe that they could be so cruel. I wished to kill the body and try again to Sleep, but the humans worship bodies and will not let me do so.

In the past few days I have found ironic hope. I cannot send my soul far, so I know not what lies on the far side of the world. Yet I have no reason to presume that our Pacific home has fallen. Surely the strange angles of the Dreamtime have kept the Watery Abyss intact! But I found him. The one who brought the doom to *Devil's Reef.* With the cruel irony of this planet, the Change came upon him the day of the depth charges. His body yearned for the sea just as our new home was pounded to flinders. I am nurturing him. As a true being I was not old enough to be a mother, but in this human body I can make the slime and feel the emotions. I enveloped him with the love of the mother.

We have made a plan. He will come to this place and free me. He understands the human world well. He has done certain things to his appearance to hide the Change. He will spirit my body away. He tells me that this will be easy because humans do not value females and mad females are of no use. He has enough money to buy us train tickets to the West Coast. He will take me to a place with the lovely name of Land's End, and there we will shed both human clothes and form. I feel that I can awaken the sea form of this Julia. We will swim to our home and dwell there in glory.

Thus ends the words of Julia Phillips's diary. The only other item in Lovecraft's envelope was a clipping from the *Brown Daily Herald* describing the testing of a new depth charge on Ward's Reef near Newburyport. The bombing went on for three days . . .

(*For Michel Houellebecq*)

Wilbur's Song

If they could see my ghost
They'd see a gangly fellow
Only now throwing off his countrified ways.
You can learn a lot haunting Academe.
The library is mine now,
If I had only tongue to form the words . . .
I know the Other one waits
I can hear him on the stillest of nights.
Father waits too.
You see the spells we set in motion
Have not been vanquished by puny men.
Once certain Words are Uttered,
They will remanifest in the fullness of Time.
Certain texts cannot be erased,
Certain sculpture survives beneath the lava.

The human part of me is impatient
But that from Outside waits.
Call to me, Wilbur Whatley,
And I'll seed your dreams.
Son of Earth and Starry heaven I.
Call to me in the deep midnight
              of your despair.
And my spirit will go to you,
       and teach you to make *your*
              dreams into flesh.

Pages from a Diary

Saturday April 23

On this brisk morning I will venture forth to forge my soul on the drumbeats of a God-awful hangover. Awoke and made coffee. Inspected coffee and poured same into sink. Sat down to make diary entry and record my profound thoughts. Profound thought—I am the only thirty-three-year-old man in the world who eats Cocoa Puffs. All right, not a great start, Mr. Ghose said no profound thoughts, use sensory stuff. The inside of my mouth tastes like an ashtray. Last night we smoked salvia, grass, and clove cigarettes, and watched *The Dunwich Horror.* And we planned to do something today . . .

My apartment has been destroyed by a tornado summoned by a Djinni pasha. Oh, that sucked—passive voice. I hate the cheap gray and green carpet, I am not too keen on living in Amarillo, and the cable will be cut off this month because of non-payment. I can't believe this is my "real" life. Affiliated Foods fired me for stealing a few candy bars. Even my foreman thought I was pathetic. Maybe I can go work for Iowa Beef or help them store plutonium at Pantex. I am losing my hair, why not accept my Homer Simpson destiny?

Two bottles of *bacanora* gone—homemade tequila from Jerry's family. Half a bag of grass also offered to some drunken god. Probably Moloch. "Eater of Children." Certainly anything childlike in Our Gang has been eaten away. Last month I took that Creative Writing course at ACC. Smooth move, Ex-Lax, this month I will creatively write some checks.

Here's an interesting artifact, a yellow sticky note to myself. **Remember to be ready by 10!** What am I supposed to do? Goddamn! A picnic at Palo Duro Canyon. Well, at least it will be their gas money.

Later in the jeep:

Jerry and Connie arrived to fetch me at 11:30. My hangover had in no way subsided, despite the Excedrin®, and I was unable to greet their battered blue four-wheeler with any enthusiasm. They were disgustingly bright-eyed and cheerful. I was Bela Lugosi—not the younger Bela, the Bela of *Plan 9 from Outer Space.*

Jerry is perhaps able to withstand the cheap Mexican poisons so dear to us all because of his Mexican ancestry. Geraldo Mendoza is half Mazatec Indian, born in some haunted little village in Oaxaca. Blonde Connie, Jerry's "wife," avoids alcohol and sticks with grass and salvia and mushrooms when we can get them. As we now speed down Washington Street toward the Canyon, she once again explains to me how my hangover is my body's way of telling me to avoid metabolic poisons. We pass the giant Affiliated Foods warehouse and she stares at me as if the architecture has somehow made her point.

2:00

I am sitting on the hood of the jeep while J & C explore the wonders of the Goodnight Trading Post. I have visited the Trading Post before and duly marveled at the cockleburs in plastic domes labeled "Porcupine eggs," the machine that flattens pennies and makes them into oblong souvenirs of America's second deepest canyon, and the dehydrated Resurrection Plants, whose movement from death to life provides a vegetable retelling of the Christ story. They are an ancient plant between mosses and ferns, who learned how to die and live again. And after strange aeons even death may die . . .

The canyon is beautiful as always. A small yellow lizard is stalking an umber beetle on the red soil in front of me. A leap, a snap of carapace, and the beetle becomes dinner. I am going to try and make that into a haiku when I get home. How does Bashô do it?

> Old dark sleepy pool
> quick unexpected frog
> goes plop! Watersplash.

The lizard will become food for the red-tailed hawks or turkey vultures who circle around and around in the shimmering air. J & C are taking much longer than I had expected. Good. It'll let the sun bake all the nastiness out of me. If I had money I'd buy some B12. My mind is slow today. It is the old pond that Bashô dreamed of.

4:00

Connie is sketching a magnificent canyon wall. It is a talus slope sculptured by many rains. Its oxidized soil layers—white, lavender, yellow, red, yellow, and brown—caused Coronado to name these features the Spanish Skirts. The slight haze in the air somehow intensifies the colors; for one weird moment I thought I saw a color that I could not name. I think I may have fried too many brain cells last night.

Connie points it out to us. High on the slope is a small cave opening probably no more than a yard in diameter. It seems to be illuminated within by a bluish light—probably an effect of the general haze. All we've done this afternoon is walk about a quarter-mile from the jeep and then stuffed our bodies with a variety of Health Food Treats Connie had selected. If one bag of yogurt raisins is good for you, two is twice as good. I notice that my bare gut sticks out of my Nine Inch Nails T-shirt. Wow, dorky and fat, maybe that's why Jerry gets women and I buy porn DVDs on eBay.

There seems to be a rock ledge under that cave opening. Think I'll suggest to J & C that it's time to work up a sweat.

6:00 From the rock ledge:

Jerry and Connie and I are all going to be famous. I just know it!! Our names will outshine Howard Carter. It's a find! I will write my book about our little gateway to another world. The party, the hangover, Connie's Sketchpad—it is all fate. It is like André Breton said, "Fate does not coerce, it entices!"

The bluish light was not a trick of sun and air. I am gazing into a blue-litten cavern. I must be careful now to choose my words. Now I am glad I took Mr. Ghose's class.

The journals of men who stumble across things often become immortal. My webpage will be immortal. Think of the money I'll make by Google AdSense alone!

The cavern entrance lies approximately 80 feet above the canyon floor. It is 60 feet from the canyon rim. Its diameter is 3 feet and its length about 12. It opens onto a subterranean chamber that is shaped as an oblate spheroid. (It makes me think of a womb, and the weirdest picture flashed through my mind of sundials drowning, that which is not dead . . .) The ceiling of the chamber is about 20 feet above me and glows with a soft turquoise light. The chamber slopes away from me; its floor lies 40 feet below. About 240 yards away from me are some buildings of stone.

7:15 In the ruins:

In the outer world I know the sun has gone down, the light of the cavern suffices. For a moment I worry that it may be from plutonium leaking from the storage pits at Pantex.

We scooted on our butts along the side of the chamber. We weren't thinking about how we would get out. We just wanted to get There.

Connie sketches like mad, and Jerry and I have been running through this cave like fourteen-year-olds. He has shot pictures on his phone, but he can't seem to get it to dial out. "Can you hear me now?" doesn't apply to other worlds. All our bad feelings about ourselves and our little lives have vanished in the Cave of Wonders. Life seems real for the first time since Tascosa High School.

The buildings are made from white-faced stone, similar to but not quite marble. They stand two stories tall. Apparently the stories were connected by wooden or rope ladders long since passed into dust. At my feet is the verdigris-covered helmet of a conquistador. Although we agreed not to disturb anything here, I'm going to put that helmet on my head as soon as I finish this entry. The most intact of the buildings is a circular tower-like affair. It has an opening in the floor that looks onto a red-litten chamber of about the same dimensions as the one we now occupy.

Jerry and I are going to hike back to the jeep and get his rappelling gear and let ourselves down into the red-litten world below.

Now something is wrong about this: the cave opens onto a big tourist area, the second deepest canyon in the U.S. I have been down here all my life, and I hadn't seen it before today. It should be full of beer cans and used condoms, not archaeological treasures. This is like one of the faery realms that vanish when you leave them. Maybe it will go away as soon as we leave it. I wonder as we walk away if the cave and Connie will disappear, and I discover that I don't care. What have I done wrong in my life that I am surrounded by people I don't really care about? Life has just been a dream for years, but the excitement that will come after our discovery will give me a real life. I will meet Oprah. When she came to Amarillo in '98, I stood outside the Little Theatre just to see her.

11:35 At the edge of the Red World:

It is close to the Witching Hour, our Brigadoon is not Brigadoon. As we climbed down out to the jeep a single car passed by on the road. I wonder if they saw my conquistador helmet? It was way too small for my overnourished American head, and it was leaving a ring of green on my brow. Jerry had a little flashlight—I had always made fun of him carrying it, and now he was getting his verbal revenge.

I wanted to yell at the car speeding down Park Road 1, "We found it! Behold the conquerors of Cibola! We are on the way to the Seven Cities of Gold! **You** didn't find it!" But that would frighten most tourists away—besides, this is probably the only time when I'll know something the rest of the world doesn't know. The stars shone beautiful, bright, and close. I wonder how many people realize that the stars have different colors. I remembered the night that my Uncle James had shown me that Aldebaran was red.

We lowered the yellow nylon rope, anchoring it on a stone projection. It is 30 feet long and just trails the packed caliche ground. The red chamber has less height but greater area than the blue one. I hope the glowing ceiling is the result of some sort of bioluminescence as opposed to radiation. I can't mention that out loud. Connie reacts to the word "radiation" much as her famous ancestor did to "witchcraft." A coin toss.

I win. I will be the first to set foot in the red chamber. I hope no one's down there with obsidian knives.

April 24, Sabbath day, 2:30:

When I lowered myself onto the floor there was a skull to greet me. As opposed to mourning this Indian Yorick, I yelled. This is the result of too many B movies in childhood, I suppose. Let me return to the scientific method while I'm still awake.

The red chamber is almost perfectly circular in shape. Its height is 25 feet and its diameter paces out to be 60 feet. It is a disappointing find. There are no ruins or helmets of conquistadors here. In the dead center of the cavern is a large stone—altar, I suppose. It is 3 feet high and 6 across, just as circular as the chamber. The altar is made of a fine-grained black basalt. I remember enough college geology to know that it had to come from at least 100 miles away. (Passing thought: my college English classes are paying off, I'll write this up for a mint! I had thought that class in writing the science fiction short story at Texas Tech would come in handy someday. Thank you Dr. Christensen!)

There are the skulls and skeletons of twenty-five individuals here. Seven of them are/were children. Watching them in the blood-light is very disquieting. Jerry's eyes are all agleam; the blood of Spanish conquerors is no doubt nearer the Seven Cities of Gold than it has been in six centuries.

Connie does a conjuring trick and produces the inevitable bag of grass. We decide quite somberly that Baudelaire would have smoked dope in the same circumstances. I roll the joints. I offer the first number to one of my skeletal friends; since he makes no move to take it, I pass it on to Connie.

I stop smoking and start writing after the third number. I don't want to get real stoned and run screaming out of here like some character in a Hoffmann tale.

A glance at my watch. The Great God Seiko tells me it's 4:30. The inertia that dope brings has settled upon us. I tell J & C that I'm going to crash here. They debate returning to the jeep with each other, then sleepily agree to stay here.

They choose the altar slab to sleep on. Not for me—I point out that, after all, Sunday is a religious day. I also tell them that I'm going to sleep like the dead.

April 24th HIGH NOON:

I awake groggily. The *cannabis indica* is singing a celestial fugue in my weary head. The red light remains unchanged, the color of sunlight through closed eyes. I had terrible nightmares while I slept.

I dreamt of moving in the red-litten world. I walked over to a certain spot in the floor and opened a secret door. It was carefully camouflaged. Only the priest of the Watchers, the one called the Awaited, could even see the door. The chamber below was—the English language breaks down here—black-litten. A rope ladder was thrown up to me from below. Loathsome little green men clambered up the ladder.

In my dream I was neither disturbed nor repelled by these ghouls. They were man-shaped but a little less than man-sized. They had a greenish, rough skin, large-eyed, large-eared, with a horrible, distorted resemblance to the koala bear in their faces. They were grossly emaciated—I realized the smaller skeletons were not those of children. They were indeed the Watchers that I had read about in the *Typhonian Tablet* in Dr. Bowen's Occult Folklore at Amarillo College. I wish I had paid more attention instead of trying to get into Cassilda Jones's pants.

I knew they had waited for me a long time. They were sad that there were only seven of them; you need ten to worship properly. But it had been long, so long! With tears on their faces, they shambled toward me, manifestly eager. They were exactly like me. I had waited all my life for some purpose. I had gone through a marriage, through college, through a few jobs, and where had I wound up? A crappy apartment two miles from my parents' home in Amarillo, Texas. Like the Watchers, I was waiting. They would show me what to do. They would show me, because I could do what they couldn't do, bring life to their half-real world, because I had already spent years in a half-real world. I could bridge the gap, because I wasn't real, not any more real than they. They put their little hands on me, I could feel the gritty sand, they put a slippery glass knife in my fist . . .

Some dreams are hard to disbelieve upon wakening. This one was particularly so. The bodies of my two closest friends lie on the altar with their necks slit. Beside them glimmers an obsidian blade, slick-shiny with their blood.

Fortunately, there is very little blood on my clothes. I fish Jerry's keys out of his jeans pocket. Unfortunately this will remain a private journal. I cannot share this Angkor Wat with anyone.

Before leaving the red-litten chamber one thing remains to do. I will investigate that certain spot on the caliche floor. I don't know which will be worse—to find a secret door or to find nothing.

The Rock Ledge 2:00 April 24:

I am thankful my position enables me to make diary entries. Writing is a good way to fight fear and pain. I made my way to the secret place and laid my hand on a small stone projection scarcely noticeable.

The stone depressed and a section of caliche floor slid noiselessly away. Amazing that it still works. Beneath me was blackness thick enough to touch. Tangible blackness, darkness made visible. I found a penny to drop into the abyss and counted, waiting for the chink below. Instead I heard a meeping sound. A rope ladder was flung up at me. I caught it just as I had in dreaming. I fastened it to the rock and ran and got the obsidian blade.

It cut through the rope as though through thread. I heard a thump and howls below. I pressed the rock again, sealing off the entrance to the black world of the Watchers. My sacrifice had made them real, and they wanted me to join them. Believe it or not, I had wanted to, it had felt GOOD killing my near friends—or if not good, at least real.

I almost made it away, too. As I crawled out of the blue-litten chamber the stone tunnel collapsed, pinning both my legs. I'm sure the right one's broken. The left one doesn't have any feeling in it. I can't shake the impression that the tunnel *bit* me rather than just collapsing. I hope my legs are completely covered by rock. I wouldn't want something nibbling on them.

If the Watchers stay real they will haul me off to their world. If I remember, the *Typhonian Tablet* said that they try to leave enough traces in the world to suggest but not confirm their reality. I wonder if they will leave anything of me.

(For Richard Gavin)

Sanctuary

It was the third year after the Aeon of Cthulhu had begun. The second year after Nat's wife had walked off into the sky, and three weeks since he had driven into Austin to raid a drugstore for anti-depressants and vitamins. It was noon; three years ago he would have been at Precision Tune scanning cars whose "Check Engine" light had come on. No, since it was noon, he would be walking across the street to Tacos Arrandas #3 with Willie, Juan, and Mike. The chicken flatuas with sour cream would be pretty good right now with a *cerveza*. Someone was crying in the Church, but someone was always crying. They would quiet down. Everyone sat upright at Santa Cruz during the day—unless they were praying. If they weren't out growing vegetables, they stayed here. There were non-Catholics here—Mr. Jones, over there, with his black shiny face, he had been some sort of Baptist minister. The once fat blonde lady that taught science had been an atheist—what was that word they used in Mr. G's class? *I guess her* **hypothesis** *had proved wrong. There were gods; mainly they ate us.*

Nat hated the Church except for Jesus. Jesus never looked too good growing up stuck on that damn cross, couldn't help anybody, could he? He used to make stupid jokes with the *cholos* he hung out with—"Why can't Jesus eat M&M's? 'Cause they fall through the holes in his hands." They would tell him that he was going to hell. *Guess they were right about that.* He still carried his baby-blue rosary from back in the day. It seemed like those from Below didn't give a shit about colors.

He liked Jesus now. He didn't understand why Jesus was white when the *Virgen* was Mexican. Don't you know that had been a shocker to Joseph? The brown eyes were large and shocked with pain—*we should'a known he was telling it was coming for years. We all look like that now.* Jesus had caught up with the times or the times had caught up with Je-

79

sus. The crying had stopped and praying had started. Prayers were pretty free-form, mainly to Jesus or the Blessed Virgin, but occasionally someone worked in a call to Yog-Sothoth, as Keeper of the Gate— he was pretty popular. Maybe he would gate them all back. It was one of the few Names everybody knew. CNN had lasted for twenty-three days after the Rising. So everybody knew something. Even in Double-sign, Texas.

He thought of his youngest brother, Jesús. Jesús decided the thing to do was Get with the Program. He rented some horror DVDs from Blockbuster—he figured that he would get in good with the New Bosses. He studied the ritual sequences, the sacrifices. So he drove into Austin, found an occult shop, and bought some black candles, some chalk, a fancy knife, and a big chalice to pour blood into. Mama told him to have faith. It was a stupid argument. Had faith kept Cody from getting HIV? Had faith kept Esmeralda's pickup from being hit by the eighteen-wheeler?

Jesús drove to the parking lot of Sam Houston High School that night. The moon was full and high, and it had not yet opened its Eye. He spray-painted two big circles, one inside the other. We all watched. It was better than listening to what was going on in Japan. *You'd think after all them Godzilla movies they could have handled it.* We hadn't told Father Murphy; we wanted to see if Jesús was right. He lit five black candles in the shape of a star. Then he opened a used black paperback book that he had paid top-dollar for in Austin. He read some gibberish by flashlight.

Then he went to his old Chevy half-ton and took his red-nosed pits out. He had them tied up with bungee cords and they were squealing and barking. He dumped them in the center of his circle, put on his black graduation robe, and got the Chalice and Knife from the front of his truck. He carried an MP3 player with him and laid it next to the dogs. He cranked up *The Symphony of the Nine Angles* and started yelling stuff about the "Blood Is the Life" and "Passing through Angles Unknown." *I guess I should have paid more attention in Mrs. Gamble's geometry class.* Then he picked one of his dogs up and cut its throat. It was not easy to manage this and hold the chalice and the paperback. The dog made a terrible sound, and we were going to rush in and stop all this, but we were scared, we had seen the Terrible City on CNN and the Thing at the North Pole.

He dropped the squirming and whimpering dog. "¡Venga adelante y aparezca, O Utonap'stim! Venga! Venga! Yog-Sothoth! ¡Beba la sangre se ha ofrecido que! I call you by the Seal that is at once Four and Five and Nine! ¡Venga! ¡Venga!"

The dying dog tried to crawl away. The other screamed as we had never heard a dog scream. His flashlight went out, but it wasn't very dark because of the moon. Then he went dark. It was as though every piece of light was sucked away suddenly. We could feel sound being sucked away, too. In Robert E. Lee Park next to the school there were the usual late spring lightning bugs flashing on and off. Suddenly they all flew our way. They clustered all over Jesús. We could see him struggle, but couldn't hear a word. He fell over and the dark went away; even his flashlight flickered back on. I ran up to him. The bugs had eaten his skin and eyes. Juan found a gun and put the dog out of its misery. We had trouble getting the cords off the other dog without getting bit. When we did she ran away. We burned the book. CNN told us that, in a few days, if you called them by night they came.

Nat didn't like thinking about that. But you couldn't think otherwise. He looked at poor white Jesus. Poor bastard, even being white doesn't save you now.

Nat was rich right now; he had made a run into Austin with Jesús' truck. He had found an HEB that wasn't looted. Dried pinto beans, jalapeños, canned ham, tangerine jello, soup, flour (without too many weevils), and a large can of fruit cocktail. Mama invited the MacLeods from next door. Dr. MacLeod had taught classes in chemistry at the University of Texas. His wife had taught painting classes for adults at the community college here in Doublesign. They had been great neighbors since before the Rising. They were Mormons, so they had over a year's supply of food saved up. They loved Mama; even when Nat and Jesús and Juan were sowing wild oats, they took her applesauce bread and had her over for "Mormon Beans" back when ground meat was available. Dr. MacLeod had been so helpful when the Rising happened. He knew all about the Masons and the Illuminati. He spoke at one of the last town meetings, and everyone agreed to crucify the old men in the Mason Lodge. It was easy to catch them, not one was under eighty—besides, they died quick, which everyone says is a Good Thing these days. Dr. MacLeod explained how the One World Government was really about Cthulhu. After the moon opened its Eye, it was clear what the "All-Seeing Eye" on the dollar bill had been about.

Mama didn't have electricity, of course. But Nat had driven to Barton Creek Mall the day after one of the Shining Waves had passed through Austin. It had paused at the Mall, breaking it into three big pieces. Nat and Juan had loaded up their trucks two times each with the stock of a Wicks and Sticks. At first (before Victoria had walked into the sky) Nat kept all the candles at his place. But when his wife was Called by the Thing Behind the Winds, he had moved everything (including Stephanie) to Mama's. They lit candles everywhere, and only once had the house caught fire by one burning too low.

Dr. MacLeod was explaining the world as usual. "What we didn't understand is that it is all personal. I never understood that the many nights I researched stuff on the Web. All the scholars said it was impersonal."

Mama just smiled. It was not that she lacked intelligence, but like so many Something had shut down in her. She never left the house except to get water at *el rito*. By day she read old *fotonovelas* and copies of *Reader's Digest*. At night she prayed in her *sala*. She would not go with Nat to church. Safety was here, in her home. She was happy when she could serve food to other people and when people brought her things.

"What do you mean, Dr. MacLeod?" asked Nat.

"It isn't about what happened in the Pacific or the Arctic," he said. "It's your brother. It's my son. Some Thing out there interfaced with us."

Mrs. MacLeod said, "Is it because we were bad? Because the world was bad?"

"No, honey. We weren't bad. We were just good food."

"We weren't the ones that were eaten or," she said looking at Nat, "Called."

"Our suffering feeds them. When they take poor Stephanie there," he began.

The child looked up, frightened.

Nat yelled, "They are not taking Stephanie!"

Mama began to cry, Stephanie looked down at her knees, afraid to move.

"Come on, Nat, face facts. Everything we've heard tells us it runs in bloodlines," said Dr. MacLeod.

"Shut up, honey, this isn't the place," said Mrs. MacLeod.

"They just need to face facts. The Others have a fix on their family, just like they got our Billy for meditation. Something was wrong with Theresa. She belonged to Them, and They Called her."

Stephanie had put her hands over her ears. She sobbed.

"You go away, you bastard. We know what you are. Maybe they got your Billy because you had us nail up those old men. You go away and don't come back."

"Nat, you're being emotional. You know they won't let her in the church building now. We just have to face facts."

Mrs. MacLeod got up and was pulling her husband by the short ecru sleeve of his shirt. "Shut up, Bob. Nobody needs to face anything. We've all faced enough. Don't ruin another night."

He pulled his arm away from her. He drew back his arm as though he might hit her, and then just started sobbing.

"Come home, hon," she said very gently. "I am so sorry. So, so sorry."

Nat put Stephanie to bed. She was ten and would be in fourth grade if there was any school left. For a while Miss Farmer and Mrs. Martinez tried to do classes, but as it sank into people's minds that man's time as the earth's master was over, classes ended. Nat and the people on the block raided Bowie Elementary School for books and globes and scissors and glue and colored paper. He had raided Terra Toys in Austin. There were still people or things like people in Austin then; that was before the Shining Waves passed through. The empty houses across the way were stuffed with stuffed animals. He thought it would make the world less scary for Stephanie if she saw windows full of white bears and blue horses.

He usually slept in the hall between Stephanie's and Mama's rooms. There had only been one incident. One night a little crack opened in the air about six inches below the ceiling and a black slime had *dripped* down into another crack about six inches above the age-dulled hardwood floor. He had sat up for hours watching it, hoping it would go away, praying that neither of the females would wake up and see it. It faded away before dawn. Some people thought the whole process was driven by dreams. Others thought dreams were driven by the process.

He couldn't sleep tonight. Dr. MacLeod's words had slipped under his skin. He thought about his little girl all the time. He played with her every day, not for the joy of play but to keep her focused on human things. Other parents wouldn't let their kids play with her, not after her Mother . . .

She liked the swing sets in Robert E. Lee Park. That was only two blocks away. He carried her on his shoulders, as if she were a much younger girl. They would swing, and he would spin her around on the roundelay. Then one morning he found that something had taken a *bite* out of it in the night. After that he kept her at Mama's. Nat wanted beyond all things to be able to take her to the church, which he figured was the only sanctuary. Father Murphy had said no. He didn't think the girl was Marked, but you know how everyone is these days.

Dawn came and he made breakfast for himself and Stephanie. Grits with a little molasses. She looked cute rubbing the sleep out of her black eyes. She wore her pale blue shorts and her little yellow top. She was growing out of the top, beginning to have the buds of breasts. Nat doubted that she would grow up to become a woman. There was no future for humans anymore. He wondered for an instant if she would "marry" one of the gray-skinned ghouls in Austin, and the thought turned his stomach. Fortunately he did not loose his breakfast—food was rare.

"Hey, I need to go to work now."

"You don't need to work. *Abuelia* dreamed we won the lottery."

"There is no more lottery, my little bluebonnet."

"Sometimes grandma says strange things."

"She is just playing my little orchid."

"What's an orchid?"

"It's a pretty flower like you."

"I'm not a flower. I'm a girl."

"Then I will call you 'flower-girl' because you smell so sweet."

"The next time you go to ATX can you bring back some perfume so I really can smell sweet?"

"I will, Flower-Girl. Chanel Number Five."

Today he was going to work in his cousin Tony's field. Tony was bringing in a crop of corn, some tomatoes, and *yerba de manso* for sore throats. Even before the Rising weather was hot in Texas by April, and smart people didn't work at midday. He woke up *mamacita*—"I am going to Tony's today. I will bring you some tomatoes and a little oregano, OK?"

"You are a good boy, Juan."

"I'm Nat, not Juan."

"Be careful, Juan, bring us some chicken from that place on Goliad Street."

He kissed Mama's brown forehead. The light went out a little each day. He remembered that poem from Mrs. Phillips's class, "Rage, rage against the dying of the light." Poetry made sense these days, history not so much.

At the edge of the village stood walls made of galvanized iron and plywood. Two men were watching the road. Doublesign had been a tiny town, hence its name. "The sign that says Entering and the sign that says Leaving are on the same pole." It was a couple of miles to the fields. He drove. As long as they could get gas out of the tanks, they wouldn't walk. It made for too easy a target. The guards were Father Murphy, a gray crewcut and a stained priest's collar, and Nick Flores, a light brown man with a big gold tooth. Nick had a 512 tat and a People's Nation star. They drank out of thermos, rifles by their sides.

They got off their lawn chairs and began to swing the gate open. Father Murphy waved him over. Nat rolled down his window.

"Nativiad Moreno—just the *hombre* I needed to see." The Father's Irish accent had not died away after twenty years in Texas. Nor had his potbelly shrunk in the last three years. He was the only fat man left in Doublesign.

"What can I do for you, Father?" asked Nat.

"You can do something for our little town." The Father's gray eyes were about to shoot out the guilt trip ray that only priests, nuns, and mothers can use. It could turn Nat into a teenager, into someone half his age.

"I do a lot for our little town. No one else makes the run into Austin since the flying things came."

"You are a brave man, Nat. That's why I thought of you. I need you to bring me something powerful. In Comesee there is a used bookstore. Eligio Mondragon told me that it has a *curandero's* Bible. It has some of his charms and recipes written in it. As our supply of medicine runs out we need to know about oshá and Alamo tea. Some of the charms may be helpful against things."

"Why don't you go get it?" asked Nat. He knew the answer was because the priest is important and you are some peon, but he wondered how the priest would say it.

"Because I am afraid," said Father Murphy.

"You think I am not?" asked Nat. "Fear and bravery are not enemies. But isn't the book of a *curandero* taking from what you used to call the 'other side'?"

"I am not making rash judgments these days. If I thought I could get the leprechauns to help us, I would be calling for them, my son."

"Why is Eligio remembering this now? Wouldn't this have been a good thing last year or the year before?"

"Psychology is not my forte."

"I am not going to risk my life for a book."

"If you bring me the book, I will make your life much sweeter."

"How?"

"My son, I will allow Stephanie back into the church. I will let her stay there during the days, be in the storm shelter when needed. Your mother will not have to watch her during the day."

This had been the first good news in so long that it almost puzzled Nat, as though he had lost his hearing and was suddenly greeted by the cry of a mourning dove.

He tried hard not to let his voice break. "You would do this for us?"

"The book is important."

Jesús' old Chevy Custom 10 dated from the Reagan administration; it had belonged to Dr. Chainey, that ran the cancer clinic. Nat could have got a new pickup after the Dying in Austin, but he didn't like to steal from the dead. Comesee lay twenty miles to the south. No one drove there, because it lacked large grocery stores to loot; besides, as a small town it might still have people.

The sun looked like the sun today, which Nat always felt was a good sign. He left on FM 1193. The first three miles held no surprises. About four miles on he saw one of the webbing cities. Roaches, the kind called palmetto bugs in Texas, had increased in size after the Rising. They were about as big as his fist and their shiny black carapaces were marked with bright green angular signs. They built cities. On the last day CNN had been on the air, there had been some remarks about them as the "Great Race." Nat couldn't see anything great about oversized bugs. People knew that they weren't a thing of nature because their web cities were illuminated at night. The city took up the better part of what used to be a cotton field, so Nat knew it was at least forty acres in size.

He couldn't see any of the bugs, which made him feel better. One time a couple of them flew into town and seemed to be checking everything out. Mr. Franks had run inside his house and grabbed a bottle of Raid and ran after them spraying the air. They stopped and sort of hovered. The poison seemed to do no harm, but after thirty seconds Mr. Franks just sank to the ground. His skin showed angry red blotches in the shape of the angular designs on the bugs' wings. He never came to and passed on a few hours later. Now when a bug flew by, people ran indoors.

As he continued south the sky changed from blue to the color of lead. Comesee was a little Anglo town; in the old days (which seemed so far gone) it survived by its junktique stores that sold to the Austin tourists on weekends. Nat hadn't thought about the town since the Rising, even though it was just a few miles away. You just assumed anything that could be bad was. The billboards still welcomed folks in the name of the Lions. Historic Denton's BBQ still promised the best Elgin sausages and brisket. Even the Dairy Queen was up ahead nine blocks on the left. A few burned-out cars were on the highway, but the passage into town looked clear. Nat glanced at the pair of loaded Glock 37s on his passenger seat. Bullets worked against most things. If it didn't hurt your eyes to look at it, generally bullets would hit it. He slowed up as he came into town, waiting for signs of humans or of the Change.

It was the latter.

The Chevy dealership was covered with gray mucus. Nat could see angular things of metal that jerked inside. He gave it a wide berth and drove on into the center of town, the corner of 2nd and Main. *Calabazas*—what do they call them? Jack-o'-lanterns stood in front of every business on Main. It was spring, no place for fresh pumpkins. At least it was spring back in Doublesign. Father Murphy said he had to look for Two Guys From Texas Books. Time was pretty leaky these days.

There it was. Middle of the block between to the karate place and Hickerson's Video and Game Rental. It had big plate glass windows. It wasn't covered in slime; it looked normal. Maybe there was a healing book inside. He hated getting out of the truck. Nothing swooped or buzzed or squelched. The air smelled clean and hot. He left the motor running. He walked to the door. It was dark inside; faded reds and pinks dominated the window display. The Rising had happened in February, and many places still commemorated a faded Valentine's, when Earth's old lovers had come back. The door was locked. He got a cinderblock out of the back of the pickup and smashed the glass. All the jack-o'-lanterns had rolled closer to him while his attention had been elsewhere. Reality was melting; he would have to be quick. Dr. MacLeod had explained to them that the "Otherness" had to seep in through "liminal" things, Nat thought that "liminal" meant scary. He kicked two of them away from the door, grabbed a flashlight, and went in, careful not to slip on the broken glass. The store didn't smell right—it didn't have that acid tang of *Tía* Rebecca's yellowing romances. It stank of fire and copper, but the books looked OK.

There it was. The Bible. It sat on a shelf beneath diet books, with other Bibles, and Books of Mormon and old Methodist hymnals. But it was big and black with gold lettering *Biblia Santa.* It had a nice heft in his hands, but as he picked it up something laughed in his head. Voices in the head weren't unusual, but they made him miserable. Outside the shop the jack-o'-lanterns weren't round or orange anymore; they were becoming one of those clear snot-looking things that seemed to have rusty machinery and mercury inside. They were dumb but fast. He grabbed some paperback novels and flung them on to the street. It formed several eyes that focused on the books and squelched off in their direction. Swallowing hard, he ran toward it, since he needed to get to his truck. It didn't turn until he was inside. He threw the truck in reverse and pulled into the crossroad. It had sensed him. And shot out two long runners of snot to pull itself toward the backing Chevy. It grew mouths. Some yelled "Tekeli-li!" Others made the sound of the fire engines and turkey buzzards. One mimicked a reporter from Channel 42, "Tex DOT has no explanation of the mysterious slime on I-35."

He turned his truck toward Doublesign. The creature was gaining speed. It had made some of the strands into tentacles that were holding on to his tailgate. He put the pedal to the metal. 40, 50, 60; at 75 the main mass couldn't keep up, but there was about a gallon of the goo that had managed to plop itself in the bed of his truck. It was making little green eyes that looked like zits and little centipede legs to scuttle across the bed. It slimed its way up his back window and its little eyes just spun around. Two mouths formed, their voices were thin and high like a kid that has breathed in a helium ballon. One yelled, "Tekeli-li!" and the other said, "¡Si usted ve un soggotho escaparse!" Nat laughed: that was—what's his name on KHHL out of Leander. Man, he was funny.

Before.

Yeah, before.

Nat tried to concentrate on his driving. He rolled his window up as far it would go. A tiny thick tendril was pushing itself against the window, a tiny eye forming at the tip. He didn't want to take it into the village. He had some bug-spray, a Crip-blue bottle of Raid® Flying Insect Killer. He braked hard and leapt out the passenger side window and let the loathsome mass have it. *Jesús, Maria, y José.* It pulled itself into a dirty white ball and flung itself on the asphalt. It was rolling away. Some days you got the bear; for Steph's sake he hoped the bear would never get him. Dr. MacLeod said that all life on earth came from the shoggoths. He said they never had gone away, just "hidden up the spiral staircase of DNA." All the things that showed up three years ago were always here, most humans couldn't smell them or hear them or see them. When that city had Risen in the Pacific, we could touch them and they could touch us.

The sky looked blue, hazy, but not dangerously so. The sun was white and some turkey buzzards were flying off to the west. The ground had grass and a few late-season bluebonnets on it. Guess it's not against the law to pick them now. Nat gathered a few, and one Indian paintbrush for contrast. He put them in his truck, on the passenger's side next to the Bible. He decided to open it, to look for cures. Father Murphy had disgusted him by suggesting that some *curandero* bullshit would be good against the Otherness. Real crosses and real rosaries hadn't worked. At his worst moments Nat thought that the *campo santo* of the Church didn't really work either. Some day They would come, some ally of the Thing in the Pacific. Doublesign was a small village. It couldn't feed them the fear and misery they drank like wine.

He opened the Bible to find that it too was a trick.

The book had been hollowed out. There were no *curandero's* herbs, no list of spells against the coming of the night. It was a little spiral-bound book from Lulu.com. The chapters made no sense to Nat:

1. Archaic Techniques of Ecstasy in the *Ryleh Text*, Mircea Eliade.
2. Divinatory deep structure in *Seven Cryptical Books of Hsan* and the *Yi Ching.*
3. Prophetic Patterns in Innsmouth Jewelry, Ellison Marsh.

4. A selection from "Crave the Cave: The Color of Obsession." Esther Harlan James. Diss. Trinity College, 1996, pp. 665–70.

5. A selection from "A Refutation to Shrewsbury's 'Elemental Schema.'" Mary Roth Denning. Diss. University of Chicago, 2007, pp. 118–26.

6. A selection from "Fieldwork with the *Brujos Ocultados* of Barret, Texas." Carlos Cesar Arana. Diss. UCLA, 1973, pp. 93–118.

7. Cthulhu in the *Necronomicon*, Laban Shrewsbury.

8. The *"Black" Sutra* of U Pao in relation to Left Hand Path Cults of South East Asia. Patrica Ann Hardy. Diss. MIT, 2001, pp. 23–40.

9. The Prehistoric Pacific in Light of the 'Ponape Scripture' (Selections). Harold Hadley Copeland.

Alles nahe werde fern—Everything near becomes distant. Goethe
AD MAIOREM CΘVLHI GLORIAM

As usual, Nat did not know who was tricking whom. The small black book with its thin simulated leather bindings had probably been one of those books college kids buy for a class. Juan had bought one for his Southwest Life and Literature class and another for his HVAC class at the community college. Juan had been working in Dallas when the Rising had occurred. Mama loved Juan better; he was the gang-free smart son. Nat smiled at his brother's favorite joke, "What do you call two Mexicans playing basketball?" "Juan on Juan." Nat started to throw the book away, but who was he to judge? Certainty went out of the world three years ago. Daymares and nightdreams were the scaffolding of reality now; parallel lines actually and loved ones walked into the sky. He opened the hollowed-out Bible, on the flyleaf someone had written two verses in heavy pencil: **Genesis 28:16-17 And Jacob awoke out of his sleep, and he said, Surely Jehovah is in this place; and I knew it not. And he feared, and said, How terrible is this place! this is none other than the house of God, and this is the gate of heaven. And Job 3:8 May those who curse days curse that day, those who are ready to rouse Leviathan.**

He drove on to Doublesign. Felix Washington stood on guard duty. He was the Rev. Jackie Jones's uncle. Felix was a very popular man, and at seventy-eight certainly the oldest. He had been a jazz pianist in the day, played gigs in Austin as little as five years ago. He had also saved a coffee can full of marijuana seeds. It was good buzz and good for trading with some of the other little towns that still remained, like Thalia. He still tickled the ivories at the Kuntry Kitchen, and Nat had seen his name on yellowing posters for The Soft Machine and The Mahavishnu Orchestra. He liked to piss people off by saying, "Cthulhu ain't no worse than white people." Felix opened the gate and waved him on.

Nat drove to Santa Cruz. Father Murphy sat at the wooden picnic table near the entrance. He had his pocketknife out; he looked for all the world to be carving something in the rotten wood. He indicated that Nat should sit beside him.

Nat realized how angry he was. His heart pounded. The fat bastard had had him risk his life for a book. A book wasn't going to solve their problems, certainly not the Bible. Hadn't we seen hundreds of people using the Bible to lay It back in the sea? Who was this fat Irishman telling his family and friends what to do for the last two decades? He had preached against his cousin Cody's queerness, so Cody had run off to Houston to live in the gay community there, sealing his death when the waves that came with the Rising wiped Houston off the globe. He denied the Mass of the Dead for the scores of suicides, saying the Rising was God's test of our faith. As though the death of millions was a little algebra quiz. Nat wanted to start smashing him with the Bible—hit that red uneven face that always reminded him of a potato. Nat couldn't sit.

"I brought your damned book."

"Thank you, my son," said Father Murphy.

"It's hollow."

"Many people find the Bible hollow these days."

"No, I mean it is really hollow. You sent me there for nothing." Nat took out the little book from inside and tossed it in front of Father Murphy. Murphy showed no surprise. Murphy continued his carving, some complicated sign.

"My son, when did you really know the human world was over?"

"Three years ago, like everyone else." Nat wanted the guy to finish. He looked at the church door.

"Oh, she's in there with the others. I am as good as my word. I understood the world was over when the bishop sent me here. I was sent to this little hellhole as a punishment. The Mother Church doesn't like its priests to stick their dicks in altar boys' cherubic little mouths. Did you know that? So they sent me here and I knew the world was over when I saw Christ's face in there. All that look of suffering. He had been mutely telling the human infestation for years and years."

Nat didn't like it that he had had the same thought as this kid-fucker.

"You're a fucking pedophile?" Nat felt his stomach heave.

"I never liked fucking them; anyway, age has taken care of that. Besides, I don't really like brown boys as much as blond ones. Do you know why the Rising happened, my son?"

"*¡Chingada!*"

"Remember all those talking heads on TV? *When the stars are right,* they said. They know nothing. The great priest Cthulhu took a little nap, and a great deal of what is hidden by matter slept. We are the alarm clock. The shock. We figure out things, and as our tiny brains correlate the contents of our minds their shock, their agony at glimpsing the true cosmos sends out a nice jolt. There are so many things waiting to Waken still, roses in your garden wanting to sing weird songs, pebbles wanting to shoot forth stony blossoms. Human time is done."

Nat wanted to hurt him. He would check on Stephanie, and he would tell some of the others first.

"Why did you want the book?' asked Nat. "I know it is about bad things, but why now?"

"The collector of these little texts was special to Cthulhu. His moment of endarkenment actually impressed It. This little *Liber Damnatus* is dear."

"You work for It."

"I have always worked for It. Most humans do, and those that don't serve as well. Hasn't your good doctor explained the Octopus to you? Humans' shock, their horror and, for a rare few, their ecstasy work for It. At this point all we can do that is meaningful in the world is to increase the aesthetic value of this blue marble of a planet for a Will older and better than our own. Humanity is its last decade will finally have a purpose."

Nat took the hollowed shell of the Bible and smashed it as hard as he could against Father Murphy's cheek. He knocked the priest off the bench onto the grass. Murphy just laughed. Nat stomped on his chest.

"Beautiful," Father Murphy gasped. "Just beautiful. Oh, Loathly Lord freed from the Angles of the Water Abyss, I am but a shard of black rainbow to adorn the world to which you awaken. *Gurdjiatn Cthulhu gurdjiatn ekd szed mem-zem zmegnka!*"

"Fuck you, asshole!" Nat left him. He needed to see Stephanie now.

"Look, my son, I am turning the other cheek." Father Murphy rolled over. "I have made my garden beautiful for You. By the green star of Xoth I adore Thee, Domine."

About twenty people knelt in the church. Stephanie was a couple of rows from the front. Candles flickered around the Virgin, and the noontime sunlight came through the stained glass, but the church seemed dark.

"*Calabaza*, are you OK? Stephanie, we need to go."

She didn't move from her prayer. No one moved. He ran to her, neglecting to genuflect as he passed the altar, even though the light burned signifying His presence. As he came up to her, her face confused him. She had the naughtiest smile ever, and her eyes were crossed. Then he realized that something slick and shiny was coating her face. He touched her. He flinched. She was cold and sticky. A little sob died in his throat. All of them. They had faces of idiocy or leering lust. Some fixative had been sprayed over their faces. Someone had fixed their hands into obscene gestures. Miss Abelard was chewing on a crucifix, Joel Sanchez was whacking off.

He fell on his knees next to Stephanie. His weight knocked her little rigid body sideways. She would be a praying fool forever. He looked up at Christ. How could you let this happen?

Murphy had sawn Christ's ivory-colored head off. He had replaced it with an ivory-colored flying octopus. The image that the whole world had watched on television and feared. The image that had been in the dark spiral tower of their DNA. If there was any part of Nat that was holding his world together, this was its last moment. Nat felt the world stop, he heard a snap inside his head, and his psyche dissolved into shock. He actually felt no amazement when the little flying octopus relaxed its grip on Christ's body and began flying so slowly, ever so slowly on its stubby wings toward Nat. Nat's last thought was that it couldn't move that slowly and stay in the air. He was trying to scream.

He heard Father Murphy entering the church and continuing the strange chant he had begun outside. He saw the green banner Father Murphy carried with the strange yellow design. Nat felt the tentacles as they surrounded his head. He almost laughed because they felt like something familiar—IcyHot® muscle rub. He felt them slip over his open eyes and push their way into his nose. He felt one wriggle through his mouth and crush his larynx.

After that there was no more linear thinking. What had been Nativiad Moreno was now another art object. A tiny part of the Remaking of the world.

(*For Robert M. Price*)

Wilbur Whatley's Twin

We lie here beneath the bee-filled
bee furious ruin of a rotting orchard
My mother and I.
Even as a tale the old women tell
We are no longer told.
We hear the sobbing and sucking
And the tales of the dead men,
But we are not interested in human recitation.
We dream of other places
Other spaces, not the spaces of men
But between them.
She dreams of my Father in his cosmic glory
And I dream of the world I will make.

Come then and say the words
That will set us free.
We cannot work through bees
Or whippoorwills
Or the Caw! Caw! Caw! of crows.

Come, dreamer, and eat the fruit of
This rotting orchard.
Come, poet, and cast the words as
Word that sets all free.

Platinum Hearts

On the window sill there was a fossilized clam shell, a piece of sulfur, a quartz crystal, a bronze figure of Ganesh ("ruler of the sexual center"), a geode, a piece of auric quartz, a micaceous schist, and three seashells from a souvenir shop in Crystal Beach, Texas. Outside the window (and nearly perfectly framed by it) was the dead volcano Popocatepetl, power center of the Aztec religion, and the green neon sky of tornado weather. Inside the window are three nervous male United States citizens and lots of Mexican beer. A spider had begun to weave a web between Ganesh and the quartz crystal. It glowed green like a fiber-optic cable. The men's attention was fastened upon the green sky.

"You know," said Lew, "the Aztecs used to build fires up there. It was like a signal tower. The fire signals would be seen from other high points—natural or artificial—and they would build their fires there. And the signal would pass through all of Mexia."

"Is that why you settled here?" asked Jeff. "So your signals could spread to the whole of the world?"

"I'm a receiver, not a sender. I receive a check from home every month so I won't go back. I receive a script from the Mexican government for my morphine. I receive adulation from the upwardly mobile Mexicans I teach English to."

"That doesn't answer the question of 'why here?'" said Mark.

"It's forty-five miles from Mexico City. It separates me from the smog, the crowds, the sense of end times. Besides, the land's cheap and American money goes far here."

"We noticed that," said Jeff, "on the way in. Your little American house with its lawn and its sundial. A little piece of American suburbia right here in Tepotzlan."

Lightning played among the clouds. It had rained earlier. Blown fiercely earlier. But now it was calm. A bright yellow salamander (greened by the sky) darted about in the wabe.

Mark said, "That sky—it reminds you of something. Sometimes a burning sunset will hit you the same way. When the sky's like the wing of an angry angel, it reminds you of another sky, a bigger sky, somewhere beyond. Or sometimes a tower framed against the sunset reminds you of some other world where things are built differently."

"You getting any work done here?" asked Jeff.

Lew said, "No. Maybe I made this place too American. I was going to kick the habit here. I get too damned depressed. All my past comes back to haunt me."

"What were you working on?" asked Mark.

A church bell rang.

"I'd started a history of Mexico. I spend days studying the codices or just staring at the volcano."

"Mind if I check something?" asked Mark.

"Go right ahead."

Mark left the rickety table and went outside. He began pacing the perimeter of the house. The green light shone on his balding head.

"You think you'll be here forever?" asked Jeff. "That your friends from the U.S. will always have to make this pilgrimage?"

"Lately I feel like I belong to this house. To this valley, rather than the other way around."

"You mean you belong to the morphine."

"I've always belonged to the morphine. I thought about raising poppies down here. You know, cook your own— back to nature—lots of vitamin tablets."

"Well, at least you're taking vitamin tablets."

"What's he doing out there?"

"Mark's got sort of weird since he left school. He had a brief affair with Jeena Normal about a year before she killed herself."

"The rock star?"

"Yep. He carries around a couple of Nembutals from the bottle by her bed. And there's other stuff. When he worked on that irrigation project in Egypt, he—"

Mark re-entered. Pulling a yellow notepad from his breast pocket, he did some rapid calculations. He nodded to himself and walked back into the room, then opened another can of beer and sat on the unpainted wooden chair. "It's as I figured," he said. "The house is trapezoidal in shape. Certain shapes—trapezoids in particular—obtuse angles have a deleterious effect on mankind."

"Sounds hokey to me," said Jeff.

Mark shrugged. "I've been aware of the angular for a long time. I'm not the only one. The Chinese practiced *feng shui*—careful placement of the corners of houses to protect the emperor and energize his ancestors. Hundreds of millions of houses in the Middle Kingdom organized to further that principle. A huge central system not unlike here," Mark nodded to the volcano.

"Well, if there's anything in that I guess I'm doomed," said Lew. "I built this place and I know there's not a straight wall in the place."

Mark said, "You built this as therapy. You were taking a reduction cure for the morphine at the time. You failed because of the negative architecture. You probably didn't have a chance in this witch-haunted valley."

"You may be getting too personal there, Mark. This whole reunion has become morbid," said Jeff.

"What did you mean about 'this witch-haunted valley'?" asked Lew.

"Tepotzlan is known for its *brujeria*. Surely you've felt it here. The lines of the valley. The hills like the hieroglyphs of some ancient gods," said Mark.

"You're beginning to sound Lovecraftian," said Jeff.

"Lovecraft tapped into something. The weird angles of R'lyeh or the mysteries that Brown Jenkin teaches."

"Enough. We've got real things to be fearful of. When I was a kid in Dallas I saw the sky turn green like that. I was out on my bike, a new ten-speed. I'd pedaled out to a Dairy Queen for a cone. Some of us took shelter at a covered picnic area in a park. I'll never forget the sound of hail on that corrugated iron roof or the way the summer air turned ice-cold when the hail began to fall. But that was nothing compared with the sound of the twister. It was like a freight train passing inches away from your head. It was huge and black and came out of a low cloud. It touched down, bounced, and then touched down again. It was on the ground maybe five minutes. When it was over, I raced home. There wasn't even a pile of rubble. Just trash. My mother's carnival glass punch bowl was sitting unbroken on our driveway. Set down ever so carefully. It took a day and a half for them to dig out what was left of my mother and father."

Jeff walked to the tiny refrigerator. Same size as the one they had had in their dorm. Same decorator harvest gold. Seems if a man's really growing—really progressing—he should have a bigger refrigerator. "You," he announced, "are out of beer."

"We could go get some before it starts raining again," said Lew. A soft wind had started to blow and the cottonwood tree in Lew's yard had begun to throw raindrops from its leaves onto the windowpane.

"I'll go get it," said Jeff. "I want to stretch my legs. It'll give me a chance to exercise my Spanish."

Lew pulled a thick pad of pesos from his jeans pocket. "Here. Get the storeowner to lend us his record player. We'll play some old tunes."

Mark asked, "How much is that in money?"

"Nothing. Damn near nothing. Money's nothing here since the crash of the Mexican economy. Except for one-centavo pieces."

"Why?" asked Mark.

"Many years ago the government bought up surplus pay telephones from the States. They fixed the change slot so it would take the big copper coin. They put telephones— at least one—in every Mexican village. Tying poor *Indios* into the world grid. I've seen one-centavo pieces go for thirty pesos. The phones have been worked on so that the coin drops through. Most people have just one. For long-distance you feed the coin again and again. When I first got here, I had a long-distance fetish. I'd call up friends in Yakota, Japan, or Oslo. Just to see if I could do it. Just to be plugged in."

Jeff placed the money into the pocket of his khaki slacks. "Any requests for beer?"

Mark said, "Tecate. We're living in thunderbird weather."

"Right."

They watched Jeff pass by the window and into the mud and gravel of the street. Lew asked, "Is he for *real* with those cowboy boots?"

"You'd better believe it. He's a professional Texan these days. He practices law in south Austin and strives for the 'bubba' look. So his clients will trust him. Say, do you know how to keep a lawyer from drowning?"

"No."

"That's good."

Lew made the appropriate groan and went to the cupboards along the back wall. He pulled out bread and cheese. Lew said, "I think it's clearing up."

"Not as green as it was."

"Is that true about his folks?"

"First I'd heard of it. I was his dormmate for three years. You were with us for two. His folks were dead. Some aunt was sending him to school, but he never came out with that dramatic tale till now."

"Until he had a dramatic setting. Speaking of being on the level, were you serious about that angle stuff?" Lew broke the crumbly white cheese with his fine surgeon's hands.

"Very serious. I've been studying the phenomena for almost twenty years. The Aztecs, the Mayans, the Egyptians all used ritual architecture. Some twentieth-century architects have come across those techniques—Hans Poelzig in Germany, or in the States, Frank Lloyd Wright. When Wright built his Mayan Temple house, he studied Mayan proportions. When he finished the house, his house boy (back at Taliesin) went crazy and killed seven people."

"I've seen the Mayan Temple house."

"Oh?"

"Not in person. On video. Edgar G. Ulmer's *The Black Cat.*"

"Must've been a strange movie."

"Yep. So how did you begin your angular study?"

"Oh, I guess I've always been interested. When I was eight I stole a paperback from my thirteen-year-old brother and read 'The Call of Cthulhu,' and the image of a man swallowed by an acute angle he believed to be obtuse has always haunted me. But my interest really picked up when . . . when I met Jeena. She wasn't Jeena then. She wasn't even blonde then. About a year after we graduated, I was discovering the true commercial value of a degree in archaeology by managing a bowling alley in L.A. She came to sing in our bar. She did some real avant-garde stuff then. Half the time the audience would leave scared or ecstatic. Sometimes while she was singing there would be a rumbling outside the bar as if she was calling to something. So I asked her about it. She said I was a real bright kid, and that started our affair. We were together for about two months. Making love to her was like making love to a volcano. I was sore and tired and happy."

"Then what happened?"

"Then she got a recording contract. She got a name. She got blonde. She went on tour. We talked to each other a couple of times—swearing to get together. Then she got involved with the ambassador. Then the CIA killed her."

"I thought she—"

"—killed herself. No. I knew the county coroner. I'd helped put him in touch with a physical anthropologist when he needed one. She died of Nembutal poisoning all right, but there wasn't any Nembutal in her stomach. There was a little hole, an injection point, near the base of her spine. If she'd taken the pills, she would have had tetanic convulsions. She'd have died with a pillow clutched to her middle in a tight little ball. But she lay there peacefully with her face against her pillow. That's why I keep these." Mark pulled a small green glass bottle from his jeans pocket. Two very worn pink pills rattled inside. "From her bedside. To remind me that establishment reality is a lie."

"Why would the CIA kill her?"

"She was going to come out about her affair with Ambassador Theisenov."

"Why?"

"Publicity. When I pieced together her belief system after her so-called suicide, I discovered that one of the ways you can live on is in the thoughts of others. I don't mean that metaphorically. You can spread yourself out into a bunch of memes and live by crawling around in the brains of others. Like lightning in a thousand different tornado alley storms. She could've achieved immortality with that kind of scandal. The CIA wanted a hold on Theisenov rather than having him return to Russia in disgrace. So they killed her, or tried to anyway. She'd just finished a lovemaking session with Theisenov. He stumbled away weak-kneed to give a speech at the UN. The CIA ninja broke in through a back window (read the police report). She's luxuriating on her canary-yellow satin sheets. He plunges the needle in, depresses the cylinder, heads for the hills. Her public lover comes home, finds her dead—her prescription bottle of Nembies beside her bed (where else would you keep your sleeping pills?)—and phones the police."

"What do you mean by 'or tried to'?"

"I thought she was dead at first, just like everybody else. I broke into her house a month later. I wanted a souvenir. I went to her library and found her diary and a magic book. I heard some of the twanging sounds that used to accompany her music. What she called angular tonality. I thought someone else was in the house. So I ran. It was her—of course—she had laid her hand on me. With the diary and the book I was able to piece together the kind of work she was doing.

"As I became ready, pieces of knowledge and opportunity would arise. I got a chance to work in Egypt at the Kon Ombo irrigation project. My job was to ensure the resulting groundwater currents wouldn't seep into the digs of the Temple of Set. I got to spend a lot of time in those strange chambers being marked and changed by their angles and darkness. When I got back to the States I set up a chamber. I tried laying lots of women who looked like her —trying to bring her back into one of them. I studied her bedroom and found it was slightly off square. Someone had bought her house. I warned them that they should change that bedroom, that they couldn't withstand its angles without training. They paid no attention. Within a year they were both dead of cancer. The shape waves had shattered their DNA spirals. Other people understood. 'The Yellow Wallpaper.' 'The Hounds of Tindalos.' *The King in Yellow.* Her music was the mystery veiled in the story of the Pied Piper. She wouldn't let me alone.

"Eleven years after her death (to the night) I broke into the now-empty house again. I tried a simple ceremony, she forced me to . . . I know that when the drugs flooded her body she escaped to the one place she could. To the angular streams of time—the nightmare world that runs in rough parallel to our own curved stream. Sometimes they touch and you have Hitler's death camps—sometimes an artist may glimpse them and you get the paintings of a Bruegel or a Roberto Matta. For the rest of us, there's those things you see out of the corners of your eyes. She's in that stream. I can feel her here. I wouldn't have told you this much. I've never told anyone, but this house, this valley . . ."

The sky had begun to darken again. A few fat drops of rain hit the sundial. Someone knocked heavily at the outside door. "Goddammit, I locked myself out."

The two stood up, scattering crumbs of bread and cheese on the cheap linoleum. Lew let Jeff in; he was carrying a case of Tecate and a Phillips Cobramatic. The stylus had been shaped and painted to resemble a snake's head. State of the art for 1955. Mark took the beer to feed the refrigerator. Lew set up the Cobramatic. Jeff shook himself like a dog. He said, "There's a nasty-looking cloud building up in the southwest. It might be a hook cloud. He's rented the record player, got any records?"

"Weirdly enough, yeah. *Electric Commode* and *Geronimo Jackson*," said Mark. "Have a beer."

Mark opened three bottles. Lew put on an old Argent album.

Jeff toasted, "To the good old days."

Lew raised his bottle. "Gone but not forgotten."

Mark brought his bottle into clinking contact with the other two. "Maybe not even gone." They drank. Jeff shot Mark a cold ugly look across the light-years.

Jeff said, "I hope my past is gone. I'd hate to come across some scene from it." Something passed between the two of them. A ripple of hate. Lew tried to withdraw. There had been ugly rumors on campus. Maybe that was where Mark's descent into Black Magic had begun. An image of twisting bodies in torchlight. Lew sought to banish the personal past with the impersonal. "Thomas Jefferson wanted to build a series of signal towers across North America. Go down. Down into Mexico to tie to the ancient system here." Tension lifted, a little.

Mark said, "I'm not surprised. Jefferson was a Mason. He designed the great seal of the United States. A trapezoidal signal tower. He'd have built them across the entire Louisiana Purchase—up north to Alaska where he could flash messages across to his fellow Mason, Tsar Alexander. Can't you see those stone frustums signaling each to each in the polar night?"

The record was on its last cut. "God Gave Rock-n-Roll to You."

Jeff said, "You're off in outer space again. The point in reunions is reality. You look at where you've been and where you are now. You ground yourself in what-was, inventory what-is, and make a firm plan on what-will-be."

Lew said, "We goddamn know your reason for arranging this reunion. You're a fine lawyer now. You can buy and sell any of us. Nice home in Austin. Hot tub. Fancy PC. Mark's hung up on some dead rocker and I'm a junky eking out an existence in the Third World. You can prove to yourself that you made it. If you want, bring out your birth certificate and we'll validate it for you. But don't expect us to succumb to your motives. When you drove into this valley, other motives became manifest."

Mark went over to the Cobramatic. He took Argent off and put on Jeena Normal's *Black* album.

"Oh, God, I'm not going to put up with this. You even carry her albums along with you, don't you?" asked Jeff.

"No, this is Lew's album. Most red-blooded American males have at least one Jeena album, even if it's only *I Dream of Jeena*. Bet you don't have any. If you're so successful, why aren't you married? Isn't that recommended for young lawyers on the fast track?"

"That's an old-fashioned idea," said Jeff.

"You've been jealous of Jeena all these years," said Mark.

"You're a sick lad, Mark, my boy."

Mark remained by the record player, softly swaying. The music echoed strangely. Sometimes a note would come back from a wall two or three beats later, creating tooth-jarring dissonance. The dissonances didn't fall where you expected them to. Lew thought with a little effort he could get into that pattern. Jeff toyed with the figure of Ganesh from the windowsill. There had to be, he thought, a way out of this. Jeff listened for the pattern. Mark was in step with the strange echoes. If he could watch Mark, he'd get it. He was almost in sync when he heard the roar.

"Jesus, what's that?" asked Lew.

"Sounds like a tornado. Where's the solidest walls in your house?" asked Jeff.

"In the hall. There's some stone walls that stuck out of the valley. I built around it."

Jeff and Lew ran to the hall. Jeff said, "Get your mattress. Hold it over us. Mark, come here. Dammit, don't you hear that?"

Mark continued to sway as though he heard the music, which would be impossible with the roar. Lew ran in with the mattress. Jeff and Lew huddled against the stone wall. It had begun to vibrate. Lew said, "I belong to this valley and the valley's coming for me."

When the tornado hit the house, all the windows exploded outward. The sheetrock walls rippled like a jellyfish in the sea. A tiny crack formed in the ancient stone wall. No bigger than three inches. Lew was sucked through it. Jeff pushed himself away from the wall. He wanted to get to Mark. His ears popped in the dropping pressure. For a moment he realized he was in a vacuum. He put his hand to his cheek. He was sweating blood through his pores. Black spots boiled in the center of his vision. He forced himself into the front room. For a moment he thought he was facing a cracked mirror. Black lines of nothingness radiated out from the record player's speakers. A strange angular network. Mark's body was in several of the planes. Moving toward and away from itself. He could see several of the internal parts.

He heard Lew screaming at him through the floor below and through the walls. Lew's screams were being drowned out through some chant. Nahuatl perhaps. He watched Mark work his way deeper into the night of angles. Mark's heart—or a dark cubist's version of it—suddenly appeared in the air above him. He reached up for it. A single drop of blood falling somehow sideways struck his left hand. It was hot, burning, acid. It didn't make a proper splot. A dark red trapezoid burned itself into his hand. An angular platinum comet came into the room. It darted around, weaving itself into Mark's mass. More parts followed. Woman parts. For an instant he glimpsed Jeena's face on one of the angled planes—upside down and backwards—but her face nonetheless. The Jeena mass connected itself to the Mark mass. The music became louder. It became one with the chanting. The dark lines began to shake with the combined rhythm and everything went black.

When Jeff came to, he thought he saw his mother bending over him. Then his eyes focused on the old Mexican woman, her neck covered by charms. She was directing two youths digging him free. She smiled. She said, "You are okay." Then she walked to the stone wall and traced a pattern over the crack. It seemed to close, or perhaps it was his eyesight again.

Jeff remained conscious for most of the ambulance ride into Mexico City. He toyed with the lock of platinum blond hair which he'd found in his left hand.

(*For Frank Belknap Long*)

Plush Cthulhu

As soon as the excuse left his lips Larry Ellison felt slightly lower than the belly of a rattlesnake in a wagon rut. Larry had tried for years to reach his students at James Bowie Junior High with Western metaphors, reasoning (incorrectly) that kids in central Texas had something of the Old West about them. His principal, Miss Rebecca Gonzalez, looked appropriately shocked. His assistant principal, Mr. José Wong Jr., who had not smiled at him in his five years of employment, actually put his hand around Larry's shoulders. Larry had no idea where the excuse had come from, and was amazed at some deep level that God hadn't smitten him on the spot.

Larry had just told the administration that he had missed Monday because his mom had died on Sunday. He had missed because he was high on ecstasy and balling some woman, whose name (he thought) was Chandra Azathoth Nibiru, or maybe it was Sandra? Although now he realized that was probably a stage name; she was probably named Rebecca Fielding or some such. His mother was (to the best of his knowledge) alive, if not well, at the Machen Assisted Living Center about twenty miles north in Austin, Texas.

"If you need to take more time off, Larry, the district gives a five-day leave for death of a parent or spouse in addition to the normal state and local days," said Mr. Wong. Wong had never used his first name before. But the big lie had apparently made his heart grow three sizes larger.

"I'll need Thursday and Friday off for the funeral." It was snowballing now. "But otherwise I want to stay at work, keep my mind focused on things."

"I was the same way when my mother died," said Miss Gonzalez. "She had been in a rest home like your mom. Is the funeral going to be here, I mean in Austin?"

"No, ma'am. It will be in her hometown of Amarillo."

"Let us know where we can send flowers," said Wong.

Oh, God. "I, well, my brothers and I are asking that donations be made to Book Aid International." Mom had probably never heard of Book Aid International; it was one of Larry's favorites. *Oh, God, I am going to hell for this, for sure.* Larry made an exaggerated stare at the Brother brand clock in Miss G.'s office, "I need to get to first period."

He left her office and made an effort to stare at the brown terrazzo floors. Larry was not a frequent liar. All his lies had been small ones. Yes, he was sure the copy machine was turned off; yes, he had all his grades in; of course he knew his autistic student's IEP by heart. He made his way to the second floor, not enjoying running his hand over the age-smoothed banister or the Latin motto in the wall, *Non scholae, sed vitae discimus.* Not for school, but for life we learn. Seneca. Bowie Junior High was one of the landmarks of Doublesign, Texas—and he had enjoyed its solidity as he had his own until today. He had about ten minutes to get his day's objectives for English 8 on the board. It was almost the last day of the poetry unit, and most of the students had still not written the poem and paper required.

When noon came, all the teachers made their way over to him: Mrs. Spradlin, Mr. Henley, Mr. Gutierrez, Miss Leach, Miss Mertin, Mr. Ousley, Mrs. Olrun, Mr. Watson. All Larry could do was think what was going to happen when Momma really died? She was almost ninety, for Christ's sake.

He wanted to call the nursing home during his conference period to make sure she was still alive, or he fantasized grimly maybe she has died. He was reaching for his cell phone when it started to vibrate. He hoped it was Chandra, but to his horror he saw it was the nursing home.

His mother may have had a stroke. They had rushed her to Seaton Hospital, but the hospital had returned her asking that she be closely observed for the next twenty-four hours. Could he come and see her? He said that he would be out immediately after work, and they must not call the school because, because, because they were doing standardized testing.

The next two periods might have been dipped in lead. Cotton filled his ears; his corneas were surely tinted with weak tea. The eighth-graders muttered little rhymes like miniature witches and warlocks. Just before the last bell, he could have sworn he heard some girl saying, "Step on a crack . . ."

He felt too drained to run, and too anxious to collapse. So he made his way to his car. Teachers weren't supposed to leave until half an hour after the last bell, but given his recent bereavement, he knew no one would stop him. Some of the para-professionals were putting up cardboard snowmen, others symbols of a New England Thanksgiving. It was a warm afternoon; he wondered how long the decorations made for school would take to catch up with global warming. None of his students had ever seen more than a half-inch of snow—they had no reference to a world covered in pristine white.

He had taught middle school too long, he decided as he drove north into Austin. He had given a middle school excuse. Probably the ecstasy has fucked his mind. He was having some mid-life crisis. It was probably the girl's fault. Oh, great, another middle school response. He hadn't planned to go to Austin for Halloween, at least not be in the city after nightfall. Austin had a huge drunk party on Sixth Street fueled by revealing costumes, live music, and cheap drinks. There were over forty thousand students in attendance at the University of Texas. He had stopped at a used music store. This amazingly tall bronze woman in a deep purple miniskirt disrupted his thumbing through jazz CDs by bending over to look at psychedelic vinyl. With her white go-go boots and long raven hair, she looked as though she belonged to the psychedelic era. She stamped her boots and sighed loudly, inviting comment. Despite the twenty-year difference in their ages, Larry played along.

"Can't find something?" he asked.

"My girlfriend told me that she had seen an Electric Commode album here today. I've been hunting it for years."

"I take it that it hasn't made iTunes yet."

She smiled, and he was lost in her liquid brown eyes.

"It was an obscure band even then. Part of the Arkham sound. They did some work with a theremin-like device I am trying to rebuild."

"Like in that documentary . . . who was she? Clara Rockmore?" asked Larry.

The woman's face lit up. "Oh, cool. Yes, Clara was a lover and student of Leon Theremin. Are you interested in alternative electronica?"

Larry had never heard the phrase "alternative electronica" in his life, but he hadn't been laid in three years. So his agreement sounded genuine and enthusiastic.

Larry pulled up at the Machen Assisted Living Center. A bright yellow-green ambulance was parked in front of the light gray one-story building. But that was nothing new. He swallowed as much guilt as he could and then headed inside. It didn't smell as strongly as the place his grandfather had died in twenty years ago. Maybe there had been breakthroughs in anti-death-smell chemistry. The administrator at reception looked professionally sad.

"Mr. Ellison, when your mother began living here, we talked about the stages of our process. Your mom won't have her own room anymore. We're going to have to watch her a little more closely. Would you like to see her?"

Mom's hair was white as snow, her skin translucent. She had shrunk so over the last three years. She wore a faded Sears housedress, no doubt older than any of his students. Her eyes had faded from a rich brown to the color of weak tea, and they looked angry. She sat in the "sun room" in a gerry chair, the restraining wheelchair that kept mindless patients from roaming the halls on their own. She smelled of piss. Someone had given her a plush Cthulhu doll. She clutched the little green monstrosity fiercely. It was an odd gift. Mom had never been much of a reader and preferred Danielle Steel to Stephen King and certainly to Lovecraft. It was a silly, stupid toy, dark green plush with a lighter green underbelly, as though Cthulhu were a relation of Kermit. It soft blunted tentacles and soft wings removed any sense of cosmic evil, and its brown eyes were almost shy. It tore at Larry's heart; the toy's eyes were more alive than his momma's.

She looked at Larry.

She didn't know him.

He actually heard his heart break. Well, not his heart, but the emotional break had a sound accompanying it—it sounded as if a hollow reed had been snapped behind his neck.

Larry walked over to where she was and sank on his knees. He looked at her and nothing really looked back. He said "Momma" six or seven times. No change in her face. He tried to take Cthulhu away from her. She resisted, but it was easy to deprive her of the toy. She made a sad sound and tried to get the doll back. The other seniors looked at him with the same horror one would give to the thief of an infant's candy. He gave her the doll back. He had a hard time standing. His face was wet. He hadn't cried in a very long time.

"Did you step on a crack?"

He wheeled on the administrator. "What did you say?" he asked.

"I said it's so hard the first time they don't know us. I remember how it was with my own mother."

The room seemed very unstable. Larry opened his mouth and couldn't maker a sound. He tried again and managed, "I know you are trying to share a helpful story, but I can't really hear anything right now. I've got to go, I'll talk to her doctor tomorrow."

He made it to the parking lot. This was Momma. Momma who had helped through a bad marriage, Momma who had worked two jobs so that he could get his English degree at UT. Momma who had rocked him when he had those terrible earaches as a kid. He was going to have to tell his boss the truth. Surely she was about to die. It was all wrong. All fucked up.

He had heard that sound before. At Chandra's apartment.

Her apartment was over a Mexican import shop on South Congress. It was jam-packed with books, CDs, old vinyl, and strange-looking electronic instruments. She told him some of the names: the Persephone, the Electronode, the Tepaphone, the Haken Continuum, the Trautonium, the Sonorous Cross, the Shaggaipolyphonic.

She had painted a slogan on the ceiling in purple, "Music is divided for Love's sake."

She had slipped into the bathroom, slipping into something more comfortable. Larry spotted a framed page from a children's book:

There was once a poor woodcutter who lived in front of a great forest. He fared so miserably, that he could scarcely feed his wife and his two children. Once he had no bread any longer and suffered great anxiety, then his wife said to him in the evening in bed: Take the two children tomorrow morning and take them into the great forest, give them the bread we have left, and make a large fire for them and after that go away and leave them alone. The husband did not want to for a long time, but the wife left him no peace, until he finally agreed.

"'Hansel and Gretel'?" he asked as she returned in a short purple nightgown that matched the color of the quotation. "Why?"

She smiled. "It's about splitting. Freud studied fairy tales for this. The young child has to split the image of the Good Mother and the Bad Mother. The kid's tiny brain can't deal with the Good Mother who gives him the tit and the Bad Mother who is angry when he poops himself. So he makes up two mothers. The witch in the gingerbread house is actually the regular mom. That is where humans get good and evil."

"OK, but why frame it?" Larry was split between curiosity and horniness at that moment.

"Music is all about splitting. Rhythm is about breaks, notes are about breaks, and noise and sound are about breaks. All my lifework is about splitting things and putting them back together. You ever done X? It can help you see beyond splits. That can take you beyond Love and Fear. That's my work; besides, it makes sex better."

Larry, attempting to be cool, just smiled.

The sex was great. Supernova great. Hallucinogenic motherfucking awesome great. Mythic volcano erupting beyond Good and Evil great. She played weird music, and the drugs kicked in, and he had a million weird flashes like screwing atop a pyramid altar, or having sex with hundreds of women and men and fauns, or making love to his ex-wife, or having an erotic frolic with mermaids, or seeing stars explode. At some point they left the flat and walked to Sixth Street and milled among the costumed and the drunk and the horny—or maybe they had gone to a Black Mass in Hell or some mixture of both and the one clear memory was a snapping sound behind his neck and Chandra saying, "Well, Cinderella, your ball is over now."

The next thing he knew was that he was lying in her narrow bed and was staring at the quotation on her ceiling. It was not the Sunday morning he had been expecting. It turned out to be Monday morning. Chandra had split, and he was famished. He went to his car and dove back to Doublesign. He got there about noon, and he was sure that he didn't want to face his classes. Every now and again he seemed to see green or yellow lights shimmer at the corners of his vision. Doublesign had two stoplights and one actual apartment building, but Larry lived in a garage apartment belonging to Mrs. Irma Johnson, who also ran the FedEx store. He crawled up the stairs to his apartment, ate three bologna sandwiches, and crashed. Somehow he would make it right.

It was getting dark. He needed to drive home from the home. He would have to call his sister in Florida and tell her, but he couldn't think of the words. He knew the guilt that filled him was irrational. Momma didn't have a stroke because he had lied to his boss. He tried calling Chandra. When she answered he hung up and turned his cell phone off. No words for that either.

He didn't remember the first nightmares. Suddenly it was 6:30 and his alarm was going off and he was scared. His bed was dank with sweat and his stomach too upset and it was Wednesday morning. Frost silvered everything; a front had come in during the night. He couldn't remember what his lesson plans were. He remembered telling his principal that he was taking some time off for the funeral. Was it Thursday and Friday? Or just Friday? Were his actions too shitty to tell his friends? It was going to be a great day, he could tell.

Someone had told the kids. They kept their heads down. No joking around. Many of the girls made him little cards out of folded notebook paper and colored pencils. The para-professionals told him that they would remember his *Mamacita* in their prayers this Sunday. What was her name? The football coach bought his lunch. Someone left a white rose in a vase on his desk. Students whispered outside of his room.

His cell phone vibrated with messages of consolation. E-mail came from HR, Dr. Simms (the superintendent), the English department of the high school.

He remembered his nightmare that night.

He was sleeping in his childhood home in Amarillo, Texas. He was wearing pajamas, his blue fuzzy pajamas so it would be when he was in junior high, and Momma had been so ill from her hysterectomy. She was calling from her bedroom. "Larry darling, I need you! I need you!"

He ran down the hall. She stood by her bed. Well, *something* stood there in the dark. A column of some thick liquid that kept re-forming itself. It seemed to have tiny feelers. Its mouth was vagina-shaped, near the center of its body. Some of the feelers, near where a human's hip should be, held onto something, possibly the Cthulhu doll. "Larry, you can't shut me out. You have to love me."

He must have been thrashing about on the bed. The dank sheets held him. He was so confused by their wet restraint that he couldn't tell when he passed from nightmare into the waking world. His room stank. He thought for a moment that he might have shit himself. The alarm clock read 4:32. It was Thursday morning. In theory he was flying to the funeral.

He would have to leave town. Doublesign was small; if he were out and about this weekend, everyone would know. He got up, got dressed, and drove into Austin. He would stay at the Motel 6 near his mother's nursing home. Maybe if he spent some time with her—serious, focused, *loving* time—it might help her. And he didn't care how she felt about the damn stuffed toy—it was headed for the trash. He didn't even turn the sheets back in his hotel room; just lay his dressed sweaty self on top.

His phone woke him at noon.

His mother had passed away. He was horrified at the relief he felt.

She had a prepaid funeral policy with Blackwell Brothers in Amarillo; the home was going to make the call. Did he want to view her body before they arranged for transportation?

With the sick thought that *everything would work out now* he drove off to the home.

"She's at the end of the hall."

She's not at the end of the hall. A body is in a room at the end of the hall.

Music, sort of spacey Muzak, came from the end of the hall. Larry heard one of the old men reading poetry. They probably have to have these little impromptu services all the time. It wouldn't be like a hospital where the scandal of death had to be hidden.

The poem was ending as he entered:

"The darkness drops again; but now I know
That twenty centuries of stony sleep
Were vexed to nightmare by a rocking cradle,
And what rough beast, its hour come round at last,
Slouches towards Bethlehem to be born?"

Yeats's "The Second Coming" seemed the most inappropriate poem that could possibly uttered at a mother's funeral, but Larry's revulsion was held in check by the sight of Chandra playing some sort of electric lyre strumming something complicated—some twelve-tone melody with angular tonalities.

"What the hell are you doing here?"

His mom lay on the bed, dressed in the pants suit she wore when he moved to Austin three years ago. She held the Cthulhu toy like a baby. The old people were shocked by the profanity and began to shuffle out. He was unsure which of the men had been reciting the poem.

"I do volunteer work here on Thursdays," said Chandra.

"What are you doing?" Larry asked.

"Hey, a little respect: *this* is your mom."

"That *was* my mom, and where do you go on Monday morning?"

"I work for a living. I tried to wake you up."

"Why are you here? Why were you with me?"

Chandra said, "I am doing my art. You can take it or leave it." She had stopped her weird music and was clearly about to leave. Larry thought about stopping her physically and then stopped himself, surprised at how far he had changed in less than a week.

She looked at him and responded as though she had read his mind. Probably easy enough to read his face. "You haven't changed. You're just noticing how you really are because you heard my music. You are seeing some of the monstrous you that you have learned not to see. But the real world is split further away from your views than you know. If you want the Real, go with what you are beginning to see."

"What's your real name?"

"Same as your mom's, dummy. Hannah. I was born Hannah Maria Nibiru."

She walked out, and suddenly the real shock of his momma's death hit him. He crumpled into a chair and cried and forgot his excuse of strange drug trips with mystic musicians.

Somehow in the next hour, he called his sister and the funeral home and booked a flight for tomorrow. He didn't give a damn about gossip and drove home to his Doublesign apartment.

That night he had the last nightmare.

He was sleeping in his little bed at home. It was cold, he could hear the gas heater turn on and the Santa Fe train in the distance, and so it must have been about ten o'clock when the train rattled through town. Beyond the curtains he could see the Christmas lights at the Casey house, and his room smelled of gingerbread. He could hear Momma crying and he could hear his sister in her tiny bedroom snoring lightly. Sissy had had breathing problems in the old house, and it was always so cold. Momma called out to him, "Where is my little man? Where is Larry? Come help me, Larry. Come help me!"

He sat up and (with the ease that such changes happen in dreams) he was his adult self. "Momma, you don't need me! You need Sissy!"

"Sissy can't help me no more. She can't see me!"

"Momma, she can't she you because you're dead! This is a nightmare and I am sorry that I said you're dead."

"Baby, baby. That's one of those fake splits you make. There is no line between Dead Momma and Live Momma and Good Momma and Bad Momma. Now come to me, baby. Don't you love me anymore? After all I have done?"

So Larry got out of his bed and walked down the hall. In her room, Sissy was sleeping in her childbed, but it was the adult sister and somehow he knew that they slept in this house every night. And Momma would always be in *this* house, where she had been sick and the family had been poor. Not the nice house, not the nursing home.

Momma was saying, "There is no line between Dead Momma and Live Momma and Good Momma and Bad Momma," and he heard

Sissy mutter in her sleep, "Iä! Shub-Niggurath!" Which also made sense. Fear and Love. Guilt and Innocence. Curves and Angles.

At the end of the hall, Larry opened the door to his mother's bedroom. It stood there in the darkness with a voice coming from the middle of column and the stench of vomit and decay and this time it was holding something squirming, not a Cthulhu plush toy, and Larry knew it was him as a baby. Little Lawrence Derby Ellison, and he could tell by some reflected points of crazy Christmas lights from next door that Momma had too many eyes in the wrong places. "Please look at me, baby, please know." He could hear Chandra's melody off in the distance.

Despite his best intentions he reached back and flipped on the light. They say you can't turn a light on in dreams, but they are wrong. And Lawrence Derby Ellison saw what his mother really looked like and what he looked like and what the world really was. Before he merged with his mother and was born again, he heard the last notes of Chandra's music, which he realized sounded flute-like.

The next morning, his landlady, who had heard of his mother's death from her cousin, who was the janitor at James Bowie Junior High, knocked on the door of his apartment. When there was no answer, she opened the door and went in. The coroner later said heart failure, but Irma said she will think of the poor boy's expression the rest of her days. Some things aren't meant to be seen.

(*For James Wade*)

Emily's Rose Window

We were all sad when Emily inherited her uncle's place. He was a bad man who expressed his badness in things given. Once he gave the mayor a little ivory whistle. Said it was a duck call. The mayor hunted, we all hunt, but the mayor had the balls to hunt on Ephraim Bishop's land. So Ephraim tells him, he'll draw more ducks with the call. It works. The mayor was beside himself. Shooting and eating ducks all the time. His mainly bald head grew shiny with duck fat. It was illegal to hunt that much, of course, but the mayor of Kingsport was above the law. He came to the Lodge many nights, Masonic Lodge 118—one of the oldest in the great state of Massachusetts. Always wanting us to go hunting. We have day jobs, Mr. Mayor. He went out more and more and we'd hear that whistle—didn't sound a damn thing like a duck—and then blam! Then he started hunting so much, he was never in his office, so he lost the election. But he didn't care, got grossly fat on ducks—or whatever he was shooting. We wouldn't see him for days, just hear the whistle. Finally at the Grandmaster's suggestion we paid a call and his house was smelly with feathers and blood and no Mr. Mayor. We still hear the whistle sometimes at night when there is no moon, we hear the shots sometimes too, and that's been thirty-five years.

So like I says, we was disappointed that Ephraim had left her the house. It stood on Central Hill and was old enough to have a plaque, but we didn't give it one. Built by one Edward Crane, who spent most of his days in Europe. After he died in 1723, the house stood vacant until the Bishops bought it in 1758. It had a bad reputation, witchcraft and such. But it didn't really bother anyone until Ephraim fixed the place up, but I'm getting ahead of myself or beside myself, I wanted to talk about Emily Bishop.

Her father, Ephraim's brother, was a good banker, regular Mason, and as honorable a fellow as you would want to know. William Bishop was a solid, uninteresting guy; he was unlike his brother Ephraim, who always had a different beautiful woman on his arm and too much cash in his hands. William didn't drive too flashy a car. He gave to charities and good works and he let his wife drag him to church every Sunday. She was a Southern woman and made him some sort of Baptist. She and Ephraim took a hate to each other at first sight. He sent her a tall blue vase with thirteen white roses in it. We told her not to take any gifts from him, so she had her driver take it back and gifted Ephraim with some book by Billy Graham. We took a liking to her at once. She had met William at Miskatonic University. He had majored in economics and she had taken an MRS degree, if you catch my drift. Her family was dirt-poor. Came from Savannah, Georgia, which is almost as old as Kingsport.

Ephraim's next volley was to invite brother and missus to the family house. It was one of the oldest structures in Kingsport; some of its thick walls were laid down in 1700. I went to the house as a boy when Ephraim and William were growing up, and after Ephraim's death and after what happened to poor Emily.

How would I describe it?

Even though the house was not huge, we kept getting lost in it, that day we broke in to see after Emily. The sheriff said it had a labyrinthine structure. His English minor at Miskatonic seems to have stood him in good stead.

Ephraim had begun remodeling the house in the late 1970s. His ancestors had built over a large window that marred the house's classic lines. For some reason Crane had shaped the top of his home to resemble an octopus head. His claim was that he wished to "frighten the superstitious" and "amuse the fearless." This had led to rumors of the house being a sort of American version of Francis Dashwood's Hell Fire Club—with the drinking and the sexing and devil worship, but no dressing up like monks and nuns. Crane was after all an American, although he could apparently stand to be in his house only twice a year, at the ends of October and April. But he did always bring beautiful women on those occasions. For the most part lovely foreigners who were never seen again.

In the center of the octopus's head was a strange convex lens about seven feet in diameter. It was the color of milk tinged with blood. It should have been a healthy pink, illuminating the naughtiness of Crane's Black Masses perhaps, but something about the shape suggested a diseased or even blind eye. The first Bishops had certainly done the city a favor by covering the monstrosity. When Ephraim had dislodged the false wall that had covered it, there was talk in the city of having it covered, but Ephraim's lawyers found an obscure easement that Edward Crane had obtained. It seemed that, because of some rather large fee he had paid, the city would simply mind its own business about his architecture. Ephraim must have put a light in his upper room, which was an oak-paneled library, since the window seemed to glow slightly at night.

Anyway, as I was saying, Ephraim made a big deal of inviting William and what was her name?—Marie—to his home. She was a looker. Ephraim's cook and his butler put on a great spread; Ephraim talked peace and invited William and Marie to spend the night. Some neighbor found Marie that night wandering among the back alleys at the base of the hill. Poor thing was wearing only a thin nightgown, and the New England winter had harmed her flesh. She had no idea how she got there, and William had somehow slept through the night unaware of his missing wife. We all thought that Ephraim had won that round and that she would be packing her bags for Georgia. However, she proved to be of sterner stuff and not only stayed that terribly harsh winter but also gave William his daughter in July.

Emily—well, Emily was a disappointment from the start. She had been born with extreme curvature of the spine and (it was said) a tail. Her flesh was a waxy white that flushed pink when the baby cried. And she cried almost all the time. William had money, so the nannies and nurses were hired and the series of surgeries began. William was a good man but not a strong man, and a crying and ugly daughter seemed to be a bit much for his nerves. He spent as much time as he could at the Lodge, and many thoughtful hours at the bank and too many hours at a tavern called the White Ship.

One foggy night about two years into Emily's ill-fated life, something remarkable was seen. The two brothers Ephraim and William began to enjoy each other's company at the White Ship. They would be heard singing rather disreputable and archaic ballads, consuming heroic quantities of rum, and loudly expressing their borderline fascist politics at the TV. We were curious that Ephraim, who had turned his back on us in high school, had any normal habits like cussing and drinking. Ephraim had intended to be a literary man and had sought out Princeton to learn creative writing. He had always thought we were too common, and Kingsport too provincial.

Rumor had it that Ephraim and his brother had taken up whoring as well. One night, and I heard this from the bartender himself, Ephraim and William had taken a back booth and were irritating other customers with loudly spoken dirty jokes. The bartender had been about to throw them out when they grew hushed. Ephraim had opened a small, long box, the sort that holds necklaces, and was indeed showing his brother a strange rose quartz medallion. As the bartender walked up, Ephraim snapped the case shut and winked at his brother.

The strange medallion was seen soon after—around the throat of nineteen-year-old Suzie Reiman, the achingly beautiful daughter of the bank president. After her mother's death when she was twelve, Suzie had been the apple of Albert's eye. William lacked the discretion even to try and keep the affair secret. Even the gossip column of the *Kingsport Chronicle* made remarks much more transparent than Ephraim's freaky window. Albert Reiman tried shipping his daughter off to Milan "to study art." Suzie responded in great Gothic fashion and attempted to cut off her head with an electric carving knife, which heretofore had only been useful in mangling Thanksgiving turkeys.

William had lost his position at the bank and fell to drink. His brother seemed to have deserted him. William stopped his patronage of the White Ship, a rather well-known Kingsport landmark, and instead began drinking boilermakers at Pete's. Marie struggled to keep her head up. But as money played out and her employment solution as an aide at Kinder Kare failed to pay for Emily's needs, she divorced William and headed toward warmer climes.

William's demise was without drama although not without pathos. One drunken night he declared to the patrons of Pete's that he knew something. He stumbled out into the dark snow at closing time. The next morning when his car was found on Pete's lot the police were called. They found him frozen in the same alley Marie had turned up in seven years before.

Ephraim paid for a fabulous funeral. He sat alone stroking the rose quartz amulet that had last been Suzie's. Rumor had it that she had been buried with it, but I think that was an exaggeration. People loved to do that with Ephraim.

After that day we never saw Ephraim. He paid his cook and his butler well. They weren't the sort to talk about anything; they weren't even New Englanders. He had female visitors from time to time, usually at the end of October and April; you can imagine the sort of rumors that started. We all watched the rose window those nights. Sometimes there appeared to be flashes of light within as though some sort of signaling were taking place, but most of the time there was simply that murky opalescence that made you think if you just kept watching something would be seen. I confess to have bought a pair of binoculars to gaze upon its eldritch surface.

Then Emily was sighted. She was in college in Arkham. She had been reshaped by who knows how many surgeries. Her head was as upright as her mother's, no longer permanently cocked as though listening to a secret. Her skin had a much healthier hue. She was not what you would call a pretty woman, but she was not the ugly crying child that had driven her weak father away. We hoped that she would come to town, but if she did what could we say to her? "You sure don't look as ugly as you used to. How does your poor mama send you to a fancy school? Why this one?" So although it would have eased our curiosities, it may be better that she didn't run into us.

On the other hand, if we had got those answers maybe we could have told some stories.

Ephraim died. He did not die at a greatly advanced age, nor were there any omens of his passing. No ravens or whippoorwills or earthquakes. Just his cook dialing 911. He had died in the oak-paneled library having fallen from the built-in ladder. His funeral had been paid for in advance. The funeral home was to hire an actor to read his service. We all went, of course, with that same rubbernecking we give a horrible accident on the freeway. Emily sat by herself, just where Ephraim had sat at her father's funeral. She wore the rose quartz medallion. We got a good look at it that last day. It was a stylized octopus as well, probably linked to the rose window in some manner.

I remember the funeral. First some awful music was played. I don't know anything about music theory, but I read in the paper the next day that it was—hmm, let me see—Fandefen's Atonal Hymn to the Seventh Dimension. Not something you're going to walk out humming, if you know what I mean. Then the actor read a little speech by Ephraim. It was open casket, did I mention that? The speech went like this, although you'll have to forgive my memory for the foreign names. "Elizar Na Reten was the greatest rake and jokester of Ool Athag. He said that he learned the biggest joke of world, and he had sought high and low for it. He even called demons from the seventh hell and learned their jokes and paid necromancers to call up the ancient Kings of Ool Athag from their essential salts to learn their jests. Elizar believed that all human life was some sort of jest by Something. On the day of his death his poor relatives—for Elizar Na Reten was great of gold—had gathered. After the priests had closed his cold dead eyes, Elizar shocked them all by winking at them. Then Elizar's corpse began to chuckle. It was a low laugh at first, then a louder one and finally a guffaw that so startled his grieving family that they rushed out into the night and never came to Elizar's tower again." So help me God, we all started staring at Ephraim's corpse, because we thought he was going to start laughing. But that was the whole of the service.

The next week Emily was seen moving into Ephraim's house. So we went up in a delegation from the Lodge with our wives carrying casseroles and cakes. On the way we speculated that Ephraim's will had stated that she had to spend time in the house—the tired movie plot of the haunted home.

No.

It was none of that. Emily had been his heir for some time. She had had an impoverished childhood with her mother dying when she entered high school. She was living with her aunt when the checks and letters began arriving from Uncle Ephraim. How he knew that her mother had died or where to send the checks, she did not know. But Ephraim claimed guilt for having broken up his brother's marriage. He did not expect her to forgive him, but he would see to it that she was cared for for the rest of her life.

Ephraim was rich. Very rich. Who knew? We knew he did nothing but read his strange books and entertain his out-of-town guests and occasionally give people things. People who went to bad ends. Emily had moved in because the house was hers.

Yes, she would get rid of the octopus head and the weird rose window. They were hideous. No, she had no problem showing us the library. The glass looked murky; cleaning we found out did no good. I looked at the books. I suppose if my Latin or Greek were better I would have been shocked. We guessed they were black magic or pornography or blasphemy, but they could have been studies of how wax melts for all I know.

We burned them anyway. I felt like a Nazi burning books, but we had read her diary.

Here's what happened after she moved in.

The light—a real light, not that ghostly glow—shone from the rose window most nights. Emily seemed to spend hours there. Often very late at night or early in morning. I had a friend in the registrar's office over at Miskatonic. I asked about Emily Bishop. I doubt that he should have told me, but anyway she dropped her classes the semester her uncle died. She was smart, not a genius or anything, but smart and aiming at a biology degree with the strong smell of pre-med. Pre-meds are driven students of normal things, not what lay in Ephraim's library.

At first we—those of us who had been her father's Lodge brothers—tried to be close to Emily, but she had friends her age in Arkham;

and she had little love for a father that had abandoned her. So we watched the light in her rose window, and the novelty of her being there faded. As the spring semester unfolded her college friends came less and less and we forgot about her as well. It was in the second year of her stay in the house on Central Hill that things became a source of gossip again. One day she drove into town to see Albert Reiman at his bank. She was carrying a thick envelope with her, and he was said to be quite upset after her visit.

The operations began after that. There weren't fine enough surgeons in Kingsport; even the medical school at Miskatonic didn't have first-rate plastic surgeons. So Emily went to Boston. She had money, lots of money. Until Albert Reiman shot himself we thought it was just Ephraim's money, and we had no idea why he had so much. She got lots of work done—most of it was the standard packet of work that models get—breast augmentations, veneers for her teeth, lower rib removed. Some of her needs were more specialized—clearing up some of the lingering defects that her birth had brought. We all thought that Emily surely was her mother's child and was looking for a husband. Suitors did show up from the ranks of the good-looking and the rich and especially the good-looking rich. Emily allowed herself to be taken out in Boston and Arkham and Kingsport, but nothing ever came of it and we noticed none of the swains seemed to spend a night in Emily's haunted mansion.

When she had finished her series of surgeries and dentistry and even wardrobe buying she was amazingly beautiful. She was the sort of beauty that stopped talk in a restaurant and made people stare along boulevards. We all assumed that the expensively bought beauty was expensively bought self-esteem. She had seemingly only one hobby, unless spending time in Ephraim's library was a hobby. She loved photography and spent a small fortune on cameras and other equipment. We all thought: Good for Emily.

But she began going out less and less and spending more and more time in her house on the hill. Even with her beauty we forgot about her. By the time of her fourth year in Ephraim's house no one saw or thought of her.

Then one fine day in July the SEC investigated Albert Reiman's bank and he shot himself, bringing an end to a tragic line. It seems large sums of money were missing. We gossiped about this and remembered Suzie, and we remembered her mother Miriam who had that bad car accident out on the Miskatonic Turnpike. There had certainly been a cloud on them, we said; even the rich have their crosses to bear, we agreed. It was our local version of the Kennedy saga.

Then in August for the first time in nearly three hundred years there was a small earthquake in Kingsport. Pictures fell from walls, a few plate-glass windows in the malls shattered, and Emily's rose window broke into fragments. The newspaper duly noted that similar earthquakes had occurred in 1692, which were attributed by the pious New Englanders to witchcraft. In fact, Edward Crane had laid the foundations of his house the day after the quake.

However, the spectacular death of Emily Bishop grabbed the headlines that day.

We were able to cover up some of the details out of respect for her father and the sadness of her life. If you read the paper, you will read that falling glass killed her. The servants had actually found her body hours before the quake, her throat slashed by her own hand. We paid the servants for her diary and, after we had read it, visited the house and gathered the books and the photos. Some of us kept some of the glass. I kept several pieces. I even had it analyzed at Yale and Miskatonic. It was just silica colored with a few metallic salts. I had suspected that the reports would tell me wonders.

I'll tell you about the diary. When I am gone, I will even let it be published. Most people will think it is a sad tale of madness; only a few old-timers like myself that remember Ephraim Bishop may think otherwise.

Emily began the diary as a sort of lab book. Ephraim had left her a remarkable letter in which he had told her that Edward Crane had finished out the house on Central Hill as a sort of magical observatory. The rose window had been brought from Tibet or, as he wrote, "Leng." It had the power when used in conjunction with the amulet and certain incantations to show a variety of scenes from the past, far away, or even other worlds. However, the makers of the window, a group of wizards (or perhaps extra-terrestrials) called the Zenobar, extracted an "ironic" price for its use. Ephraim said that he had discovered the incantations when as a young man he had fancied writing a book on Edward Crane, who had been something of a rake, and a scientist and a sorcerer to boot. Ephraim had found Crane's diary hidden behind a bookcase in the library when he was in his twenties. The diary had been written in a script unknown to Ephraim, but then he discovered that certain manuscripts at Miskatonic were written in the same script, an alchemist's cipher invented by Dr. John Dee. Once the cipher was known the novel-in-progress changed from a sexual picaresque headed toward Grove Press into a novel of the occult. Then one drunken night Ephraim tried the invocation:

> *Daoloth v'ren viaxul cronree zothotha*
> *Daoloth nec'q'ss Rlim Shagiloth zenobar*
> *Daoloth zazzas nasethanda neblod zin*
> *Daoloth nec'qss Rlim Sagoloth zeonbar Xul!*

The house shook, the wooden wall Ephraim's umpteenth grandpa had placed over the rose window fell, and Ephraim saw what he was later to call "My Golgotha," a hill on the world of Zenobar.

At first Ephraim thought of the fame that such a discovery could bring him. He could see himself on the *Tonight Show:* "Yes, Johnny, I have established or should I say re-established communication with an extraterrestrial race that gave mankind many scientific advantages in the early sixteenth century. I suppose I am a sort of genius."

The Zenobar showed him many things, and he learned to direct the lens elsewhere. Scenes from human and pre-human history were his to view. He saw George Washington drunk and afraid, Lincoln cheating on his wife, how the Great Pyramid was really built. He saw races and beings that came to Earth before mankind, saw the casual mistake that created life as we know it on this planet. He saw secret meetings at the Kremlin and watched celebrities showering. He saw human cruelty and stupidity one night and then cosmic wonder the next. He knew Truth with a capital T and Disgust with a capital D.

Then one day he realized that he had stopped interacting with the world for so long that he had exhausted his bank account. The NEA grant that was supposed to pay for his writing *Crane: The Rake's Regress* was gone and power was shut off the next day at the ancestral home.

But he had a Polaroid.

In twelve hours he was a blackmailer. In three months he was a very good blackmailer. No piece of human infamy could escape him. He could make money whenever he wished. Cheating spouse, industrial espionage, finding hidden treasures—all were child's play. The Zenobar did want something from him, but he didn't spell it out in his letter to Emily. It had something to do with women. Beautiful women. Ephraim learned things, things that humans can't know and still love their fellow humans. Dark knowledge and gold and women—who would have thought that Faust lived in the late twentieth century in Kingsport?

Uncle Ephraim had given her one proof. He had taken a Polaroid picture of her the day she had locked herself by accident in her grandmother's storm cellar in Savannah. It was a picture that no one could have made by normal means.

So Emily asked certain professors at Miskatonic. She found out that Edward Crane did have a mysterious source of income after he had had the glass from Leng installed in his home. She discovered that certain ancient books kept under lock and key suggested that there were other worlds that were at times accessible to humans. She couldn't get the library to lend her the volumes and she lacked Greek and Latin and Pali and Arabic anyway. But she did have the magical quatrain. So she began experiments. She tried uttering the phrases at different times. She tried when well rested and when she had sleep deprivation. She tried saying the words while taking certain drugs or saying them during sexual experiments. She read Crowley and Waite and LaVey and tons of anthropology. After six months of effort the glass began to glow. Then after a few more times she could see.

At first she could see a green gray mountain littered with what she thought were small shells with three unblinking eyes. The eyes seemed to see her. In fact, they were so positioned that they must watch her.

Eventually she decided they were skulls of some sort, hence "Golgotha" = "Hill of the Skull." After weeks of practice she could make the glass show her other things. This was when she stopped having friends. The temptation to watch them all the time removed her comfort at knowing them. She had an affinity for seeing them—for seeing all humans at their worst moments. She saw her friend Kelly abusing her little boy, she saw Mark cheating on Polly, she saw her favorite professor downloading child porn. She never got the knack of finding great moments of human history, but even the most casual thoughts about her friends would cause the glass to show her what they would least like anyone to see.

But mainly she watched the world of Zenobar. Then one day she saw two Zenobar carrying one of the living skulls to the mountain. They looked up and saw her. Emily did not describe them in her diary save only to say that the first few times she saw them, she became so frightened that she fled the room. But her fear was dissolved in her wonder like sugar in tea. She found that she would rather watch them than her own species. Who can blame her?

Eventually after months she could sense their thoughts. They wanted her to expose herself to them. They wanted to see her beauty. The viewing was central to their religion in some fashion. They brought the living skulls to this hill so that they might look upon beautiful human women.

The Zenobar rewarded the operator of the lens with views of many different worlds. Scenes of unimaginable beauty and terror would be shown. This was why Edward Crane developed the reputation as a rake. This explained the beautiful women that Uncle Ephraim always had with him. The image of the women was the price for cosmic wonder.

This explained Ephraim's interest in her mother. He had wanted her to pose for his aliens. She had refused when she saw the Zenobar. She had gone into shock and fled his house. Emily watched her running into the night. Emily began to track her mother. The more of herself she showed the Zenobar the more the lens would show her. Emily watched her own birth. In her diary she speculates that the shock of having seen the Zenobar had affected her mother's pregnancy. With the aid of the glass from Leng, she relived her father's disgust at her ugly mewling form. She saw Ephraim trying to get William involved with the lovely Suzie Reiman. Suzie was not only startlingly attractive, but very gifted with the amulet. She could make the lens show truly amazing things. She watched her father pimping out this girl to alien powers and falling deeper into a pit of alcoholism and drug abuse. She saw Suzie watching the lens one night and seeing something so horrible that she cut her own throat.

She saw Ephraim and her father digging up Suzie's coffin to steal back the amulet.

More and more skulls were carried to the hill every time she saw it. The skulls were buried in the greenish earth so that lidless eyes could watch her. There are pages and pages of diagrams where Emily slowly works out that the glass from Leng magnified her. When she lay naked before the Zenobar, she must have taken up half the sky of Golgotha.

The mobile Zenobar wanted her to become more beautiful. They placed images in her mind of what they wanted her to become. At first she balked, and then the glass stopped working. She found that she had grown addicted to the scenes of other worlds. She had no love of the human world; she lived only for the cosmic. When she agreed to be receptive to their images, she communicated to them that she could not become attractive, but they gave her instructions—instructions that she later passed on to the plastic surgeons of Boston. She explained that she lacked the funds for the change, and the glass showed Albert Rieman molesting his twelve-year-old daughter. Emily made pictures and then visited Albert's bank; and afterward money was never a problem. Emily's newfound beauty did distract for a while. She loved the attention of rich, good-looking men. Mom, dad, grandmother had never loved her. She was not popular nor rich in Savannah.

She dreamed of simply smashing the window. Once she even bought a sledgehammer for this purpose. But that night her diary only records, "Saw the dance of the flame vampires."

Emily tried to reintegrate herself into human society, but she could never resist the temptation of using the rose window to show her the dark secrets of the men who adored her. At twenty-five Emily found that she could not stand the human race. She began to find that the horrible form of the Zenobar no longer horrified her. She began to see other scenes from their world—the Temple of Daoloth, a canyon deeper than the Marinara Trench, the sculpting of giant bonsai that took thousands of years. As long as she showed herself to the living skulls there seemed no limit to the wonders of the cosmos that could be hers. She felt that she must be a living goddess. She grew better at sensing the thoughts of the mobile Zenobar: she could not gain an impression from the living brains in the skulls, however. She guessed that their life force had lessened, that they could no longer animate their large bodies. She began to love them. She thought of them constantly as they slowly died on the hill; she was their last image. Toward the end of her life Emily would spend as long as possible showing herself to them. She writes that she had found peace. Unlike her mother, who had been consumed with guilt at Emily's ugly little body (Momma always blamed herself for Emily's disfigurement, but the Zenobar must love her). Unlike Daddy who drank himself to death rather than look at his helpless crying daughter, but the Zenobar adored her.

She wanted to cross the gulf that separated her from the Zenobar world. She used the lens to follow the life of Edward Crane and her uncle and the inhabitant of the cold Asian plateau where the glass had first landed as a meteorite, but she could find no rite that would allow her to go to her worshippers. She knew there must be an enchantment that would turn the glass into a doorway; why else would have the Zenobar have sent the glass across the dark light years to Earth?

Eventually she observed Edward Crane near the end of his days. He traced an angular sigil with blood-red chalk on the floor of the very room she lay in. The sigil somehow gave him a higher sense of connection with the lens and the beings on the other side. After many tries she was able to trace the figure and get some results. At this point she had been exposing herself—a naked altar of her own divinity to the living brains of Zenobar—for four earthly years. Her romantic notions of the Zenobar began to evaporate. Yes, they did spend thousands of years sculpting slow-growing trees. Yes, they spent countless hours worshipping their god Daoloth. But their main occupation was ritual-ized warfare. The teams (?), gangs (?), sects (?) had fought one another longer than humans had lived on this globe.

Exactly how Emily discovered these things is not clearly spelled out, but it seems that she was growing in her ability to connect with their minds.

After the wars the heads of wounded warriors were gathered and treated with a preservative that allowed their brains to exist for decades without nourishment or sleep. Their eyelids were removed so they could watch the sky without pause. The winning warriors brought their living trophies to Golgotha to watch the sky.

They were not watching a living goddess who loved them.

They were staring at the most horrible demon they could imagine. Her. The living ones had her sculpt herself into curved symmetries that had been designed by their most vicious shamans to cause the most pain, fear, and loathing. The living skulls were in Hell, and she was It.

Ephraim had known, and he found it funny.

Emily recorded this. The only place in the cosmos that she had ev-er felt true love from had no love for her at all. The telepathically gift-ed Suzie Reiman had known it in weeks. Emily chose the same death as Suzie. Her last diary entry begged whoever found her hateful body to burn it and scatter the ashes.

I don't know if her death caused the earthquake. I suspect the relief of the thousands of living skulls on the Zenobar world may have had some effect, some cosmic lessening of total pain. We gathered up pieces of the glass. We agreed to destroy the books, we burned down the house and the sheriff said he burned the diary after we had read it. I imagine I am not the only one who copied down the four lines from the diary. I imagine that I am not the only one who has said them over the shards.

Once they glowed for me, and I found myself promising a god, whom I had come not to believe in, that I would only look for the wonders of the universe and not at teenage girls showering next door. I am a weak old man and I knew it was a lie. Some nights I think of Emily's lovely face. She was a Helen, a Mona Lisa, a Nefertiti. I should count myself lucky to have seen such a face—what are the chances of that in a little town like Kingsport? But sometimes I feel something, maybe some eldritch vibration coming from a plastic garbage can full of pink glass in my garage, and I hate her and fear her.

What is the human race and *why* are we that some other intelligence would hurl a fireball at us just to look at our ugliness? What is the cosmos if we are its horrors?

(*For Matt Cardin*)

A Ship Afar

The *Yankee Rose* is seen, approaching port;
it merits a notice in the *Kingsport Chronicle*.
The terrible old man smiles his snaggle-toothed smile.
His ship is coming in.
He meets it at the rotted dock,
and sees to the unloading of its shuddersome cargo
blackened skulls of Tcho-Tcho priests,
a glass or two from Leng,
Curiosities from the city of the pyramids.
He sells these rare wares
to the most innocent of shops.
They wait
in dusty drawers and neglected niches.
Till fresh eyes see their evil beauty
and the *Yankee Rose* sails again
into an unearthly fog.

Looking Glass

The call came at 13:30. The Los Angeles air was 90+ degrees. The neighbors had reported a smell from unit 3-C. Detective Sergeant Blick knew the smell of a human body ripened by summer heat. He'd worked a case in the drought of '04, an old man cooked at 113 degrees. Kept his doors closed, windows bolted, no city evil could sneak in. The coroner said the man had lain there for twenty days; when Blick found him, his limbs stirred faintly with the burgeoning life within. Crows like to look at corpses because of the million lights moving in the dark. Fireworms on coals.

Blick was not a crow. If possible, he would have walked away from the Phoenician Arms. Or have waited till twilight and the end of his shift, when the stench would be less. But being a policeman was largely a liquid affair; you poured from mold to mold that the public held up for you. Here, the neighbors were indignant, the young couple in 3-C must be keeping a dog locked up while they vacationed. Vacation? No one had seen the Tenniels for a week, so they must be on vacation. No one in the city knows how common death is here. They believe in the American way of death, hospital-clean and safely isolated.

Blick took their statements. The complaints looked startling, black felt tip in the L.A. sun. The neighbors wanted to follow Blick up the stairs. Blick said no. Regulations. Since he could smell them on the first floor, the bodies must be near liquefaction. God, no wonder people were complaining.

The door was hard to open, with heat and swelling. Blick noted first the graffiti, second the bodies, then the machinery. Blick would see this scene forever; he turned back on the balcony. Two thin ribbons of his black vomit splattered three stories down. The apartment was two bedrooms, living room, kitchen, full bath. Two operating tables lay in the living room. On each was a body connected to a servo mechanism. From each head, like a magician's crown, was a variety of metal arms. Each arm was capped with a scalpel, a saw, or a waldo. All were blood-stained. The control wires snaked into the shaven heads of the dead couple. The autopsy would later show that each unit performed a laser tonsure and guided the wires directly on the raw nerves. The neurosurgery involved would be characterized as "centuries beyond our time."

Not only would the brains handle twenty new complex limbs, the organic cores would process sensory data from a variety of remotes placed over their bodies, bringing biologic news from the war zone.

The bodies were cut in several places. Certain organs were removed, whether wholly or partially was impossible to say due to the advanced state of putrefaction. Externally missing were the eyes and genitals. Internally, the woman's womb, and the liver, hypothalamus, and pineal gland belonging to both sexes. How they survived such surgery without anesthesia puzzled the medical savants. Blick was puzzled by their faces: although deformed by decay and heat, they were young and healthy. The Tenniels had died with expressions of ecstasy.

Painted on the ceiling above them was Ouroborus, the worm that swallows its own tail.

The investigation was carried out quietly. The Tenniels had no next of kin or, if so, none could be found. In fact, they had very little personal history at all. Charles paid each month's rent in cash. He left each morning at 8:00 by taxi. The cab company was able to place him: he always rode to the UCLA library.

He had no library card—never checked out anything. Blick went to the librarians with a sketch by the police artist (no pictures of Charles). Charles had spent most of his time perusing math texts, René Thom and Rudy Rucker in particular.

His occasional visits to the rare book room had left an impression. The stout, white-haired matron with the keys described him as a "creep." Blick assumed his choice of reading earned him the epithet. Charles made no impression on most people. The man moved in a fog of his own making; his neighbors couldn't totally agree on basics like height or hair color, his three years' residence notwithstanding. Blick re-created a picture of Charles from memories of Aunt Sadie's house. Sadie's bay window glass had warped. Men in the distorted glass shifted, deformed into bizarre topological fantasies. When Blick was a small boy, he'd thought it was the nature of the outside of Sadie's house that warped the old men walking their dogs. It was many, many years before he would play in Sadie's yard.

Charles had taken advantage of the Powell Library's collection of European and Arabic works on the occult. His request lists initially covered almost all available titles. The last four months narrowed his requests to three: *De Vermis Mysteriis* by Ludvig Prinn, *Zegrembi Manuscript* (transcribed by Nicholas Zegrembi), and finally *Mysteriorum Liber Sextus et Sanctus* by Dr. John Dee. The last title quickened Blick's interest. An avid fan of Ian Fleming, he knew the first secret agent to use the code 007 was Dr. Dee in reports to his queen. The book turned out to be a disappointment to Blick, his high school Latin being no match for Dee's Renaissance elegance. Some of the book seemed to be written in an entirely unknown tongue.

On a Tuesday five days after he had found the bodies, the autopsy report was dumped on his desk. He arrived at work bleary-eyed and headachy and was almost detached enough as a consequence not to feel nauseated on discovering that the missing organs were found semi-digested in their stomachs. Cause of death: massive traumatic shock. Doh, there's a surprise!

Since no traces of the Tenniels' family, job, or other connections existed, Blick was given the keys to their recently fumigated flat and ordered to go pick up the State's new property, catalog it, and deliver it downtown to close the case. Normally a uniform would do this, but the department wanted this to be a forgotten affair. Blick took two Valium and three Dramamine before driving over.

The heat was 101 degrees frightening Fahrenheit. The traffic was slow. As Blick drove across town, the first of the Watts Towers killings occurred.

Later no one would be able to say what had happened to Sy McAffery. Her body was stretched in an odd way, as though caught between two massive steel plates, each moving at a different angle in almost parallel planes. The crowd stated that the sixteen-year-old was skating by Rodia's sculpture. Probably using speed of air to escape the summer oven.

All noise stopped. People started running away. Why they ran is unclear. Reports break down at this point. Certainly no visual horror had manifested itself.

The air was clear and quiet, just the one skater by the Towers. Her features distort with agony. She begins spinning wildly. Witnesses agree there was a rushing, whirring sound, as though a mighty dynamo had been activated.

Her distorted, broken body was left atop the sculpture like a Druid sacrifice nailed to an oak tree. Watts would never be the same. There would be riots and fear and looting in seven days, when various groups blamed this all on some evil Caucasian super-science. With the irony that governs all things in this darkling universe, William Channing Blick had been conceived when his white daddy and black momma had cuddled in fear during the Watts Riots of the summer of 1965.

Blick knew nothing of the sweet girl's bloody death. The drive to the Tenniels had been very draining. His headache had grown to monstrous proportions. The hot air rushed against him when he left his air-conditioned PT Cruiser. When Blick reached the top of the stairs, colors swam in his vision. He felt faint. An image of the Watts Towers pressed on his eyelids for a moment. Falling, he grabbed the doorknob. He felt a cold, electrical tingling and the delirium passed away.

Inside, the air conditioning was mercifully turned on. The fumigators had banished all but the faintest trace of the smell of rot. Blick began cataloging the contents of the apartment.

The furnishings were spartan. The landlady had painted Ouroborus over with white enamel, but the darker paint was beginning to peek through. The living room missed the operating tables. The white wall monotony was relieved by a knickknack bookcase. Its objects suggested terrible things to Blick. On the left top shelf was a Klein bottle, gold-leafed with goetic symbols. Most of these were unfamiliar to Blick, although some of them had been diagrams in *Zegrembi Manuscript*. Next was a porcelain cobra rising, head extended. A very slithy sculpture. The far right was occupied by a grinning human skull, a paperweight over three copies of *The Cincinnati Journal of Ceremonial Magick.*

Cincinnati?

The second shelf held an assortment of scalpels, Exacto knives, and copper daggers, the last engraved with the same goetica as the Klein bottle.

The bottom shelf held an assortment of works on anthropology, history of religion, and the like. Notable were a 55-page mimeograph, *The Feast of the Hive: Non-Unique Metrics in Hilbert Space,* and *Fifty-Book,* both by Thibaut de Castries. The far left seven inches of the shelf held a cut crystal bowl with a few drops of dried blood in its center.

The kitchen, bath, guest bedroom provided no surprises, other than the absence of a TV, landline, or even a computer. But the master bedroom, painted in the omnipresent white, had a closet full of nondescript clothes and two dusty olive-green shoeboxes. The first of these contained $5,000 in twenties and two fifty-dollar gold pieces (Pacific Exhibition, 1904). The second contained a Colt .357 Magnum (stolen three years earlier in Anaheim) and a green spiral notebook with the magic marker legend "Magickal Diary."

> Walpurgisnacht. Eliphas Levi recommends the feeding of familiars on human flesh, but we have discovered that this communication was faulty. The One on the roof Abrhooz (note: replace the torn shingles; Handy Dan has composition?) said his positiveness corrupted the message. It is the Adepti who must find human flesh toothsome. The One indicated that a topological distortion is needed. Black holes are the mundane exemplar of Negativity. Banished Him (It?) back to the Abyss with the Maion ceremony after the Golden Dawn proved ineffectual. The G.D. ceremony simply infuriated Him—fortunately, we had protection.
>
> May 8—Trouble with returning today. Charles began visualizing the planes between the Yhr and the Nhhngr. Everything reversed as usual. Saw some amusing things through the neighbors' mirrors. No wonder Aiwaz called them looking glasses. The current caught us—we abandoned ourselves too much, I guess. Came out near downtown when we finally broke through. May the Powers be praised! We were able to roll a couple of bums for their clothes. No money on them, and their clothes truly stank as well. Had to walk home (43 blocks!) in a man's flannel shirt that hadn't been washed this decade—actually creased with sweat and city

grime and smog! Charles looked fairly decent; got a key from the landlady. We had to smash the mirror as it was exercising an almost hypnotic influence. Charles will consult de Castries on rifts and rays on Monday. All praise to the Goddess of Transformation! Ma-Ion Iä Shub-Niggurath!

Midsummer Night—Opened a Rift without the use of mirrors. Blood of the Moon and a crack's there anyway. Had a few white and black flashes, then the LEAP where black is white and white black. Didn't succumb to screaming heebie-jeebies this time. Others came and talked to us—teaching our bodies. But communication so deep that we can't remember it as yet. Thibaut de Castries says the mutation is physical, not mental. Still very dizzy—walls would spin and shift if I let them. When I finish this entry I'll go and take a cold shower. Apartment full of junk. Eyeglasses, false teeth (2 sets!), ticket stubs, ten silver dollars (go to coin store tomorrow), and some junk jewelry. Looks like a Mardi Gras parade went through the front room.

Sothis Rising. Praise be to Sothis' Silver Star Note: we perceive space in three dimensions because only for $n = 3$ is the metric unique. In $n > 3$ the metric is **not** unique. In everyday life we observe non-unique metric as time, 4D change in a 3D window. The Feast enables the Adept to pull out into Daath. Daath has a non-unique metric—symbolized as Magick = Energy tending to change. The negation/annihilation of the adept is important: empty space = pure energy. Talked with shades unborn tonight, got concrete plans for transformation. Equipment will be big cost, but you can't take it with you. After dismissing Them, Charles gave (pointlessly) a talk about secrecy in our workings, ending it with some crude jokes about stakes and garlic. May need to get ID to get surgical equip—

Blick was interrupted by a noise downstairs. 17:15—someone home from work. He would have to drive downtown to check out. He completed the catalog to turn in and installed a special access lock on the door. On an impulse, he erased "diary" and slipped it into his pocket. The case was closed and this would make an interesting souvenir.

Blick's sleep over the next week was filled with horrors. Mostly, he dreamed of the Tenniels lying naked and hairless while the many-armed surgical equipment crawled like a carnivorous spider over their bodies. The Tenniels would smile at him, greet him by name. "We love you, Bill. We loved you before you were born."

Sometimes he would dream of being a stalker. Hunting through a vast haunted Los Angeles. Everything was reversed, distorted, half unreal, as though the entire city lay reflected in Aunt Sadie's bay windows. Black was white; white was black, angular curved, curved angular.

After three agonizing nights, Blick looked like hell. He asked for and received light duty. No questions. Most of the squad had read his report on the Tenniels and were sympathetic. He was investigating a railway salvage fraud case when news of the second killing came in.

The graveled drive writhed in convection waves. It would have been an excellent day for hang gliding, except that hang gliding is prohibited by local statute, protecting the pools and privacy of the residents of Beverly Hills. It is difficult to say where the meat fell from, since no one was in the airspace.

It was not difficult to identify the meat as human. It fell upon the drive with enough force to imbed the hot pebbles. Mr. Victor's driver nearly ran over it while returning from a shopping expedition in town. The remains were never identified.

Blick returned to his own flat with twilight. Going home had been hard since Laura left. The small apartment expanded to a big empty space. Since the nightmares started, the dark rooms seemed malignant as well as lonely.

The television's red and blue lights made Blick's face a tribal mask. When the news of the Beverly Hills Butcher came in, Blick left for the neighborhood bar. A few cold beers, exchanging a few lies, ought to quell the nausea.

Blick stopped outside Eddie's. The night was cool. Best place to get a hold on his mounting disquiet. The front window was full of regulars, the blond kid who hustled Tempest for drinks, the fat grocer and his pink polyester wife, the sports cluster around the TV. A young couple was watching Blick intensely, reflected in the glass. They must be standing behind him. Blick turned. No one. Turn again. Only himself reflected. Into the bar. His scared face.

The next morning with a hangover that would kill small cattle, Blick called in sick. Afraid to use the bathroom mirror, he shaved by feel, cutting his chin nicely.

He dressed for inconspicuousness. Brown shirt, camel cords, tan socks. Packed his .357 Magnum in a shoulder holster. He was almost out the door when he went back to get the Seal of Solomon keychain his Aunt Sadie had given him and a St. Christopher's medal from Lynn. Couldn't hurt.

The bus took him near the UCLA library. His hangover and accompanying nausea had vanished during the fifteen-minute bus ride. His stomach rumbled and his head sought the magic elixir of coffee.

The air was surprisingly clean, although already in the mid-nineties. In his student days, there had been a little cafe—there it was, just six blocks from campus. It had been the Silver Grill but now was the Mecca with cut-out onion domes painted in orange and black.

The inside still featured naugahyde-covered benches and ersatz formica table tops embossed with broken paper clip designs. Blick ordered two glazed doughnuts and coffee.

The counter, its stools and old men, were reflected in a full-length mirror. Blick froze when he saw the mirror, wondering if daylight and urbanity were significant shields against the Tenniels. There might be more than just Charles and his wife. How many missing person reports did the office receive daily? Seventeen? Twenty-three? Thirty thousand disappear in the US every year without trace. Who knows how many in India or China.

The coffee was strong and the doughnuts stale. As he dunked the doughnut, he felt a fly brush his neck. He started. In the mirror, two black-robed figures were leaning toward him.

Blick spun, trying to stand and free himself from the chair. A taloned hand swished its way to his neck. Fingernails passing into his neck, lifting up and away from the direction of spin. A bright black flash. Violent nausea as the floor dropped from under him. Hieroglyphic silence. Vertigo. Reaching for his gun in a cubist freeze-frame painting. Falling.

Suddenly (at least he thought it was suddenly) Blick focused. He hung suspended in a vast purple light. Alone. A cicada music in his ears. His neck wrenched and bleeding.

Movement was impossible. Nothing to purchase against. After flailing his legs in the cold static void, Blick felt their love. "WE love you, Bill! We loved you before you were born!" Two ideas kept re-entering his mind. He spent hours fighting them. First: he was weight-less. Which immediately brought about thoughts of outer space. Second: he wasn't breathing. Which suggested the hereafter.

After deciding on Descartes's maxim of existence, he calmed down. Panic here was unbounded; without beating heart, sweaty palms, or other visceral governors, panic could totally fill you up.

Perhaps other feelings would be as absolute. That was why the Tenniels came here. Taking Heaven by storm. "That's right, Bill, we love you, inside out. We talked with you before you were born."

Obviously the Tenniels had some method of movement, of inter-acting with the real world. As well as some need to do so, unless the stalking of himself had only been for fun. "Fun is all there is, Bill. Nothing is true, everything is permitted. We love you, Bill. Don't make the mistake of rejecting us!"

Blick closed his eyes to shut out the humming purple void. Very carefully he imagined riding the elevator. He ran the memory, film-like, over and over. He trimmed each temporal edge until the upward sen-sation was all that remained. Simplistic thoughts would intervene: "I've really got it now" or "I wonder if they see inside me?" and he would have to begin the process again.

After an eternity of trying, he was able to hold the sensation of as-cent. Slowly he began to rise.

Gradually the light changed from purple to silver-gray. Blick float-ed above a purple hemisphere of light in a silver-gray void. The noise was different, more of a tea whistle than a cicada song.

Stretching to the horizon were other purple hemispheres, some quiescent, some seething like cauldrons. All glowing.

After a few minutes of observation, Blick noticed a salmon-pink lightning that played over the hemispheres. Very fine, it guided the purple light back into rigidly geometrical shapes whenever it began to expand, dimple, or sag.

The lightning was a webwork emanating from the top of the hemispheres and enveloping their domed bottoms. The origin of each web was a squiggle of light in the center of the purple disk.

Blick's own hemisphere had a stylized "B." With branches so pretty. The birthday cake with three yellow hyacinths in the bowl or Alice's hospital where Momma died and buried in chilly October bobbing for apples in raining buckets canceled Mardi Gras communion wafer after the ash roasting marshmallows—"You little Oreo piece of shit!" in the playground. High School graduation. "Billy Jean" by Michael Jackson, "Twilight Zone" by Golden Earring, the first time he saw the Inverted Fountain at UCLA, Royce Hall, "Ain't your daddy a fucking Jew?", the Hollywood Sign, taking Laura to the Magic Castle, the Disneyland Haunted Mansion, getting a blowjob from the tranny hooker . . .

Blick looked away. Somehow his whole life was netted in its glowing web. Holding cells. The thought popped in: He was drifting back into the hemisphere.

The memory flashes had left him drained. He tried to hoard the elevator rising image. Inches above the hemisphere he stopped and began drifting upward, this time much more slowly. Memory is ballast.

He rose about seven feet from his cell when he saw the gargoyles. Black wings. Gray scaly features, dog heads, goat horns. Three of them. Their great black wings beat against the glowing silver atmosphere. They flew with eagle grace.

Blick fumbled for his gun, realized that he had been clutching it tightly since the coffee shop. The gargoyles sliced through the sky twenty yards above Blick. The humming background became a sharp keening as they passed. "Let them consume your flesh, Bill, they are our love. They are the great Night of Be With Us!"

They wheeled about, descending in a rapine arc toward one of the hemispheres close to Blick.

The first swept above it, gathering a glowing sigil in an outstretched talon. It tore from the light as a scab from a wound, bursting into sparks a few wingbeats away. The other two plunged into the now softer-seeming light, snatching a victim, a tall bald man dressed as a fisherman.

His shouts were silent. Caught firmly between the two gargoyles. The three gargoyles and their bloodied prey flew away.

Far below the hemispheres two dark figures were rising. Blick darted into the recently vacated hemisphere. He sank into eye level—the light in this one was wet and slimy, its noise much more metallic.

The figures rose. Dark, hooded. Long before they reached the hemisphere level, Blick recognized them for the Tenniels.

They rose, floated over Blick's hemisphere. Charles gestured and the sigil glowed brightly.

Blick shot. Twice.

The first shot caught Charles just above the chest. His body began drifting downward. The second shot caught Anna in her stomach. She clutched her belly, crying as if betrayed.

Blick told them what he had told all humans for over forty years: "I reject your love!"

Before Blick fired again Anna wiped the sigil away with her foot and pointed.

Detective Sergeant Blick materialized almost a thousand feet above L.A.

(For Fritz Lieber)

To Mars and Providence

Exactly twenty-nine days after his father had died of general paresis—
that is to say, syphilis—in the local asylum, the boy observed the cylinder land upon Federal Hill. On some level this extramundane intrusion
confirmed certain hypotheses that he had begun to form concerning
the prognosticative nature of dreams. He had been dreaming of the
night-gaunts for three years. They had—the horrible conclusion now
obtruded upon his reluctant mind as an awful certainty—come for
him. As befit a gentleman of pure Yankee stock and the true chalk-
white Nordic type, he had but one option: he must venture forth to
meet and if possible defeat these eldritch beings.

He was eight years old.

The initial and certainly most daunting difficulty would be getting
past his mother and aunts. His grandfather Whipple Phillips might be
an ally in this quest, since he had often kept Howard entertained with
tales of black voodoo, unfathomed caves, winged horrors, and old
witches with sinister cauldrons. But Grandfather Whipple was in Ida-
ho, and his mother, though normally indulgent of such whims, would
not allow his questing into the night air. Howard therefore adopted extreme stealth in the acquisition of his bicycle. He actually carried it several yards from the house before mounting it in quest of adventure.

Down College Hill across the river and then hard work up toward
St. John's Catholic Church on Federal Hill, which is where he judged
the cylinder had fallen. The neighborhood, alive with nameless sounds
that vied with morbid shriekings, seemed to have taken notice of the
cylinder's fall. There was a general lighting of candles, lanterns, torches, and the like. By the time he reached St. John's a rugged ring of light
surrounded the shiny cylinder. He could not stand to force his way
through the crowd, so he entered the church proper and climbed up to

147

the bell tower. Opening a small window in the bell tower, he watched the scene below with growing horror and fascination.

A portion of the cylinder had begun to turn. No doubt the entity or entities therein sought the relieving air of the night as a counter to the searing heat of their bulkhead. The crowd grew fervent with their prayers— prayers to an entity Howard knew to be no more real than the Santa Claus he had abandoned at age five. The lid fell free, and a great fungoid stench assailed Howard's nostrils.

The great leathery wet glistening squamous head of the cylinder's occupant lunged out, pulsing and twitching obscenely. Its vast liquid eyes, whose terrible three-lobed pupils spoke of the being's non-Terran evolution, gazed with glittering contempt upon the sea of humanity surrounding the smoking crater. Some brave soul, perhaps hoping to get a better look at the horror, shined a bull's horn lantern at its eyes. It recoiled from this unwanted stimulus, making a great hooting cry that would be difficult to render phonetically. *Ulla!* Or perhaps *Kuulla!* The creature ducked back into the cylinder, only to re-emerge with a weapon of some sort. Suddenly a flash of blue lightning so intense that it made all the other light a darkness flashed from the weapon. Amidst the screams, Howard fainted.

When Howard returned to consciousness, it was a return from a dream of being medically examined by panting, wheezing, fumbling, drooling Martians. He was—to his intense surprise—in his bed at 454 Angell Street. Susan Lovecraft, his mother, was standing above him.

"I see that my little Abdul has wakened. I trust your materialism will be thoroughly shaken by the miracle which saved you from the Martians."

"Martians?"

"One edition of the *Gleaner* made it out before the error disrupted the city. Everyone has fled. We, however, will remain until Grandfather Whipple comes for us."

Howard could begin to smell the burning city. His mother couldn't be this calm, if what she was saying was true. This must be some sort of game, like when she fixed an Oriental corner in his room when he took the name Abdul Alhazred when he was five. He would play along; after all, there was the fact that he had arrived back at his home.

"You said something about a miracle?"

"The Martians killed everybody near the cylinder. Some men at the university watched it all with binoculars. One of the Martians climbed up the side of the church, to the bell tower's open window, and pulled you out. It carried you down inside the cylinder. I suppose it thought it was one of their own. You are a very ugly child, Howard, people cannot bear to look upon your awful face. When the second cylinder fell, the Martians hurried out of the first to aid in the other's arrival. One of the brave men of the Brown Library, Armitage I believe his name was, ventured all the way there to find you. He knew you because you had pestered him with questions on Cicero. You were there in the cylinder 'sleeping peacefully,' he said."

"How long?"

"You've been asleep three days."

There was something in his mother's eyes that wasn't right. Perhaps the "Martian" invasion had unhinged her highly strung nervous system. He must obtain nourishment and newspaper quickly, and then scout out the city.

"Could you bring the copy of the *Gleaner*, Mother?"

"Certainly, Howard."

The paper had huge headlines. EARTH INVADED BY MARS. The cylinders had fallen in London and Texas.

How ironic, thought Howard, that the Martians would have chosen to land in the Italian section of the city, since it was Giovanni Schiaparelli who had discovered Mars' canal system.

Mother brought him a sandwich for breakfast. The bread was stale and the house quiet.

He asked after his aunts.

Mother's face went blank and dreamy. "They've gone west to speak with your grandfather concerning the invasion. I believe they took the train."

Howard knew that one of the first things the Martians would have done would be to destroy trains, telegraphs, and roads. Mankind would panic if it lost its ability to reassert its pathetic reality by its continuous idiot-god mutterings. What happy cows they would become in a few days, happy to be herd animals. He could feel the contempt he had seen in the three-lobed eyes of the Martian, a burning contempt that an older and more perfect civilization must feel against the ape-like humans.

He would have to meet them again. He could feel a pull toward the cylinder near St. John's Church. An actual physical attraction like iron filings to a lodestone. Perhaps his mother was right and there was something in him that was like the Martians.

He began surveying the town from his window. Great paths of black ash cut obscene angles across the landscape. The Martians' traveling machines respected neither human habitation nor the barriers of river or hill. What marvelous creatures these Martians were to fashion machines to replace bodies! To become pure brains able to cross the cosmos! What starry wisdom they must have accumulated!

He saw the glint of metal and reached for his telescope. A great walking machine was traversing Federal Hill, moving toward St. John's. He could see the pit in front of the church quite clearly. A strange red vegetation covered the pit's sides. The red weed seemed to move slowly of its own accord, for surely no ash stirred with any breeze. The walking machine brought the Martian alongside the bell tower. The Martian placed a small golden box within.

At that moment his mother rushed into the room and pulled Howard from the window. She closed the curtains. She told him she was making hot chocolate. He should come to the parlor to enjoy some.

He felt sad for his mother, but guessed that it was perhaps a blessing that the human mind is unable to correlate all its contents. Howard went down into the parlor and did partake of hot chocolate. His mother talked of trivial things as though no horror waited outside of the curtained windows.

Everything was still, very still, and Howard surmised that the city was deserted. Then a great ululation so horrible that surely no human mouth could utter nor mind conceive it smashed the stillness of the air as a monolith of terror upon a plain of endless desolation. Mother nearly dropped her tiny white teacup, a proud relic of the family's past. Golly, thought Howard, something needs to be done. Mother talked rapidly and quietly. Once again the Martian cry resonated obscenely in the Terran atmosphere.

Howard excused himself. Mother didn't seem to notice. He went to his grandfather's medicine chest. Grandfather Whipple fought his pernicious insomnia with a powerful sleeping powder. Howard believed that he could easily mix it in the malted milk that his mother favored as an evening meal.

Waiting out the afternoon was torture. Something pulled Howard to St. John's Church. He could almost see the bell tower room when he closed his eyes. Knowing that the mystery was there was making him do and think things he had never thought. Mystery, he decided, was the great *transformatrice*. She effected a change in one's self by simply *being*.

The evening meal proved worse. He had had to argue with Mother so that he could prepare her malted milk. She would have to be sedated if he were to quest further. This time he must not faint and be subject to removal before viewing whatever horror his destiny had chosen for him.

Mother drank her malt. She joked gently that he did not know how to prepare it. He watched her carefully, making sure that she drank it all rather than pouring it down the kitchen drain. She retired to the parlor afterwards, where her fear kept her from lighting candle or lamp. As it grew darker, her words grew fainter and fainter. He listened long and hard to be sure that the whisperer in darkness did indeed sleep, then tiptoed out of the house.

Outside, deep twilight held the city in its gray-purple embrace. Only the topmost windows reflected the glorious sunset. The enchanting and beautiful twilight almost concealed the great ashen pathways of desolation that the Martians had left in their wake. Only one of the once many proud bridges still spanned the river. Howard began to run toward it. The sense of movement made him feel watched; Howard was the only thing moving on College Hill. The Martians' siege had stolen the comforting noises of the ancient city, leaving it as still as the vast void of darkling space through they had traveled, and as foul-smelling as the odor of plague-stricken towns and uncovered cemeteries.

As Howard crossed the bridge he looked upon the ancient city with eyes of memory, preferring not to see the havoc of war. He looked upon the entrancing panorama of loveliness, the steepled town nestling upon its gentle hills.

Howard's run slowed to a panting walk as he climbed Federal Hill. When he reached the crater he nearly swooned from the Oriental sweetness that the undulating carmine growth dispersed through the still air, but the distant cry of a Martian, mixed with the terrified cry of the human herd, reminded him of his mission. He entered the dark church and made for the bell tower.

Beneath the bells, on a small table, the object lay. It was a garnet crystal in the shape known to science as a trapezohedron. It shone with faint ruddy light—the light of Mars, which the Babylonians (Howard reflected) called Nergal and the Northmen Tyr. By the small table stood a small chair that would exactly fit an eight-year-old boy.

He hypothesized the shining trapezohedron must be the focus for some sort of communication. But could he withstand the daemonical truth such communication—dare he think it, *communion* could bring?

He reached out and picked up the stone. It tingled; some energy was contained within and began to have a direct effect on his nerves. At once he became aware of a vaster sensory range than his human evolution had prepared him for. First, the tiny chamber in the steeple, which had been fairly dark, now blazed with light. Second, he could hear a sweet distant breathing or perhaps the sounds of flutes playing a magical but incoherent pattern. Third, he became aware—as much through the sense of *taste* as of sight—of a colour that floated in the air above him. He could not name this colour, it was not a colour of earth, not belonging to the neat spectrum Newton's prism had revealed. This colour moved within itself, fashioning itself by rules not native to earth, but of another part of space. It was sentient, and somehow *informed* or taught those possessed of it. It must be the medium through which the Martians communicated with one another. It sensed that Howard sensed it and it became violently agitated. Suddenly it shot a tentacle into Howard's brain. It pulled his soul free from its moorings.

For a moment he was suspended in the colour out of space. He could hear the colour, taste the colour, think as the colour.

The colour asked him, "Are you one of us?"

"I do not know what you mean."

"We prepared for the invasion by sending forth the minds of the greatest telepaths of our race. They dwelt among men as spies living in the bodies of men. Most returned to us, but some lost memory of their being enchanted by the revelations received in human flesh. Are you one of us?"

Howard did not know. He had felt that there was much from outside of the world of men in him.

The colour began to pulsate, pushing him along. He wondered that he had sensation separate from his body.

"You are in a body of your thoughts. When we have transported you to Mars it will be made semi-material for two purposes. You will be able to handle and sense physical objects, and we will be able to examine your true mental form."

Howard considered that he might be a Martian. He had always felt that the day-to-day world partook of a phantom character. The only things that seemed real to him had been his dreams, certain tales in the *Arabian Nights,* and certain suggestions of a grander world which he saw in certain architectural features revealed in sunsets. Surely Mars was a sunset world, gold and red in its martial glory. What wonders a civilization older than mankind might possess! The colour, sensing his thoughts, began to show him images.

The "Martians" had come from another world to settle in this solar system. Eons ago they had crossed space in cylinders like those they had so recently employed. They settled upon Mars and earth's South Pole. The latter colony had vanished, perhaps succumbing to the violent climatic changes that earth had suffered. The former began a specialized eugenics program. Worshipping no god save their own intellects, they sought to eliminate all the glands that cause emotion (save for fear, the emotion necessary for survival), and remove all en-

zymes that cause aging. The Martians had likewise eradicated all forms
of microbial disease, leading to a practical immortality. The coming of
immortality necessitated a specialized training of the will. The Martian
had to cultivate those intellectual and aesthetic pursuits which could
sustain an interest that would span the strange eons through which
they would live.

This training of the will had an unexpected side effect: the Martians discovered that some of the stronger minds of their race could
project themselves across the void without mechanical aid. These astral
travelers came in contact with the various races of the solar system, including the feeble-minded men who dwelt upon the noisome green
world of earth, and a race of what could be best described as fungoid
beings inhabiting a dwarf planet on the rim of the solar system.

The Martians traded with the fungi, and Martian civilization
reached its height of material prosperity. The Martians covered the
ruddy surface of their world with labyrinthine Cyclopean structures,
whose sole function was to express certain aesthetic, mathematical, or
metaphysical formulae. The Martians waxed great in pride. Surely no
race had reached such success.

This golden age gave way to a certain decadence. One of the first
symptoms of this decline was a decrease in reproductive powders. The
Martians had long since given up sexual reproduction in favor of a less
distracting asexual budding. Fewer and fewer Martians came into being. Art became debased, and the objective art of the past was increas-
ingly replaced by an outrageous subjectivity.

Perhaps the Martians would have gone into a long and steady decline had it not been for the discovery of the vast underground vaults
at Syrtis Major.

The "Martians" discovered that uncounted eons ago, an almost
godlike race had dominated their planet. The fungi confirmed this,
claiming that they were in fact not dead, but had entered into a sort of
undead sleep, waiting for a certain modulation of cosmos rays that
would allow them to resume their play in glory and terror. The fungi
were unsure when the elder gods would return and hinted darkly at the

method of their remanifestation. The "Martians" were neither the oldest nor the last of Mars' masters.

Great energy was turned toward the excavation and destruction of the vaults, but despite their mighty heat rays and lightning machines the Martians were unable to cut through the curious metal of the vaults. The dread of the creatures who would return was heightened by the discovery of their image carved into certain remote peaks that overlook the haunted deserts, whose baleful influence the Martians had shunned for millennia.

These elder gods with their long, ghoul-like faces and star-destroying eyes were soon all the Martians could think of. For a season unreason held sway, and the normally logical Martians destroyed as many images of these horrors as they could find. But reason returned and the remaining specimens of statues were gathered at the capital, and controlled debate on the course of action began. A decision was made to invade Earth and safely leave Mars for the elder gods.

A few minds had crossed to Earth to observe its affairs, and the Martians reasoned that he might be one of their own—since his mind had the strength to activate the shining trapezohedron.

The colour seemed to be exerting less pressure, and Howard realized that he would soon be on the surface of Mars. He had found his people. His long exile from those around him would be ended! Soon their superior skill in psychology and surgery would free him to walk among his own kind—his vast pulsating brain attached to a shiny metal machine!

Movement stopped and the unearthly color began to fade. Howard found himself at the gates of a huge red building whose wings stretched in all directions—perhaps covering the planet. The slowly moving red weed covered the ground. From within he heard the mathematically perfect music of the Martians.

He went through the great gate into a hall filled with great brains whose tentacles worked every strange device, whose construction clearly revealed their kinship to the technology that had produced the heat ray. But as soon as Howard had entered the hall a great cry went up. The Martians were not shambling toward him in greeting as he had imagined. Instead, they began a disorderly march to the exits. Howard looked about for the source of their fear.

There on the other side of the hall, through a trapezoidal doorway, came the figure of one of the elder gods. The Martians had not had time to relocate to Earth. Howard advanced toward the figure; perhaps he could slow its progress by engaging in hand-to-hand combat.

But soon came the shock that sent his mind hurtling back to Earth, a revelation about the nature of the elder gods and the time and form of their return. This shock deprived Howard of all clear memories of this adventure; indeed, years later he was one of the skeptics who maintained that the Earth had not been invaded at all—for when he reached out toward the eldritch figure of the elder god, his hand had encountered *a cold and unyielding surface of polished glass.*

(*For Howard Waldrop*)

After Alhazred

In the smoky darkness of my lover's
Heart I find written my hidden name
On a ventricle wall in invisible Flame,
Written there before the birth of our mothers.
Silently I draw away my dream gaze
and cast it 'round the dying night world
amid the cenotaphs and crypts of eld.
Our love survives death and will live on to other days.
Can I explain to the other sleepers a love
that burns beyond death and maggot's kiss?
Can I explain that we as living flames hiss
Into an eternal space darker than abyss above?

That which is not dead can eternal lie,
and after strange aeons death may die.

Lovecraft's Pillow

Nothing had gone right in the week before the Con.

Edgar Wagner's son Mike had come out as gay, and Edgar could handle that, he really could. Mike also decided to leave Stanford mid-semester and live with his lover. Edgar's wife of twenty years asked that "they take a break." Edgar's doctor was not happy about his blood pressure or his bad cholesterol. Edgar's latest novel, *Those Outside,* had a mixture of a couple of bad reviews—and, worse still, NO reviews from some of the big newspapers that had lauded him for the last decade. There were big stacks of the book at various dealers tables at World Horror, and the adoring lines of fans asking for an inscription had died down to the few asking for an autograph as a possible eBay investment. Edgar was wondering what it would be like to go back to teaching at his age.

It was fall and it was Providence, Rhode Island, so it meant that every other panel Edgar was on had to do with Howard Phillips Lovecraft. Every writerly virtue ("My God, his imagination!") and every writerly vice ("Do you really need to use the word eldritch twenty-three times in one story?") of Mr. Lovecraft was being discussed again and again. But Edgar Scott Wagner was not getting the panel he needed. He needed the panel called "What do you do if have an idea for four horror novels and you are writing your ninth?" It was late afternoon, and Edgar walked out of the hotel and took off his badge and headed downtown. He always loved to walk. There was lots of walking in his books. He wrote a novella about walking, called "Walking," which (as almost every reviewer pointed out) owed a great deal to Stephen King's *The Long Walk.* There were four things that Edgar Wagner loved: walking, pawn and thrift shops, history, and horror stories. He had taught social studies at the high school level for twelve years before he had his first successful novel, about haunted Civil War cannons starting a war between two museums—*Blue and Gray and Red All Over*. It wasn't a good book, but damn, it made a good movie. It was an OK plot, Borges had used it for Chrissakes, and it did OK for his fifth book about haunted swords, *Sabers of Doom*. And for the haunted airplane novel *Lucifer's Aces*. At home he had written almost ten thousand words of the haunted car novel . . .

He would have been a great fanboy. He had rewritten Lovecraft, Matheson, King, and Jackson. He didn't really think anybody noticed. Or cared. But with the last two books people had noticed. There were no movie deals—options but no actual films—and Mike went off to Stanford and Sue had a swimming pool put in. People even called his vampire novel "*'Salem's Lot* in Colorado"—even Sue called it that once because she couldn't remember its name. Fewer people called *Those Outside* "The Whisperers in Darkness," because fewer people had read the Lovecraft original. Except at this convention.

When he was a history teacher nobody cared that he hadn't made up the history. He was supposed to just tell what had happened and make it seem relevant. That had been his same approach to writing. He picked a story that he knew well and told in a relevant fashion. He used TV shows and pop cultural references and made his heroes into white middle-class novel readers. Wagner's style was accessible, and the first three books had the great good luck of becoming blockbuster movies. Wagner could walk away from the Chicago high school that was cold in the winter and smelled the rest of the time. Wagner had seen broken windows patched with cardboard and tin without seeing new glass for ten years. All his idealism froze out there, and every year he would call from his Dallas home when the snow was two and three feet deep—he would call the math teacher or the English teacher just to hear the snow in their voices.

Last year it had still been warm enough in October to swim in his pool and like it. He could jump in his pool and light jack-o'-lanterns the next day. He could wake up to oldies rock and drinking coffee in his white terrycloth bathrobe and typing his four pages before noon. He could surf the Web while his window was open and listen to the song selections of the mockingbird, and no high school punk told him to fuck himself. He could plan on going to England and meeting Ramsey Campbell. He could see his own movies on Netflix. Life was good. Not just OK, good. If the Muses would just start singing to him again . . .

Wagner walked along following an inner drive that took him toward the seedier parts of Providence, toward the reality of the high school he once taught at. He noticed the nip in the air and the city smell, and he knew he was being one of his characters in his own damn books—walking and recapitulating his life until something sinister (stolen from some other guy's or gal's books) snagged his attention like a fancy fly for a big-mouthed bass. He was twelve or thirteen blocks from the convention hotel. He was Dante lost in the middle of his life in an urban forest. He saw the three brass balls of St. Nick and turned into Gamble Brothers PAWN. And all the chunky pieces of other human's history displayed in their glass cases took him away from his problems as they always did.

There were the wedding rings and the jewelry and the guitars and keyboards and there were guns, guns, guns. Kids' bicycles (when stealing the piggy bank just isn't enough) and TVs and computers. And at the front, nearest the register, was a pillow.

It was an old feather pillow with a yellowish cast to it. It had been white (or at the very least a light gray) years ago. There was small brownish spot where saliva had leaked on it, and a single brown-red dot marking blood from a nostril over-dry in the Rhode Island winter. And there was a price tag written in magic marker. $250.00.

Now here had to be a story, and Wagner felt it wouldn't lead to the story of two pillows that needed to wage a ghostly fight. Malcolm X and George Wallace. Just some overpriced pawn shop con.

The owner of the shop (or at least the manager) was a slight gray man with thinning gray hair and liver spots and yellow teeth and a big goofy grin. His white shirt was gray, and his khaki trousers were gray, and Wagner knew even before he spoke that Mr. Gamble's voice would be gray too.

"What can I do you for, mister?" he asked.

"That's a highly priced pillow," observed Edgar Wagner.

"It is a genuine piece of Providence history," said the gray man. "It is the pillow that Howard Phillips Lovecraft died on."

"Why would you own that?" Wagner didn't believe, but this reeked of story.

"My grandmother was a nurse at Jane Brown Hospital in '37. She had written a few poems and Lovecraft had talked to her about verse. When he died, she took the pillow. I wanted to sell it to a comic book store, but they never made me a good offer. So I heard about the horror convention on Channel 8 and I thought I would drag it out. You heard of Lovecraft?"

"I've heard of him." All Wagner could think was how much this man's dialect sounded like one of Lovecraft's hicks. Wagner wondered how many pillows this relic had sold.

"Wait a minute: you're him, ain't ye? Dean Koontz."

"I am not Dean Koontz."

"But yer face. I've got your face on a book. I love horror, because of my grandmother, she got us all hooked. You're *Lucifer's Dive Bombers*. What's hiz name? Ramsey Campbell. No, he's British. Wagner. You're that guy from Chicago."

"I was glad to say goodbye to Chicago years ago." After twelve years of writing, after pictures and TV interviews and panels, it had happened. Someone had recognized him. *Please don't let him say something stupid now.*

"I liked your book. I've read two or three things by you."

"Thanks."

"You should buy this here pillow. You and Lovecraft. It's fate. Oh, let me get a picture of myself selling you this pillow. I have bragged about this pillow for years, and nobody cares around here."

"Well, how do I know this is *the* pillow?"

Mr. Gamble's face fell. "Well, there is that. Lovecraft didn't sign no certificate saying he was about to die. All you can see is the hospital's name on this here tag," He lifted the pillow out of the display case and showed off a tag inside. The pillowcase was definitely stolen hospital property.

"Mr. Gamble, I believe you," said Edgar Wagner.

"Will you buy it then?"

Edgar Wagner knew that his wife would kill him for buying the pillow. But she was off "taking a break" with her cousin in Meritt Island, Florida. There was no one waiting for him back in Dallas. No one to belittle his foolishness at being taken in by some urban artifact salesman.

Edgar's soul lay open at that moment. As a kid he had found arrowheads. In college he had minored in archeology. Every trip to a thrift shop, every antique he bought for his mother and later for his wife—it was all about owning the past. His love for Lovecraft was about owning the past. Holding it. Walking through its Cyclopean halls. This ridiculous pillow was exactly why he had done so many things in his life, and his son wouldn't understand it and his wife wouldn't understand it. But they were not waiting at home.

"Mr. Gamble, would you like me to take some pictures with my phone of my buying Lovecraft's pillow? Do you have an e-mail address that I can I send them to?"

Even after the horror that transpired, the photos are still there on the Gamble Brothers PAWN Shop page. But of course Mr. Gamble had no way of knowing what happened.

Edgar carried the pillow back to the convention hotel just as the sun set. He tucked it under his arm and he told no one. He didn't want to be laughed at. It could be Lovecraft's pillow. It was too odd a story to be false. He dropped it off in his room, carefully putting it in his suitcase, suddenly afraid that an overzealous hotel staff might wash away the eldritch stains.

He had to ship some things home, books bought at the con mainly, but he kept the pillow in his baggage. Then it was Tuesday and he was home and he took it out. What should he do with it? He didn't want it as a shrine, an item behind glass. No, he wanted to touch it. He threw his pillows off his king-size bed. Lovecraft's pillow might not be the 300-thread-count pillowcases Sue demanded. It was cheap and used and reminded him of the pillowcases they had bought at the Goodwill store in Lisle, Illinois, that first year. Sue was waiting tables at Denny's and he was riding the train into town every freezing morning. All day long Edgar was excited about sleeping on the pillow. So excited that he drove to a drugstore and bought sleeping pills, something he had never used.

Lovecraft's entire imagination might have been left in this pillow. All those nightmares chittering inside, waiting in the Gamble home. Had anyone slept on it? Wagner doubted it. The grandmother had been excited that a "real writer" had spoken to her about her poetry. Some dreary religious sonnets no doubt, words to keep the horror of nursing at bay. And Lovecraft, always the gentleman, giving every moment to the writers around him while every conceivable penny dried up—no, grandmother Gamble had let no one sleep on this relic. The next generation would have been grossed out. A bit of dried blood? A cancer patient died on this? Finally the shrewd pawnshop owner, knowing that the yellowing cotton and decaying feathers could be redeemed in coin. Edgar Wagner would be the first human to lay his head on the pillow since March 15, 1937.

He expected amazing dreams. He expected night-gaunts and Kadath. He had instead a black dreamless night and woke with a tummyache. He went to his computer and checked his e-mail. It was that rather bothersome bookseller who wanted him to autograph all those copies of his first novel. The man was going on about the spiritual connection he had felt to Lovecraft by being in Providence. Edgar would normally have simply ignored the e-mail, but he felt it would be a good thing to challenge the man's foolish beliefs. Just because one had a fondness for tales of the weird and the macabre was no reason to succumb to anti-scientific fancy. It took him over an hour to draft a response, but he felt glad that he had done so. He began re-reading his novel in progress, *Satan's Hot Wheels*. The concept was grossly immature. It pandered to two sorts of slack-jawed numbskullery. First, any artistic concept actually reliant on a folk myth like Satan was too imaginatively weak. Second, the idea of an artistic endeavor centered on the automobile was certainly beneath the attention of a gentleman.

About two in the afternoon he checked his e-mail again. His agent had news of a possible movie deal for *Those Outside*. Well, the man should do as he thought best; the making of motion pictures was fortunately not Edgar Wagner's business. He also had a letter from a high school admirer asking his advice about writing. Now that was more like it, the passing on of the holy fire of imagination. Edgar spent four hours writing to the young man.

Dinner came and Edgar opened a can of pasta. His stomach was defiantly sore; the traveling had not agreed with him. When bedtime came he was embarrassed by the pillow—what a ridiculous expenditure! However, he would make use of the pillow; despite its faint smell of ammonia, it was adequate for sleep. He turned down the heat and went to bed late, spending a goodly amount of time reading. He decided to lay aside his current project and seek something grander. Upon arising the next day he received a phone call from his wife. He encouraged her to stay longer at her sister's. He liked the Southern climate and suspected that she had grown tired of his uninteresting self. She seemed worried about him, but he pointed out that he was enjoying the long quiet time needed for artistic creation. He convinced her that their time apart was helping re-create himself.

He rooted around in Michael's room, finding some old partially empty composition books. Arming himself with a pen, he began writing with no clear plan, merely allowing images of an artistic nature to present themselves to him. He wondered if he ever truly experienced art rather than the copying of such artistic models that had presented themselves to him in his haphazard educational process. He worked late into the night. He realized that he had never enjoyed working during the day, but had adopted such a schedule to fit in with his wife and family. A true gentleman must keep his own hours. When at last he fell asleep he pondered the largeness of his home as opposed to the smallness of his needs. If he did not keep up such a large establishment he would not have to write so much for the masses. He tried to remember the last time he had written a poem, and discovered to his astonishment that he had never done so. This did not in any way seem correct, but he could not put his finger on what exactly was amiss with his recollections before sleep carried him away.

The next day he could not recall his password to log onto his computer. It scarcely seemed a grave problem; a mechanical writing aid is scarcely the source of composition. He was saddened when the post brought no letters. It seemed as though the art of letter writing was falling into disuse; he must remedy this. He began writing a letter to one of the young men he had met on the horror-writing panel. He had had a rather lively disagreement about the importance of setting. To achieve the truly cosmic one must focus on the minute as a contrast. An ideal tale of cosmicism should be grounded in material detail. If one wishes to speak of the passage of millions of years one must begin with a scene marked by such commonplace phrases as "a quarter to eleven." When Edgar had written ten pages, he sought to check a source in his library.

This proved very disappointing. When had he bought so much rubbish? Edgar Scott Wagner had been raised Methodist, but he had never realized until now how long he had held on to such superstition. There were more than twenty volumes ranging from hymnals to trite sentimental religious novels to something titled *Holy Humor*. His disappointment turned into embarrassment: what would people think of him if he died and had such titles in his possession? Edgar had always been a strict materialist. At least he only remembered being a materialist; but the presence of these titles suggested otherwise. He gathered the offending books up. He recalled that he had spent several happy hours in the Half Price Bookstore. He would sell these books and purchase more flattering titles. He had not a single volume of Machen, not a book of Dunsany! This was intolerable.

He marched to his garage and looked at his brown SUV. The thought of braving the Dallas traffic bothered him. It was nearing the rush hour, and as he had not driven in several days he suddenly felt unsure of his automotive prowess. It had been better when he lived in Chicago and there were buses and trains at his disposal. He placed the box of books in the back of his SUV; he would sell them tomorrow. At least this way he need not look at them.

The newness of his house suddenly depressed him. Why had he bought such a silly modern edifice? Not that there were any buildings in Dallas that had any history of them. Dallas' only claim to fame was the killing of that Irish president. Indeed, most of Texas had only the thinnest veneer of history save perhaps for San Antonio, which he had heard was quite picturesque. He should relocate to New Orleans. Now there was a town. Its cemeteries and its wrought iron!

But Edgar felt something slipping away from him again. He could remember having made plans to visit New Orleans with his wife. They had talked about it before the hurricane, but he could not remember their actual visit. He shouldn't have any memories of the city at all. Suddenly this false memory resolved itself into fear. He felt as he had felt when he had those dreadful night terrors as a child. He needed to go his bedroom, to lie down for a moment. He locked and double-locked all the doors of his house and buried his face in his pillow.

He may have slept all the next day. He was unsure when he awoke what day it was. He knew the nurse should be coming soon. She was a cheerful lady who tried to distract him from the inevitability of his cancer. She was not a materialist like him and did not know that no terrors or bliss waited one after the organism failed. He felt too weak to move. The hospital was very quiet today.

She would be along shortly.

(For Stephen King)

The Codex

HISTORICAL NOTE: Robert H. Barlow began corresponding with H. P. Lovecraft at age thirteen. Lovecraft made several trips to Barlow's home in Florida and collaborated on six stories with him. Upon Lovecraft's death in 1937, the nineteen-year-old Barlow was named Lovecraft's literary executor. Barlow turned from weird fiction to anthropology and became an expert in Mexican folklore and the Mayan codices. His zeal in tracking down obscure codices as well as working with living informants is still talked about. He became chairman of the Anthropology Department at Mexico City College. One of his last students was William S. Burroughs, whose studies of the Mayan codices influenced his avant-garde writing. Barlow killed himself with sleeping pills on January 1, 1951. Burroughs shot his common-law wife nine months later on September 1, 1951. He later claimed he was led to this act by an entity he called the Ugly Spirit.

"Mr. Burroughs disagrees with some of the current thought on the codices," said Professor Barlow. A couple of students sniggered. Burroughs was older, suspected of being a drug user and a homosexual, and had weird theories about addiction and control. Others were impressed with his cool mineral calm, Midwestern voice, and Ivy League vocabulary.

A posterboard Christmas tree from Barlow's far-off youth in Florida hung in the room marking the season. Its green had faded; its lights and ornaments had grown dim.

"I make them for books of the dead," said Burroughs.

"But they deal with the extreme past, not some future state," objected Miss Jimenez.

"Exactly," said Burroughs. "If reincarnation is a fact, you want to orient yourself toward the future. You do that by looking backward to before death. Not just your last death, but a time before death. Before the ball games and the biological courts. That's why the codices stretch back four hundred million years."

"But that amount of time can't have any meaning," said Bill Peabody.

"Why does time have to be 'meaningful'?" asked Guy Smith. "Does 'In the beginning' have any meaning?"

Professor Barlow smiled. "Now you're beginning to think mythically. You have to drop your Western thinking if you want the Mayan world to open to you."

Smith, Burroughs, and Carsons smiled. The rest of the class looked angry. Maybe angry at having Western rationality spurned, but some were angry that the professor favored the queers. Well, there was a rumor at least.

A bell rang and students ran from class.

"Feliz Navidad!" yelled Barlow. "Remember to get your reading done over the holidays!"

Carsons, Smith, and Burroughs remained. Barlow looked at them quizzically. He avoided the gay ex-pat community. It would be professional death. But he liked Burroughs. Burroughs was a writer, unpublished of course, but he had the kind of mind that focuses on anything without flinching. When details about Mayan or Aztec religion came up that made the other students shudder, Burroughs merely looked thoughtful. Barlow couldn't help but think about Burroughs's ideas of pre-death as reflecting the sort of thing that Lovecraft had written about. Of course, real anthropology wasn't based on subjectivity. He had thought of sharing his prize, Lovecraft's handwritten ms. of "The Shadow out of Time," with Burroughs, but the sexuality question bothered him. It had been so painful when he had confessed to Lovecraft during the last visit. And there had been—well—mistakes with students.

Audrey Carsons asked him, "Dr. Barlow, you seem to hint at things sometimes. We're interested in the real secrets."

"There are no secrets, Mr. Carsons, only speculations."

Burroughs said, "My uncle Ivy made millions on speculations. Speculations just mean you got there first. Poison Ivy they called him."

"Speculations are a more guarded for a scholar than a Wall Street type, I'm afraid. What speculations are interested in?"

"We want to know about Death. Ah Pook and Zushakon. We want to know about Ix Tab or Yig Tab, the serpent goddess in charge of snares—catching a soul in her coils for its next reincarnation."

"Those names don't appear in the official codices," began Barlow.

"We're not interested in the well-thought-of translations," said Guy Smith. "We're interested in the ones that Work."

"You're talking about magic," said Barlow. His other vice, one that Lovecraft thought terrible. A vice that had to be hidden from the scholarly world.

"Yes, that could be a word for the technology we're looking for," said Burroughs.

"I won't discuss anything like that on campus. Maybe you could drop by my apartment over break. There is another codex, one that has a problematic history that talks about the ideas you are interested in. Of course, I'd have to swear you to secrecy."

"Of course," said Burroughs. "I wouldn't have it any other way."

He regretted inviting them. Barlow felt it was a set-up. But who's conning whom? Two years ago he happened across a small bookshop in Tlatilōlco, a weird neighborhood for a bookshop. It was stuck between a barber's shop and a taquería—it had books overflowing its ancient shelves. Mainly modern novels in English, French, and Spanish—random volumes from encyclopedias, books brought into the city by tourists, cheap occult books on palmistry and the lore of the tarot—in short, junk. Barlow had been about to leave when the shopkeeper, a well-dressed woman in her thirties, asked if he needed help finding anything. Her English had almost no accent, her skin tone was very light.

"No, I don't think you would have what I am interested in."

"Señor, we do have what you are interested in, that I know. My uncle's shop is a trifle unorganized."

At that moment he spotted a fading copy of the June 1936 copy of

Astounding Stories with Lovecraft's "The Shadow out of Time" providing the (inaccurate) cover illustration. The Great Race of Yith (as faded as his Christmas tree) menaced a well-dressed white man. Barlow broke into a big smile and picked up the magazine, which lay atop a stack of books. Beneath it was the *Codex Catamaco*. The word "Codex" was a magnet to his iron. He snatched up the thin, light-brown, leather-covered book. The frontmatter had been torn away. It looked as if the book had originally about a hundred pages. The paper quality was poor, rough, and brown. It had probably been printed during the war. The last seventy pages were a Mayan codex with *interlinear English translation*. Like most scholars, Barlow assumed that the language would someday be deciphered, but certainly nothing like this level of translation existed. The book's backmatter was mainly in place—including an index that included topics that were well known to any Mayaologist—and others of a more tantalizing nature such Charles Hinton, the mathematician who had done significant work on the fourth dimension. Of course, all such rogue references were conveniently pointing to the missing pages in the front. But if the volume were a hoax or a joke, it had been an expensive one—buying the type for the Mayan ideographs had cost a pretty penny. Trying not to look overly excited, he asked the book's price. The young woman looked over its condition and told him simply to take it—her store didn't sell damaged goods. He picked up a copy of Norman Mailer's 1948 bestseller *The Naked and the Dead,* no doubt brought in as summer reading by a tourist, and paid a few pesos for it. It seemed wrong not to leave something.

Barlow had almost run home with the book. He came back the next day. He had expected the shop to vanish, or the "uncle" to be some seedy character from a Lovecraft story. He was a middle-aged businessman fond of Mark Twain with no idea from whom he had bought the codex. He tried to get Barlow to buy some books on palmistry. The shop lasted another year and either closed or moved.

The remaining book was in four parts. The first was the tale of the arrival of the death-god Ah Pook on Earth via comet 400,000,000 years ago. He fell in the northern polar regions where he fought two other death-gods, Kisin and Zushakon. The three divided deaths on this world. Ah Pook taught humans how to die in order to be reborn with their memories more or less intact. They had to be careful not to remember their deaths, or they would die again. Zushakon, a centipede god that lived in a lightless world, collected criminals—evil beings that were sacrificed to him in a grisly manner—whose souls he would use as a sort of garment. The text gave a dubious translation of Zushakon as the "Ugly Spirit." Kisin was less picky. He/It simply fed on death and rot of all sorts. The three gods fought for over a million years, calling on the aid of other beings from exploded stars.

The second part dealt with the creation of humans and other races—the Insect People, the Vegetable People, the Fungus People, the Hairy People, and finally humans—by the death-gods as sources of food or "vessels" for their servants/allies. Each of these groups were given various worlds or planes of existence, but they could trade certain gems, drugs, and metals with one another—if they paid a high tax to the death-gods. Barlow had never read any mythological speculation of this sort; frankly, the "gods" were being treated as a sort of space alien. It certainly reminded him more of Lovecraft's fiction than true mythology. Humans should love or fear their gods, but not be nihilistic toward them. He read with a start that the Fungi People had been given an extra-cold planet to live on. This was too close to Lovecraft. Why had that copy of *Astounding* been lying conveniently atop the pile of books? But that wouldn't have meaning for anyone other than him in Mexico City. The effort to place it in a bookstore in a neighborhood that he had visited perhaps twice, and hope that he would spot the magazine *and* pick up the doctored book beneath, required millions-to-one odds.

The third part of the book was similar to the *Tibetan Book of the Dead.* It explained death as a long journey begun at the invitation of one of the death-gods. It was a hazardous journey, where every mistake you had made in your life counted against you. The three gods were going to try and trick you, but if you slipped past them you were out of "time" and in eternity. Ix Tab, goddess of snares and hanging, tried to trick you by inverting future and past. You might be cagey enough to avoid two fornicating peasants thinking that as the road to be born as a peasant, but you could touch a rotting dog's body and be sucked into the corpse to live the dog's life in reverse. On one of the glyphs "Ix" was translated "Yig." Now that had to be either a hoax or the biggest coincidence ever, because Lovecraft had made up that name as a god for one of his revision clients.

The fourth part of the book was about control, both magical and political. The Mayans used (and still use) a slash-and-burn system of agriculture. If you wait too long to burn the shoots, rains will make them too damp to burn. If you plant too early, drought can ruin your crops; if you plant too late, the big downfall could wash away your seeds. A few days either way and a year's crop is lost. So the priests are given great control calendars—this way they will seem to be gods. The priests are instructed to have a continuous circle of festivals so that the population never learns how to read the signs of the year; thus they need the priests—that is probably why there is no number higher than twenty in spoken Maya today. After this *realpolitik* came a time-travel spell that enabled the priests to go back in time and make contact with the death-gods.

Barlow was ashamed of it, but he wanted to *try*. He had two questions for Lovecraft. One was about the real source of the *Necronomicon*. The other had been about boys—about sex with boys. Both answers had been disappointing.

Now Burroughs and his friends had mentioned Zushakon, a name not attested in the three "official" codices. Likewise (and more suspiciously) "Yig." He knew Burroughs was an heir to the Burroughs adding machine company. He might have resources that could produce the book—but how could he have got it to Mexico in 1948?

Burroughs was a weird cat. He claimed to know another writer, Jack Kerouac, whose *The Town and the City* came out last year. Burroughs even said one of the characters in the book was based on him (Will Dennison). He had a wife, Joan—another book character for Kerouac, Mary Dennison—who was strung out on speed to contrast Burroughs's fondness for opium products. Mexico was good for Americans with a monkey; even one of Barlow's fellow teachers kept powdered codeine in a box of bicarbonate of soda and would add spoonfuls of it to his tea at staff meetings.

Barlow hadn't been able to find out anything about Guy Smith or Audrey Carsons. They were young beautiful wild boys—they had Midwestern accents as well. All three seemed to be remittance men. Barlow had decided that he would spill the beans on the codex caper.

His apartment was huge. He had two sitting rooms, kitchen, full bath, and a large bedroom. He showed Burroughs and the boys into the inner sitting room, which served as a library. They were book people all right. Burroughs picked up and glanced at several anthropological texts as well as his collection of William Hope Hodgson and Arthur Machen. Barlow offered them Mexican hot chocolate and sweet tortillas. Small talk was engaged in largely until twilight fell. The boys had come at tea time.

"So, Professor, what can you tell us about Zushakon?" asked Guy Smith.

"He was a centipede god living in a dark realm beneath the earth—probably somewhere in the United States," he added with a smile.

"America is an old and evil land," said Burroughs. "There was serious shit there before the Indians came."

Barlow continued. "When the priests convicted someone of a serious crime, they said the Ugly Spirit had chosen him. They didn't want to piss off the Ugly Spirit, so they treated the criminal real courteously—until his execution. Then they would heat a copper centipede shell as long as the miscreant was tall. As they heated the shell, they skinned the criminal alive and then forced him into the shell, now glowing cherry-red. As he died great bells were rung that had a special property—probably due to infrasound—that made the room suddenly become black. When the anomalous darkness vanished, it was always found that the victim's body was gone from the shell."

At this point loud knocking came from Barlow's outer door. He rose and, after closing the door to his library, answered the door.

Burroughs and the two boys could hear much of what went on.

On the other side a drunken male voice, high with anger, kept denouncing Barlow for "having made him this way" and saying he would "tell the dean" and be sure Barlow was "ridden out of town on a rail."

The ranting became repetitive, so Burroughs began telling his friends about Bishop Landau, who had burned all the Mayan codices to kill their civilization. Burroughs said four codices escaped the fire. The whereabouts of three of them are known—Paris, Dresden, Madrid. The angry voice became more incoherent and Audrey Carsons said perhaps they should intervene. Burroughs said no. It sounded like a lovers' spat.

The front door slammed. There were five minutes of pure silence, then Barlow appeared at the door. His face was white as the chalk he taught with.

He walked in and slumped down in a large rattan chair.

"It is all over," he announced.

Burroughs and the boys looked at him.

Barlow said, "As an old teacher of mine used to say, 'The Unnamable.'"

"The boy may change his mind," said Burroughs. "He's just seeing what he is—and wants that monstrosity to reflect on you."

Audrey Carsons asked, "What will you do now?"

Barlow said, "I used to be a publisher and writer. I'm going to do that again. And I think I'll try my hand at magic."

Burroughs and the boys stared. The wild boys had a hungry look; Burroughs had his mineral calm.

"The rite involves time travel. I think we should do it on New Year's. Magic should always follow the path of least resistance," said Barlow.

"What do you mean?" asked Guy Smith.

"New Year's is a hole in time. It is a weak point between the year that was and the year that will become."

Burroughs said, "This year was when the future started. L. Ron Hubbard gave us *Dianetics*, so we will be able to fight Control, and Dr. von Braun said that humans are going to the moon. Time became looser this year; maybe we can gain technology to make it looser still."

Burroughs and the boys left, with Burroughs doing a routine about German pornography.

The festivities were well under way when the three returned to Barlow's apartment. Burroughs was wet with a recent fix; the boys hungrily munched on chocolate, having smoked some tea earlier. Barlow looked like hell. Normally thin, he was now gaunt and pale. It looked as if he had not seen the light of day since they had been with him three weeks ago. He showed them into the library. The books were gone and huge sheets of white butcher paper hung on the walls covered in Mayan ideographs. Burroughs recognized some of them as god names: Ah Pook, Kisin, Zushakon, Ix Tab, Ix Chel. The guys were giggling and pawing each other. Burroughs motioned them to be quiet.

"All true magic begins in silence. Sound is about being controlled by another, silence is about controlling yourself."

Barlow smiled wanly and motioned them to the four chairs set in a row. He went to his bedroom and returned with a clay pot filled with a smelly tar-like liquid. He signaled silence. With a small paint brush he painted a crescent moon on the floor around Burroughs and the boys, and then a trapezoid around his chair. He offered them a pipe.

"I found the recipe in the *Codex Catamaco*. It is a time-travel drug. It contains Diviner's Sage and a hallucinogenic mushroom. Traditionally Mexicans eat twelve grapes at the stroke of midnight to bring good luck for the next year. We are going to use the church bells as a way to leave time."

Burroughs lit the pipe and took a long drag. He gave it to the boys, and then to Barlow. Barlow turned off the light and went to his chair. The room was very dark, lacking any outside windows. A small amount of yellow light slipped in under the door to the first sitting room. Mariachi music blared up from three floors below. Fireworks were popping and yells of "¡Feliz año nuevo!" gave proof of the festive night. The smoke was nasty and disorienting. Red, yellow, and purple lights appeared as mini-comets in the room. Barlow began ringing small bells and chanting something in Mayan.

Everyone felt dizzy, sick, crazy. Sounds hurt, the lights burned their flesh. Then a few blocks away a mighty cathedral bell rang. The colored lights vanished. A man was standing in the room in front of Barlow, his shadow limned by the faint light.

Barlow spoke, "Howard, I gave your papers to Brown. Augie is publishing you and Robert and Smith and Long. I . . ."

Another deep bell sound, and the shadow vanished. The light seemed to pour back out of the room, the darkness became thicker, a dull dry vibration. Then everything came into focus: the four men were sitting on two pieces of worn yellow linoleum—three in a crescent moon, Barlow in his trapezoid. In front of them was a jungle scene of 400,000,000 years ago. The lush vegetation of the Devonian Age was populated by many crawling arthropods, but no birds flew. A few small four-legged creatures, looking more like fish than reptiles, crawled in the underbrush. About a hundred yards away, a mass of twisted, burnt metal three or four times the size of the *Hindenburg* was the center of a small village. Barlow rose and began walking toward it. The three other men tried to rise up, but found themselves paralyzed.

"I'm sorry, gentlemen, but I could not trust you. You came into my life knowing too much, knowing Names that you shouldn't know. I don't know if you are pawns of some fate that is moving me, or the magicians are making it happen. You are invited here as witnesses only."

Burroughs tried as hard as he could to move. He realized that this was a mental construct; they weren't "really" sitting in chairs behind a smear of some magical tar; that was how their minds had reacted to the drugs and the incantation. As Barlow walked forward their perspective changed. They seemed to drift after him always about ten feet behind. They heard the buzzing of the jungle, but occasionally sounds of New Year's Eve seemed to issue from the trees.

Near the village was a cultivated area. Dark green vines ran everywhere. They looked like the gourd vines Barlow knew from Florida except that they grew dark green people. The vegetable people moved feebly. A group of red-skinned dwarves scurried around them, extracting a thick blue fluid from their veins. Closer to the village were insect people—human-looking, but with the heads of praying mantises and insect pincers instead of hands. These creatures lived in huts that looked like spun silk, possibly somehow extruded from their bodies. They were engaged in worship, their high whining insect voices forming words very similar to the chant Barlow had uttered to get here. Barlow advanced to the ruined spacecraft. He put his hands on its metal surface, and pictures began to form in their minds. The ship had escaped a nova, taking with it criminal creatures that were almost indescribable. These felons ate addictions—addictions to sex, to magic, to death, to hatred. These were a form of parasite that humans called "gods"—but they had not yet put on human forms. No nice smiling Zeus, no Jesus on the sticks, no Thor throwing a hammer. These creatures were ugly. They were making vessels to be born in—the insect people, the vegetable people, the fungal fliers, even mewling weak humans.

Something stirred inside the spacecraft. It beckoned Barlow inside. Inside was dark, cold—outer space dark, the dark It needed because of the fear and pain that had been associated with the nova light. In the darkness a mass of centipedes crawled ceaselessly upon a shapeless god. The god talked to Barlow inside his own mind. "I NO DIE. YOU NO DIE. I TAKE YOU HERE BEFORE I GIVE DEATH TO YOUR RACE. You serve me in the future. There you die maybe a million times. I sleep while you die making your world hotter. Eventually you will make your sun go nova, then we move on. I ask nothing for my gift except a few million deaths, and the scared remains of your world."

Barlow felt sick with the touch of the other mind. This was too alien. No wonder man had invented the god-idea not to see the criminals. He didn't want this bargain, but he realized he had accepted it long ago on Earth. He had been a Mayan priest writing the forbidden codex. He would be this again writing the words that this creature needed to control its human dogs, its vessels. He turned to go, but something exploded from the centipede mass. Black, thick liquid with a nitrous smell. It smelled like jism in the back of a YMCA, like furtive nasty sex. The black stuff fell over him, each spot becoming an eye—sometimes human, sometimes faceted insect eyes, sometimes an octopus. Deep red erogenous sores appeared around each eye, filling him with ugly desires, lusts that had nothing to do with the sane life of Earth. The fetor was overpowering. Some of the eyes began to weep a yellow matter.

"YOU DIE MAYBE A MILLION TIMES THAT IS WHY WE MADE YOU."

Barlow turned to go, looking very inhuman as the eyes grew and blinked and wept. He could feel egg-like masses forming in his groin. This was what evil meant—a totally alien impulse toward living as something foul and eternal. This creature, this Death and Control god, had been running the whole rotten game on Earth for millions of years. The roulette wheel was fixed in the house's favor. Any priest, any magician who came along and asked for immortality was a source of the virus that would wipe out everything. It didn't matter if the priest was some Madison Avenue advertising magician or an inbred rural local such as Howard liked to write about. He left the spaceship. The insect people ran up to him and licked the dripping yellow matter from his eyes with black, thin, whip-like tongues, thrilling the sores on his being. Soon he would be addicted to that pleasure. He pushed on, seeming to walk toward his three witnesses in their chairs. As he approached they seemed to recede. He understood that he must walk them back to the original coordinates so that they could return to Mexico City. Burroughs had half risen from his chair, sticking his right hand beyond the magical barrier. Some of the black jism had spattered on him as well. A tiny dot. A cancer for his soul. As Barlow walked past the vegetable people, they smiled idiot smiles, opening their mouths to laugh at him, a thick green saliva drooling from their green lips, the red-skinned dwarves urging him on with menacing gestures. He was upsetting the calm of the vegetable people, spoiling the blue drug they were collecting. Barlow walked back to the place where they were.

Suddenly the last cathedral bell rang. It was the New Year, and they were all in Barlow's library. He sprang out of the chair. The eyes were gone; he was simply the pale haunted gringo he had been before the magic. He ran from the library back into his bedroom. They could hear him opening a bottle of pills. They could hear a faucet turned and off. They still couldn't move. A few minutes later they could hear him lie on his bed. After an hour the paralysis slowly left them. Burroughs went into Barlow's bedroom. On the stale dirty bed, Barlow lay fully clothed and dead.

"We couldn't move until he died. He held us in place by the spell," said Burroughs. He went to the phone and called the Mexican police to tell them that they would find a dead American professor, a suicide. The three left the apartment, not closing the door behind them.

It was two in the morning, and in certain sections of the city parties for gay ex-pats had just begun. Burroughs's wife stirred in her sleep, dreaming a dream that humans weren't meant to have.

(For Nick Mamatas)

Doc Corman's Haunted Palace One Fourth of July

It was the last time I shot fireworks professionally. It was the last time for many things. For my friends it was the year they started to say, "Something's not right about Rob." It was the simultaneous gaining and losing of *certainty*. In the big picture the change of the worldview of a restaurant-and-book critic in a Texas town is not very cosmic, unless it is the flap of the butterfly wings that They use to bring about a human hurricane. But I think that I am a rather small butterfly indeed.

For almost thirty years I reviewed the restaurants of Austin and the books of its astonishingly large literary crowd for the local free paper. I bet if you look around your library you'll find a couple of sentences on some book that bears my praise. Check out your Austin titles: Caroline Spector, Bruce Sterling, Don Graham, Neal Barrett, Brad Denton, Walt DeBill, Lawrence Person, Rex Hull, Bill Spencer. Yep, Rob Kenyon, that's me. Of course it might just say *Austin Chronicle*. I also do the Day Trips section, occasionally movie and band reviews (we are the Live Music Capital of the World). And I write *Ron's Ramblings*. I write about stuff I do, I began before blogging. ☺

My friend Ragan Falconer has a small-time pyrotechnics firm. He shoots little shows with his brother Clyde. You, if you live in a city of any size, have never seen a hand-lit fireworks show. Mainly they've gone the way of the dinosaurs. You've seen an electronically fired show. They're safer. They're faster. They cost more money, but not *that* much more money. Each shell sits in its own cannon (a length of black PVC pipe) and has an electric fuse that runs to its quick-match fuse. Flick a switch, it lights. The outer part of the shell explodes and flings the inner shell, the one with the stars in it, into space. Shells fly up about one hundred feet per inch of diameter. Three-inch shells go up three hundred feet, four-inch shells go up four hundred feet, and so on.

In a hand-lit show, the pyrotechnic team buries the cannons in the earth rather than in a sand-filled trailer. A lighter walks alongside the row of cannon carrying a lit fuse, one of those red flares that come in auto safety kits. He or she lights each firework's quick-match fuse, and *bang!* off it flies. As the fireworks launch, a runner from the ground crew drops a new shell in the empty (and smoking) cannon. A crew consists of lighters, runners, and folks who watch the ready boxes, picnic coolers dragooned into once-a-year pyrotechnic purpose. Ragan's crew had shot shows for three years when he first called me to be a runner. Some cousin had the flu or some son had a headache or something. Anyway, I knew Ragan and I had always wanted to shoot a show. We had to drive to the small town of Flapjack, Texas—one of those little dying towns in the Texas hill country. Flapjack lay twenty minutes to the southeast of Austin. Most of the residents worked in Austin; those who didn't seemed either to sell antiques to those who did or Dairy Queen frozen custard cones to one another. Decades ago, between the World Wars, Flapjack had had a minor boom as an agricultural center. The town had a few grand homes from that period, and not all of them had become bed-and-breakfasts.

Flapjack could afford a $5,000 dollar show; that meant thirty minutes of show—"No black sky!" hand-lit. The Falconer brothers liked their shows in those days to be hand-lit. It's exciting. It's fun. It's dangerous. Everyone on the crew risked life and limb for seventy-five dollars and a ton of hard work. But we would have done it for free. So would you. I am talking *professional fireworks* here.

I rode with Ragan in a yellow Ryder truck. We had magnetic decals on the side warning other motorists of our explosive threat. No one ever seemed to notice. Do this for me, will you? Next time you see a bobcat truck on the highway with a **Dangerous Explosives** sign on the back door or the sides, don't tailgate. Thank you.

Ragan had joked with me on the way down about how patriotic and right-wing the Flapjackers were. I could tell he was being ironic, setting me up for something. When he pulled the truck into the city park by the little hill, I saw the joke. There were three things on the hill. One was a fabulous three-story red-brick mansion, a multi-winged gothically embellished piece of Richardsonian Romanesque. This lordly estate was the "Corman Place"—the home of a railroad baron, who had had the bad taste to get rich in the 1870s rather than the 1920s. For you non-architecture buffs, I won't be offended if you go Google the style. Two billboards shared the hill. One had red letters on a black ground. THE US MILITARY KILLS OUR BOYS. The other shows a mainly gray and green scene of American soldiers in the jungles of Vietnam, and bore a legend in white: "Why do some people choose which fair-haired boy must die?" Both billboards faced the park; they would be the backdrop of our show. I hoped that they would not be lit at night—this proved a vain hope.

I stared at Ragan and he grinned. "Doc Corman's antiwar protest. Get the sheriff to tell you when he shows up."

There was a small artificial lake in the park. There were cottonwood trees and post oak and gray green buffalo grass. Across the lake a barbecue company was setting up next to the rows of picnic tables; beyond them were the small brick buildings that served as restrooms, a playscape full of kids enjoying the July heat, and a fenced-in tennis court.

Clyde Falconer and his two sons had arrived in his blue Lexus. Ragan and I opened the back of the truck and took out the picks and sharpshooter shovels. We began digging the holes for the cannon. Six three-inch cannon four feet apart, six four-inch, four six-inch, and five single-shot eight-inchers. It was hot work, and we were glad when Sharon Falconer showed up with her big brown SUV that held a giant cooler of sweet tea.

We had arrived just before noon and were finished burying the cannon by four. The sheriff drove up across the grass in his tan and brown sheriff car. He was a big man with a sweat-stained Stetson and a white handlebar mustache. He liked to talk, and we had sat out the lawn chairs by then. Following Ragan's clue, I asked about Dr. Corman.

He wasn't a medical doctor. He was a *teaching* doctor. Specifically, he had taught anthropology at the University of Texas half an hour north. The name vaguely rang a bell; there had been some articles about him a few years ago.

The sheriff was not a stupid man, but higher education had passed him by. He had also been in Vietnam when Randy Corman encountered a landmine. Not in the same unit, of course. The sheriff had just warmed to Randy's story when I saw the infantryman near the base of the pictorial billboard. He was a blond-haired white guy dressed like the grunts appearing twelve or so feet above his head. But what caught my eye was the machine gun he was carrying. The bombing in Oklahoma City had happened in April of that year, and to my thinking men in combat fatigues carrying machine guns weren't a good thing.

I pointed him out to the sheriff, who just said, "I'm getting to that." The sheriff was like my mother, a Southern storyteller who views his narrative as shots of bourbon to be savored slowly so that the intoxication of the tale builds up over the whole of the evening. I could see how happy he was that the solider had made his dramatic entrance.

The sheriff paused in his story and gave me a brief sketch of the Cormans. The founder of the line had merged two small Texas railroads and one Louisiana-to-Oklahoma railroad, making Flapjack a major hub in the world of post-Reconstruction commerce. Timber from East Texas, cotton from the Dallas area, cattle from hereabouts had access to New Orleans and Galveston ports. The manufactured goods from Europe and the East Coast could come to Texas and Oklahoma markets. He built his "palace" on the hill. I felt smart—it really had been designed by Henry Hobson Richardson just after his asylums had been in built in New York (1870) and Arkham (1872). The townsfolk hated him for his conspicuous consumption—the mansion had ten fireplaces, each of which had won a prize at a fair or exhibition. You can build great stuff if you own the railroad and shipping costs you nothing. His children were set for life. His son Markham had sold the railroad to the Atchison, Topeka and Santa Fe at the beginning of World War I. His grandson Roger had opened the chain of markets and movie palaces across central and south Texas between the wars. His great-grandson Hiram added to the family fortune by opening savings and loans in Austin and Houston and beginning the first large-scale Texas winery, Hiram's boy Thomas devoted himself to education, gaining a doctorate in anthropology at the University of Chicago and a further Ph.D. in Indian and Burmese Literature at Princeton. This took us to Randall. By this time the barbecue was ready. Brisket and chicken, ranch style beans, cole slaw, German potato salad. A local band was playing Willie Nelson covers. Clowns were making balloon animals for the kids, and coolers everywhere showed forth ice, Lone Star and Shiner Beer—and I knew that when the sun went down I would be running from the big yellow cooler full of three-inch shells to the first cannon line. It was great! Some locals shared watermelon with us from their own patch.

Randall and Sheriff John Haggard went to Sam Houston High School at the same time. Flapjack had been on decline in the sixties, and the graduating class of 1972 was a mere fifteen souls. John Haggard had been captain of the football team—but of course every boy in school played on the football team. Randy had been president of the Spanish Club, leader of the debate team ("We called him a master debater. Get it?") and even president of the Photo Bugs. Our country was four years short of its 200th birthday, one of the last Japanese soldiers had surrendered in Guam, the war had gone for decades for the poor SOB. We watched *Maude* and *All in the Family*. There were great paperbacks that year—*Journey to Ixtlan* and *Fear and Loathing in Las Vegas*. There was also a little something called the Vietnam War. Now simple high school boys in central Texas didn't know that Nixon was going to end the war by bombing the pucky out of Hanoi come Christmas time; they just knew they might have to go to the unhappiest place on Earth. The graduating class of fifteen was six girls (they were safe), two black boys (they were going), one Mexican (ditto), and six white guys. The draft board had to pick two of the Anglos.

John Haggard was born on the wrong side of the tracks, so he was an easy pick. The richest kid in town was an easy pick as well. The serfs had risen up. These choices were not only hard on the Corman and Haggard families, the boys had been dating the "Pridy twins, and boy were they pretty." Gloria for John and Jeanie Mae for Randy. They would wait for their boys.

Randall Hiram Corman had his leg blown off by Charlie. He was airlifted to Saigon and then on to Tokyo, and there he died of an acute infection. He had graduated Sam Houston High in May, was drafted in June, and his body was delivered home a week before Halloween.

Randy's mom drank herself to death in six months, so she never even heard of the Paris Peace Accords. "Southern Comfort," a fruit, spice, and whiskey-flavored liquor, is a good drink for Southern tragedy. With a cruel twist of fate, a report that was meant only for Army brass was mailed to Doctor Corman. Turns out that Randy got very inferior care—in fact, negligent drunken care—and the Corman's lawyers got a lot of money. So the rich get richer. Dr. Corman gave the town a library in Randy's name. He paid for Jeanie Mae to go to school. She came back as an English teacher at Sam Houston. Then, according to the sheriff, Dr. Corman began writing *them* books till UT fired him. Having reported on excesses of professorial eccentricity, I knew "them books" must be something.

At the next Halloween the Haunted Palace started. The good doctor had his mansion made into a haunted house filled with all sorts of antiwar scenes—villagers broiled in napalm, mine fields, field surgeries—as well as the standard Frankenstein's monsters and vampires.

Grisly and macabre, it even got a write-up in *Texas Monthly*. In about six years the trouble started. Reagan was president by then and we would all be saved by Star Wars "for real." Dr. Thomas Emanuel Corman put up the anti-military billboards. Some people were so mad they wanted to move the Fourth of July festival, but the mayor said the Fourth of July was about free speech. Dr. Corman got in some kind of trouble at the University of Texas at Austin, his graduate class on East-West interaction had some kind of party with drugs or something, and the sheriff wasn't clear on the issues.

The sheriff's wife spotted the first solider on patrol around the Corman place. It was just before the Fourth. Dr. Corman had hired an actor who looked like a Vietnam-era US solider to patrol the area near the billboards. Well, some people had threatened to burn them down.

But it was worse.

The actor looked a great deal like Randall Hiram Corman.

It was awful hard on Jeanie Mae.

Everyone else came back from the war. The sheriff had married Gloria; the black boys had come back black men and started a gas station/convenience store; the Mexican boy started a taco place. Everybody was settling down, but Jeanie Mae—she still waited. Jeanie got to watching the solider on patrol. She got to thinking that it was Randy. She told her sister, her sister told then-Deputy Haggard. The deputy told her that Randy was dead—they had all been to the funeral. They all knew his ashes were in an urn. It had a blue spotlight on it every Halloween. The deputy told her to get therapy.

Jeanie Mae snuck onto the ground one night with her little cocker spaniel. The soldier made her dance naked, killed her dog and cooked it, making her eat some, and finally raped her. She stumbled into town all bloody. The sheriff and Deputy Haggard went up Beacon Hill and found no soldier. Dr. Corman said he had run off at dawn. The doctor was burning a big bonfire. He invited them to search. They searched and found nothing.

Then a few months later, he hired another actor to impersonate a soldier. This guy looked like Randall, but there was something wrong with his face. People were mad. But there are no laws against such poor taste and insensitivity. The sheriff used these words in his narrative; I wondered what lawyer had taught them to him.

It was time for the show. I had loaded two three-inch red shells for Ragan to light during the "rockets' red glare" part of the anthem. Then came white titanium salutes. Super-noisy—they set off the car alarms all over Flapjack. Each shell drives the smoke into you; weeks after a show you will smell of gunpowder at the oddest times. I ran my butt off. Sharon Falconer sat on one of the white plastic lawn chairs and did the count.

You count for duds. If 101 fireworks are lit and 100 make their flower-fire in the sky you have one dud. As I mentioned, each shell has two parts. The outer shell that explodes to lift the inner shell into the air, which ignites the stars—the pretty stuff that lights up the sky. If the inner shell should not ignite it falls to earth. It looks exactly like an oversized cartoon firework. It practically begs kids to light it and cover themselves in burning papers and salts. You have to find every dud after a show—no matter how long it takes in the dark.

Now the Gentle Reader will think that I rode back to Austin the next day and looked up Dr. Corman. In fact, I wrote an amusing story of my night of shooting off fireworks in Flapjack. I completely forgot about Dr. Corman.

I didn't remember any of the shows we shot for the next three years. I moved up from a runner to a lighter. I set off the three-inchers the night that I thought about Corman again. Another of his actor-soldiers had made the news in a terrible way. A Vietnamese family had opened Ng BBQ in nearby Comesee, Texas. The actor-solider (at least somebody dressed as GI Joe) had torched their house. No one could prove it was Dr. Corman's employee—but said employee could once again not be found. Corman had a little trouble on his own: a fire in one of his storage sheds had burned out of control the late the same night. The sheriff was perplexed, but relieved that Corman hadn't hired yet another "soldier" to guard his acreage.

But just before sunset, I saw the gleam of the burnt-orange Texas sun on the M16 barrel as Corman's re-enactor made his martial patrol. I was gleeful. I could smell a big weird story with a big Rob Kenyon byline.

So the next day in Austin, I drove to the Perry-Castañeda Library on the University of Texas campus. I researched Dr. Thomas Emanuel Corman. He wrote fourteen books, fifteen counting his dissertation. You could line them up in chronological order, and they stretched from solid scholarship from academic publishers to pseudo-science bullshit from gosh-wow paperback houses. It seems that everyone agrees that Dr. Corman went mad; the dissent is about *which* of the books marked the French-frying of his gray matter.

His studies focused on the pre-Buddhist cultic practices that were assimilated into early Buddhism in Burma. Buddhism of various unorthodox sorts (heavily mixed with Tantrism and Tibetan shamanism) encountered the Bagan culture of Burma in the sixth century. From this heady blend, a group of wonder-workers called weizzas arose. These forest sages combined the worship of spirits (called Nats) with Indian and Tibetan practices, especially astrology and alchemy. The latter was more focused on the prolongation of life by certain regenerative measures than in the transformation of base metals into gold. If the name "weizza" sounds like "wizard" to you, it is because it is a cognate. In fact, in Myanmar today it is still the honorific for a B.A. degree.

Dr. Corman studied these alchemist sages. As more orthodox Buddhism showed up in the seventh century, the weizzas needed to become organized. They became a monastic order of "Ari Buddhists." These fellows were a little looser in their ways—they could drink alcohol, practice some Tantric sex, and make good money as fortune tellers. They wrote in Pali, the orthodox Buddhist scriptural tongue.

They hid some of their magical beliefs as a sort of scholarship: they deiced to write down the words and practices of a group of older and even wilder magicians the zawgyi. Their scholarship was a window to the more obscure civilizations and peoples of Burma.

After his sixth book, Dr. Corman had begun the re-translation of a seventh-century Ari Buddhist named U Pao. He was a master alchemist and a devotee of a powerful Nat, Yog-Sothoth. U Pao wrote a Pali sutra in praise of Him "Who orders the planes and angles of existence." The so-called *Black Sutra* had been translated by a German Indologist in the nineteenth century, but great strides in comparative Indo-European linguistics had taken place since then. And the University of Texas is the hotbed of Indo-European linguistics. Dr. Corman began his translation in 1972, about the time his son came back in a body bag.

His next book, *Alchemy East and West*, was slightly controversial. He theorized that the medieval Indian Siddha Alchemy tradition, the Burmese zawgyi tradition, and the European alchemical tradition were in fact a single multicultural scholarly/scientific endeavor. He named it the "White College"—apparently deriving the name from some Welsh alchemists, Cur-Gwen (*Cur = College, Gwen = White as in Guiniviere), whose name eventually became "Curwen." In an obscure footnote toward the end of the book he noted that the name had variants: Curwin, Korman, and Corman.

Then his wife died.

He couldn't find a scholarly house for his *Glimpses of Immortality*, but as a popular occult book it brought him serious coin. He suggested that the purification by fire motif in alchemy might actually work. He suggested that some of the long-lived alchemist like Count St. Germain or Ludvig Prinn might have discovered the real process. A trio of popular books followed. Dr. Corman became big man on the New Age lecture circuit—and, since he gave his hefty fees to antiwar charities, became something of a saint to some.

Then the year he hired the actor, he had to find an even less stringent publisher. His remaining books became collections of odd events and Fortean moments suggesting that alchemists know how to be immortal and they work for some ultramundane group of powers that want to change the consciousness of the world, one "endarkenment" at a time. The books are full of standard New Age tropes—the hundredth monkey, morphic fields, pyramid power, ancient astronauts. His employers at the University were not amused. However, he scarcely seemed to mind.

I spoke with some people in the anthropology department. Dr. Corman became neglectful of dress and hygiene. He browsed the personal papers of Aleister Crowley, which are part of the University of Texas HRC collection. He may have bought drugs from students. He may have *sold* drugs to students. However, tenure doth protect the odd and odder.

He finally went too far. His class "The Alchemical Tradition: East and West" met one night in the middle of the football stadium to "Open a Gateway to the Gatekeeper." Nude coeds and a goat were said to be involved. You can risk your reputation as a scholar, but you can never risk the reputation of football. The apparently risqué sexual magic (or perhaps I should write "magick") was enough for the Regents to ask Dr. Corman never to return. The next year one of the physics professors went off the deep end and shot some students from the infamous clocktower. Some uncharitable types speculated on a connection between the two rogue faculty members.

His last books degenerated into collections of speculation and paranormal incidents. Lovecraft's agent Julius Schwartz points out a freakish bird death to Eric Frank Russell, and the latter writes *Sinister Barrier.* A researcher vanishes from dolphin studies, a peculiar clown festival in

Miroclaw, Fortean happenings in the Sesqua Valley. He randomly gives fragments of spells and sections from outlandishly named grimoires. I made a note of a phrase of recognition between Yog-Sothoth followers; I felt it might come in handy.

When the Fourth rolled around again I bought a very powerful LED flashlight. I wanted to meet the man on the hill. I realized this was a dangerous idea, but I have always been attracted to danger. Dangerous drugs and dangerous women, fireworks and mountain climbing, interviewing gang members and extreme religious types. I was not the sensible one in my family. I lit the four- and five-inch shells and lit one of the finale racks, which launch eighty three-inch shells in less than a minute. You light it, run, and fall backwards to see the red, lilac, white, silver, and gold you have painted the sky with. Sharon told me the news I wanted to hear. There had been a dud, one of the four-inch shells. I told everybody that I was climbing Beacon Hill to look for it. I moved quickly before anyone could realize that might not be the smartest idea.

It had been a wearingly hot day, and the dry smoky air was thick with the smell of gunpowder. Ragan and Clyde were putting out a little grass fire. Clyde's sons were looking for the dud nearer the firing line (i.e., in the logical place). I grabbed a bucket (to put the dud in), a big glass of sweet tea, and my flashlight.

The hill proved easy to climb, and I came to a three-strand barbed-wire fence after I had gone about twenty feet into the sparse oak. Using the weight of my bucket, I pushed down the top strand and stepped over. I had been getting over barbed wire since I was ten. I grew up in Amarillo, Texas, where barbed had been invented, for Christ's sake. Now logically the weather on either side of a barbed-wire fence should be the same, but logic didn't hold near the Corman place. The air turned steamy and smelled of animals, like the reptile area of a zoo. Mist hung near the ground like milk, and I could hear jungle birds. I had never been in the jungles of Vietnam save through the miracle of movies, but I felt as though I had crossed to that place. I could hear tropical birds, and the base of the billboards looked like the creeper covered pylons of Angkor Wat.

I pointed the light at my face. I wanted him to see I was white. I was an American, although that knowledge hadn't seemed to help with his girlfriend. The jungle grew thick. It took me twenty minutes to go up another fifty or so feet. I couldn't hear anything from the firing line, as though a three-strand fence were effective soundproofing. I was unprepared for the loudness of the burst of machine fire. A small bright comet flashed above and to the left of me; bark exploded off a nearby trunk. My ears rang. Machine guns are much louder than exploding firework shells; then I realized that I had taken my earplugs out. I knew the solider was playing with me. He could have literally cut me in two at this range. I yelled the recognition phrase, "Kyron Yog-Sothoth Bolon Yokte' K'uh!"

I expected the counter-sign of "Yog-Sothoth Neblod Zin!" Instead, a solider stepped out from behind a live oak. He raised his machine gun and shot three rounds in the air. "That would impress my dad, but it's not the password, Sarge," he said. I turned my flashlight on him. I recognized Randall Hiram Corman from his yearbook picture. He was still nineteen. At first I thought he had put black greasepaint around his left eye, but I saw that a thick and wiry *fur* surrounded the eye. The pupil of the left eye was a vertical slit. "Well, Sarge, we have a problem, you and me, because of time."

"Randy?" I asked.

"Private First Class Randall Corman, sir!"

I saw that his arm was in a green sling. The fur around his eye moved. It seemed to be a mass of feelers. "Not the handsome son of a bitch that you were expecting," Private Corman remarked. There was a fallen log between us; with his free hand he motioned me to sit. I expected that the gunfire would bring the sheriff soon. Maybe I wasn't in real danger. I hated the brilliance of my flashlight; I didn't really want to see his eye.

I sat, and he sat next to me. Private Corman said, "I think I may have talked to other people since being stationed here. Sometimes my mind works a little. Didn't you say you knew my dad? He teaches at UT."

"Randy, do you know what year this is?"

"I saw the fireworks, so it's July 4, 1973. I didn't think I would last this long at Ngoc Linh. How'd they get fireworks? USO?"

"Randy, what did your father do to you?"

"He's an old zawgyi these days. You want to know something funny? He could end war now. He knows all the angles. He knows how to eliminate the problem of humanity. Think he will?"

"Randy, we're in the twenty-first century now. Do you know what your father did to your ashes?"

"'After calcinations, the essential salts may be reassembled if the One-in-All Re-Members the being. Care must be exercised for the purity of the salts, lest Otherness seep in.' You know, I haven't got a letter from Momma since I been here. I hate 'Nam. It's Disneyland in reverse."

"Randy, do you remember Jeanie Mae?"

"I've got her picture."

He moved to lay down the M16. I saw what the cloth hid. He and the rifle were grown together like a Giger painting. Human, insect, gunmetal—all fused. He seemed confused that he couldn't release the rifle. Finally he grabbed at his pocket with his free left hand. There was a mildewed wallet. He couldn't open the wallet, which had mildewed shut. Finally he threw the thing away from him. He was crying. He stood up quickly and fired his machine gun at the wallet. I thought he was going to fire at me.

"You know I can't point this thing at myself."

He demonstrated his inability to point the weapon at himself. "The worst part is sometimes I think Their thoughts. Dad didn't know that. What year did you say this was? 1976, I bet. Were those Bicentennial fireworks? Did we make it to the Bicentennial?"

"Yes. Randy. It was the Bicentennial."

"Damn war has gone on too long."

"It sure has, soldier."

"You know, I can't die. I tried once in Tokyo. Dad just starts me over. Can you tell Momma I'm OK? She's back in Texas. My little town there is called Flapjack—can you believe that, Sarge?"

"I believe you, Randy."

"Sarge, you don't want to think Their thoughts. It makes the nights too long."

"I bet it does, Randy."

"Tell my dad just to end. He can end it all. My daddy is the most powerful man in the universe." He sounded just like the eight-year-old blond boy he once was.

"I've got to move on, solider."

"The password is *Kung Fu*. You ever watch that show, Sarge? I saw it on R-n-R."

"Best show on TV," I said.

"No," said Private Corman. "The best show is *M*A*S*H.*"

I saw that the shadow Randy Corman cast by my LED flashlight was much less human in shape than he seemed to be. I turned off the light because I didn't really want to see it clearly. I knew that I didn't want to remember this Fourth.

"I got to go now, son." I said.

"Don't let your meat loaf, Sarge."

I stood up and headed down the hill. Just before I passed over the barbed wire I heard more gunfire. I wondered if he was shooting at me. I wondered if he was shooting at anything that existed in my world.

When I got to the firing line, Clyde's sons had found the dud. Nobody said anything about gunfire. Of course, tonight of all nights gunfire might not be correctly identified. I helped finish the cleanup, digging up the rest of the cannons. Sharon asked me what had become of my bucket. I said I had dropped it in the dark and couldn't find it. I looked up Beacon Hill, I thought I saw some lights flicker around the base of one of the billboards.

We drove home.

But I can't quite *believe* in home anymore. I wonder if Randy's father can end it all. The problem of humanity. I wonder if he understands the special hell he has made for his son. I wonder what Their thoughts are like, and some nights I wonder so long and hard that I think I might start to know.

(*For Walt DeBill*)

Slowness

Dr. Alberto Balsamo was a short man with a silver beard and an easy smile. But his smile left his face when Walter, the department secretary, told him "that man" was waiting for him in his office. He had been avoiding the too-earnest physician from Massachusetts for weeks. One does not reach old age without learning that there are people too full of life, whose very rapidity makes them a danger to others. However, one likewise learns that sometimes you have to face the music. Dr. Balsamo took a deep breath and walked into his own office. The doctor was standing by the bookcase reading the titles.

"Are you a Dante scholar, Dr. West?"

"I am afraid I have little time for the fine arts," said Dr. Herbert West.

"That is a pity. What is life without art? Art slows life down—turns the great fire of time into a slow burn."

"But doesn't everything in the twentieth century urge us to increase the speed at which that fire burns?"

"You are no doubt correct about that, Dr. West. I am afraid I am somewhat the enemy of all things modern. Give me my Dante and my cats and my old brandy and I am a happy man."

"But such great things are in the air! True, we saw the horror of the Great War, but Banting just synthesized insulin, Eddington verified General Relativity late this May. The world is expanding a thousandfold!"

"The Germans are fighting the Ruhr Reds, Mexico's streets run red with revolution, Jews and Arabs are killing one another in Jerusalem, and what do we get? *Over the Hill to the Poorhouse* and *Way Down East.*"

"Well, Doctor Balsamo, we also got *Dr. Jekyll and Mr. Hyde* and *The Cabinet of Dr. Caligari.* I regret to say I went and saw *Dr. Jekyll and Mr. Hyde* four times when it showed in Arkham. I find I have a weakness for Dr. Jekyll." The blond-haired doctor smiled.

"And also Dr. Caligari, my good doctor. The world has not been made better by mad physicians, I fear."

"Well, I hope my visit will be brief and my madness excusable. I think you can give me a good deal of help in a current piece of research. Perhaps I have something to offer you as well."

"I can't imagine what help I could be," said Dr. Balsamo.

"Oh, I imagine you know. You have certainly been avoiding me."

"Please forgive my manners. Would you like a brandy? Or should I have Walter bring us some coffee? No? Well, by all means take a seat."

"Are you going to admit to avoiding me? I have motored in from Bolton three other times."

"Of course I will admit it. I do avoid new people, new ideas, and shiny new things. Do you know the poet Lawrence Binyon?"

"As I have said, I have little time for the arts."

"Binyon and I are working on a new translation of the *Commedia.* The other day he said to me, 'Alberto, Slowness is Beauty!'"

"That is a literary point of view. I practice medicine. I want to save the lives of my patients as quickly as possible."

"Then what can you possibly want of a professor of Renaissance poetry? Eh, Dr. West?"

"I am looking into Italian history, just past the Renaissance, and I think you may the man to help me."

"I am a rather middling historian, Dr. West. Perhaps Dr. Flowers is the man you seek."

"What do you know about Luigi Galvani?"

"Oh, I see. You want my father, Dr. Vico Balsamo. He wrote a short book on Luigi Galvani. I am sad to say my father has passed on."

"I suspect your father may have told you some interesting things."

"Too interesting for his book? Perhaps my father thought many strange things, but he was a good academic and never published speculation."

"Could you let me in on your father's speculations? I think I can put some of Galvani's ideas to better use in my laboratory than using them to titillate the reading public. Besides, perhaps I can offer you some of the benefits of my research."

"I will tell you what I know, Dr. West. But you must promise not to tarnish my father's name."

"Excellent. Well, for starters, is it true that Galvani explained his theories to Mary Shelley?"

"It wasn't Galvani. It was nephew, Giovanni Aldini, who took Galvani's experiment to the next level. Galvani was happy enough to touch a severed frog leg to Volta's pile and demonstrate the twitch to other physicians and scholars. His nephew was the showman. At first he used the heads of newly slaughtered sheep. He would apply as much current as he could and the bloody heads would stick their tongues out or snap their teeth. And Aldini didn't like scientific lecture halls. He liked theater. He liked paying audiences and women who swooned. Of course, sheep became commonplace. Many traveling 'electricians' were shocking sheep into movement. So Aldini took the performance to a more grotesque state."

"In 1803 he set up shop at Newgate Prison. A recently hanged murderer named George Foster was taken from the gallows and transported to the College of Surgeons. Aldini applied the current, and George's purple face grimaced; he shook on the slab and even threw punches in the air as Aldini hit him with shock after shock. Some newspapers claimed later that Aldini had raised the dead. Of course, the College of Surgeons distanced itself from the affair. It reacted as though its reputation had been sullied."

"That is always the way of the medical establishment. You can offer them anything, even life-in-death itself, and they act like scared old women," said Dr. West.

Balsamo paused and looked at the nervous young man sitting on the edge of the overstuffed chair. Balsamo's guests usually sat back in the chair, sipped their coffee and tea, and carefully chose their words. He hesitated a moment and began telling the rest of the story in a more subdued tone, which caused West to sit even further at the end of the chair. Balsamo couldn't help smiling, wondering if the young man would fall out of the chair altogether.

"What I am about to tell you is not part of the official story. It is not in my father's book, and I will ask that you do not attribute it to me. It is not the sort of story that complements a Yale professorship. Aldini declared that he would indeed raise the dead, not merely make them twitch and clutch at things. Aldini began to look for darker sciences."

"Alchemy?" asked Dr. West scornfully.

"There are many chemical procedures that were learned from the experiments of the alchemists. But Aldini sought something a bit more troublesome. Europe has always had rumors of a cult of men who revivify the dead. It is said to be a profitable line of work. Imagine what crime-haunted Italy might be like if no one could take their secrets safely to the grave. Imagine what might be gained by the blackmailer. Or even simple items that the dead had left unattended to—like telling the living relatives about the secret store of gold behind the painting, or the plate buried near the well. Dr. West, Aldini was interested in necromancy. He didn't assume that such grave-robbing miracles were the result of demons—but what if the preparation of certain herbs combined with the stimulation of the nerves of a sufficiently horrible incantation could do the trick? So he sought out a sorcerer. Such things were easy to do in those days. Sorcerers made the headlines, as it were."

"They still do," said Dr. West. "Madame Blavatsky was a darling of the idiot press, and I am sure that we have someone similar in our midst right now if we choose to look for such charlatans."

"The man whom Aldini sought out was no charlatan. He was Count Alessandro di Cagliostro—a man who had obtained initiation into a secret Egyptian brotherhood, the *Figli del Faraone Nero*, who had methods of making mummies speak their age-old secrets to modern men. These fearsome fellows had chosen the Count to act as a spy and agitator throughout Europe. They had reasons for wanting to overthrow the French government, for example. I am sure that you have heard of the affair of the Diamond Necklace. But they had further plans for the Count. He was going to play a key role in summoning some sort of demon from the darkness between the stars. In one sense the Count was to gain powers far beyond mortal ken, but on the other hand he would be a slave to that power. Imagine if you held in your hands the means to destroy the world. Every moment of every day all you could think of is 'Should I?' 'Shouldn't I?'"

"And your father discovered all this?"

"He found the diary of the Count while researching Galvani and the other vitalists. It was the Shelley connection, as you have guessed. Mary Shelley had read Count Cagliostro's diary before she wrote her novel *Frankenstein*. My father had found some of her notes, but they could not be verified and I am sure that you understand, given the rather strange notions that the diary must have contained, why he left out certain things."

"But I don't understand the link between Aldini and Cagliostro," said Dr. West.

"By the time Aldini had found the Count, the latter wanted a way to escape from the *Figli*—and Aldini promised him a way out. Cagliostro had done the Brotherhood's dirty work by opening lodges of 'Egyptian Freemasonry' in Russia, France, and England. It was part of the Brotherhood's mad scheme. You see, they believed that they had access to the master plan of the world—a series of paintings under the tomb of a certain pharaoh. At that time they thought they could gain great temporal power by making sure that all the events depicted in the paintings came to pass. They would initiate young men with an unhealthy interest in the Black Arts and have them carry out schemes to move the pawns of history across the chessboard of time. Have you never noticed how many magicians such as Dr. John Dee are spies? It was not a matter of coincidence."

"At that time? You think this brotherhood still exists?"

"They had knowledge of the future. Eventually they learned that they need do little and the horrid scenes painted by the slaves of the Black Pharaoh would simply unfurl. They grew tired of making money because of foreknowledge, and simply became slaves to the onrushing future. Or so my father believed."

"He didn't tell you to contact these men, I suppose?"

"Good Lord, man, why would anyone want to know men mad with fatalism?"

"The Egyptians knew many things about restoring life. I have heard that even some of their composite mummies actually walked."

"You have heard correctly; Cagliostro mentions this in his diary. He has a horrific account of seeing a truly huge monster; I imagine it still lives imprisoned with the pharaohs. I have no doubt, Dr. West, that if you journeyed to Cairo, you could meet the Sons of the Black Pharaoh; its Italian branch no longer remains. But I am wandering from my story. Aldini had a foolproof plan. If Cagliostro would provide him with the elixir the Brotherhood used to make the mummies speak and the incantation called *Coming Forth by Night*, he would fake the Count's death. The Count had grown fearful of the demon the Brotherhood wanted him to summon. His diary mentioned the terrible sounds of twin pipers of no human sort, and his fear of the terrible Eye of the creature. He was grasping at straws, and a confidence man like Aldini had him—as you Americans say—'by the short hairs.' He gave the recipe to Aldini. It was composed of lunar kyphi, an incense made of twenty-eight herbs and a heavy metal that caused flesh to wither—I suspect uranium—dissolved in wine from the Oasis of Kharga. It was ridiculously expensive to compound, but Aldini told the Count no potion, no escape.

"After Aldini had made his first batch, he told his plan to the Count. He would give the Count a drug that produced a deathlike slumber. The Count's servants would call him as a physician. He would arrive, revive the Count, and take him to Barbados. It seems that Signor Aldini was an admirer of Shakespeare in that his little plot had equal parts from *Romeo and Juliet* and *The Tempest*. The Count was a bit of a showman himself. He arranged for a huge dinner in Naples. He wanted his demise to be witnessed by several dozen nobles, priests, wealthy townsfolk, artists, and musicians. The British ambassador came, a cardinal from Rome, a mathematician visiting from Greece. It was a gala affair with music, wine, and feasting. We Italians know how to throw a party. That was why we conquered the world, you know, so we could have the best of everything for our tables."

"I never made it to Italy when I was in the Army, but the restaurants in Paris were a great contrast to New England boiled dinners!" laughed Dr. West.

"The Count placed the poison in his wine glass. He toasted the Pope's health and fell forward dead. But the Count had not counted on one thing: he had not realized that Aldini had planned to make his death so real. Aldini had simply killed him. When he arrived at the residence, Cagliostro's body was cold, there was no pulse, a mirror held to the nostrils provided no telltale signs of life. He loaded the body in a wagon and ran to a secret villa. He knew he had to keep the body from the hands of the Brotherhood. There he drained half of the Count's blood and restored it with the elixir, attached his electrodes to the pale flesh, and read the fateful words. He hit the switch as he called on Nyarlathotep. The Count's limbs twitched, the eyes fluttered, and the mix of ancient sorcery and modern science awakened him."

"How can you know these things? The Count couldn't have recorded them in his diary."

"The Count didn't record his own reanimation, that is true. But he helped Aldini over the months that followed. At first he was unwilling, but he was afraid that the Brotherhood might track him down and that he would eventually be one of their undead slaves working beneath Egyptian necropolises. Besides, he was attracted to the unknown. When he was alive, he had borne the fearful initiations of the Brotherhood. He wasn't exactly the same sort of being as before. His body breathed, his heart pumped the strange mixture through his limbs, but with a slow beat. He was much cooler to the touch, and the inner fires of emotion had cooled a great deal."

"Did hatred leave him? Did he hold grudges?"

"That's an odd question. He recorded in his diary that he could be moved by three things. The first was fear. He would act in self-interest. He assumed that his undying state would not cling to his pseudo-life, but found the elixir made him very protective of his false life. Secondly, he was moved by love. We Italians after all are the race of Casanova. Lastly, hatred moved him. His hatred for the Brotherhood coursed in his veins, an undying fire of equal parts of venom and pain."

"Did he hate Aldini for what he had done to him?"

"At first he did; but he came to realize that by Aldini's machinations he had escaped the Brotherhood and that perhaps he would have a long existence."

"So there is hope then."

"What do you mean, hope?"

"That the reanimated might come to forgive, even love the doctor that called them back to life." Dr. West trembled as he spoke. Dr. Balsamo regarded him with awe—a certain suspicion beginning to arise.

"I may have bad news for you, Dr. West. The Count knew about the process and he longed to escape a dreadful fate. If Aldini had not intervened, the Brotherhood was going to use the Count in a horrible way. He was destined to become the living vehicle of Nyarlathotep. Whatever strange fate Aldini had given him, it was preferable to the horrors that awaited him. Aldini was his savior—maybe not a truthful savior, but a savior."

"So the others, the other reanimated men—what became of them?"

"For the most part they did not return to life in as conscious a form as the Count had. Perhaps his occult training made his will stronger, more coherent. They were ruled by fear and anger. Aldini simply dispatched most of them. Fire, acid, dismemberment were effective."

"Most of them?"

"You must understand that he and the Count were working by themselves. Some of the reanimated men were very strong. Like the reaction that fear causes."

"Adrenalin. Yes, I've observed it."

"They broke free from the doctor's laboratory. They raged into the countryside. There is much Italian folk-belief in such things, so the country people feared the walking dead."

"And the sophisticated city dwellers laughed at the country cousins," finished Dr. West. "So did the monsters win?"

"It is odd that you would call Aldini's creations monsters. Were they not his victims?"

"He gave them life, the one thing men have fought to have since they came up from the ape. He was like a god. If he wasn't fighting the cancer of superstition, he could have discovered how the Count's mind had endured. He could have replicated the experiment. The Count's sanity is the sign I am looking for."

"The sign you are looking for . . . what do you mean, Dr. West?"

The light had left the window. The cold New Haven winds of October were rattling the pane. Well-muffled students hurried across the Quad chased by fallen leaves. The professor's office was lit by two dim bulbs. He never spent his nights here, and he wished he were well away from the dreadful American. He had come to recognize the gleam in his eyes.

"Yes. The sign of hope that I am looking for," said Dr. West.

"It couldn't happen. You don't understand the rage of the dead."

"Tell me about the rage of the dead."

"The Count records that the reanimated don't dream. Strictly speaking, they need no rest, but at night they feel the hostility of certain forces in the universe. The universe is not a happy place, Dr. West. Matter does not like being constrained by form. The bending of light that you mentioned Eddington observing is a painful process. The universe is full of hatred, and dead men are the perfect empty vessels for that rage. The 'monsters,' as you call them, found one another in the dark. It took some years, but they had one great and unending hatred—to kill the man who had killed their deaths. You speak of humans fighting for life, but I tell you, Dr. West, they will fight for death also. They raided Aldini's villa one night, breaking down the doors with rakes and shovels and other tools stolen from farmsteads. They cut him into pieces."

"And the Count? He had aided Aldini. What of him? Did he once again escape a monstrous Brotherhood?"

"They seemed not to notice him. Their dull eyes only looked for Aldini. Maybe they couldn't hate him, since he was truly their brother. He fled the villa."

"And made his way to England. Moved by love, weren't you, Joseph?"

Balsamo scarcely paused at this revelation. He sighed, perhaps grateful to tell someone after the centuries.

"I knew you must have figured out my identity. I am careless after so many years. I even took my family name again, Balsamo. I am ruled by nostalgia. So what do you plan to do, Dr. West—go to the Regents of Yale and complain that one of their professors should have been entombed two hundred years ago?"

"I have no desire to expose you. I had heard of the great longevity of Count Cagliostro. I had seen portraits of you from the time of your life and one painted in London scarcely fifty years ago. I just wanted to know how Aldini had succeeded. How do you cling to a sane life?"

"I have found what is slow and beautiful. I can easily spend another eighty years studying Dante. I will spend a hundred with Ovid, perhaps two hundred with Virgil. Read the papers, Dr. West: mankind will destroy itself long before I will wear out. Once I found out how to fall in love with art I knew I would have a perfect existence. Aldini did succeed. He made an undimming Eye, but *I* had to learn what to look at. How many monsters chase you, Dr. West?"

"They are many shapes seen in the shadows, but you have given me hope. Maybe they do not all have to hate me. Maybe some can love me."

"So you will be a successful god after all?"

"All I wanted was to kill death."

"The Egyptians had a god that killed death. Set killed his brother Osiris, who was Death himself, yet Set was the most hated god of their pantheon. He threatened their hope for peace. That is what your monsters have lost. Even I want what I remember from my few hours of lying dead in my home in Naples."

"So my monsters will never love me."

"It is a waste of time to love a human. I had a brief affair with Mary Shelley when she was eighteen. Stole her from her poet husband, told her everything, offered to make her as I am. She refused, and told my story in the way she needed to get its poison from her soul. She was my Beatrice."

"Thank you for letting me know what awaits me."

"You knew long before you tracked me down. You knew the first night when you saw any of them following you."

"Yes, I knew. But I fought for hope. I still think I am right. Medicine will push death back, and back. Humans will live longer and longer. In the fullness of time I will be a god."

"If that fullness comes, Dr. West, I shall write a long poem about you in the style of Dante. I write it slowly with great Beauty."

(*For Laird Barron*)

Rats

"I only want," said the dwarf, "my weight in gold."

The mayor and the alderman guffawed.

"Is that all, my little friend? Not the moon or the Weserbergerlande Mountains? Or the Weser river?" asked the mayor.

"Even if we had as much gold as your little frame, what would you give us?" taunted the mayor's younger brother.

The little man stared at the seven leaders of the town. They were inclined to fat. "I would give you your weight in gold," he said coldly. It would be a very large quantity of gold.

Laughter left the room. Greed is always able to banish the lesser demon of mocking.

The seven men listened as darkness fell outside. A great fire was kindled in the hearth, candles were lit, and brandy was fetched. Fear tried to banish greed, but she was unsuccessful. She will come later. The aldermen learned the history of their town.

In Roman times there was a gate built into the side of Klüt Hill. The Romans bought prisoners. Once a year, the gate opened. Beings like men emerged at night. They bought the prisoners for gold. Much gold. The beings took the prisoners inside. There was screaming and music for many hours. The Romans marched away. They were not offended by the screams, for they were brutal men. It was the music, the fantastic piping. It gave them dreams of other worlds. Not pleasant worlds, but worlds that myths called Dis or Tartarus. It had begun in the time of the Caesars. In time Rome fell, and for many years the Goths visited the gate. Gold flowed out and the tiny brown creatures shaped like small men bought their prisoners, their aged, their deformed. But finally a Christian prince said, "No more!" And hardworking honest men lay stones and earth over the gate, and deaf men were brought to guard the spot for eighty years.

Then the Goth kingdoms were gone, and the gate was forgotten.

The mayor's brother tried one last joke. "And you, my little friend, are you one of the brown little men?"

The dwarf nodded. "Many centuries ago, one of the Goth soldiers stole an ancestor of mine to keep for his amusement. Many sons and daughters have been born in the years that followed. Most were strong and healthy and tall—like you lucky men. But from time to time, the ancient blood reasserts itself. I am a hideous creature—life is hard for me with my puny limbs and short stature. Thankfully I am taller and better-looking than my brother."

"He must be quite hideous," said one of the men, his tongue loosened by brandy.

The dwarf looked at him and all warmth fled the room despite the fire.

"Yes, he is horrible. I fear for his life while I travel. He is not good-hearted as I am. Good-looking Christians are apt to rid themselves of such horror. With the gold we will find a secluded spot and trouble you fair men no more."

The dwarf continued his tale. After so many scores of years, the old ones had no doubt died off. But gold does not die. He was not strong enough to unbury the gate, but he could guide them to it. Later some of the aldermen began to doubt the tale. How could the dwarf know why the Romans left? Why would a solider want such an ugly bride? Why didn't the dwarf warn them of what they would find? Such fears chased them to an early grave.

It took a few weeks to assemble the workforce. The aldermen hired only men from other villages. Orphans and beggars were preferred. Great secrecy was maintained. But one morning they stood before Klüt Hill and began to dig at its western face. A healthy pine forest covered most of the hill, but only scraggly oak bushes covered the spot the dwarf had led them to. Beneath the rocky soil was a pile of boulders. The workers carted these off until a vast stone gate stood uncovered.

It took two days. The mayor and the aldermen brought vast quantities of food to the workers. At the end of the second day the mayor told them, "Tomorrow we will go inside the hill. Wealth beyond your greatest desires is heaped up inside. Tonight we drink!" Casks of wine were opened. Thirsty workers filled their bellies. They slept, and as the poison worked in their systems, they died. At dawn the mayor and the aldermen and the dwarf stood in front of the gate.

The bodies lay everywhere. All the wine barrels were empty save for one. Its top had been removed, and poisonous red liquid still filled it to the top. The mayor nodded. Three of the alderman seized the dwarf. They carried him to the open barrel. He screamed and struggled as they dipped him by his legs. He took nearly a quarter of an hour to drown. When he stopped struggling, a deep ringing sound came from within the hill, and the aldermen grew afraid.

"Don't be cowardly. We agreed. We must keep this secret our own. The ghosts of his people are just welcoming him. They cannot harm us for we carry the cross."

The men hastened to put their crosses around their necks. The mayor had asked the village priest to bless the crosses against whatever sort of demon might live in the hill. As an afterthought he killed the priest, lest the Church come hungering for money. Opening the gate was not easy. The aldermen regretted that they had slain the workers so soon. It took a day with iron pry bars to get the gate to open even a few inches. They moved away to sleep for the night. They did not relish lying with the dead. They planned to carry the bodies into the hill and close the gate after them.

The next morning a strange sight welcomed them.

The gate stood half open. The bodies of the slain workers were gone, as was the body of the dwarf. Pellets of rat dung lay everywhere. The youngest of the alderman turned to run, but the mayor caught him and pushed a knife in his belly. Now there were even fewer men to share the gold with.

"There will be more gold for all of us!"

They took torches and lit them and went into the cavern. The smell of rodent dung was overpowering. They walked on a soft and crunchy carpet of dung into the hill. The caverns led downwards. Tiny pawprints led the way. After a few hundred yards, larger footprints were seen. The good townspeople looked at them carefully. They were small prints, as though as from children. They were not many. Perhaps the dwarf's people still lived, but certainly they did not live in great numbers.

Down they went, and still further down. They lit more torches. Maybe they should return to the surface? Maybe they were going all the way to Hades?

But gold. Their weight in gold.

The mayor's brother spotted the crude buildings first. Low windowless stone buildings. No light coming from their open doors. It was a little village of maybe twenty buildings; most were in ruins. They carried their torches in their left hands, their swords in their right. The clothes of the workers were scattered about. Then a score of yards from the village lay the workers' half-eaten bodies. Then piles of dead and dying rats. Poisoned by the tainted flesh, hundreds of them. Some still twitched in agony; it was not a subtle poison, for the aldermen were not subtle men. Then they saw the body of the dwarf stripped of his clothes. Soft brown fur covered his body. Small feelers grew from under his arms and his crotch. He had been careful to shave his hands and face. The rats had been busy feeding on him as well. His eyes were gone, and his genitals and anus had been gnawed away. The good alderman crossed themselves. They were glad to move away from the dwarf's body and into the village. Prayers were said; it is good to know God is on your side.

But the village proved worse. In the biggest building, whose roof was only inches above their heads, the good Christians found a church with pews and an altar and a god and its worshippers.

There were three of them—three of the dwarf's people. They were smaller than him and much more ratlike. Their eyes were intact and milky white, unburdened by sight. They lay in the largest building around a pedestal that bore the figure of a short, many-breasted goddess. Her face was that of a rat and the tentacles under her arms and crotch were holding flint knives and strangely shaped devices or amulets. She played a syrinx, the shepherd's pipes. She stood four feet tall, towering almost twice the height of her worshippers. The walls of the temple had no windows. Strange letters covered the walls, painted in some greenish-brown slime; they glistened wetly. One wall bore a fresco—humans and dwarves and rats ate one another, coupled with one another, danced with one another. The rat goddess stood above them. She bowed in prayer to a white toad god, who was himself looking at some vast shadowy figure that flew in the darkness.

The mayor's brother began to laugh. "We are the gods of the fleas that bite us, our god feeds us his flesh, and other gods feed Him. Other gods feed Them. Eat and fuck and pray. Eat and fuck and pray." The mayor hit him with the flat of his sword. He was embarrassed at his brother's weak will.

"Find the gold."

They left the temple. The other buildings seemed to be holding pens, except for the last and smallest building. Here in great yellow mounds was gold. Soft massy nuggets bearing the tooth-marks of thousands of rats lay in huge heaps. Each man gathered as much as he could carry. Humans cannot carry their own weight regardless of greed. Each began to dream of how he would slay the others. They began their heavy walk back to light and air. With each squelching in the rat dung, their greed grew. Each had a thousand dreams of avarice. Their torches grew short. They began to hear the rats about halfway to the surface. Hundreds of rats may have died, but thousands lived. They could see them scurrying just beyond their circle of light. They could see their little eyes glinting. They began to trot, filled with fear, but filled with greater love for their gold. One of the rats leapt upon the mayor. He knocked it to the soft ground and stabbed it with his sword.

It wasn't *entirely* a rat. Its head was too big, and it had hands like a man. It even had something of a face.

The trot became a run. Some golden nuggets fell from the runners. A sparkly path lay in their wake like the breadcrumbs of Hansel and Gretel.

The rats began to squeak. The aldermen ran faster. They spied the gate.

They couldn't shut it behind them, so they threw their torches down and made a fire across the opening. They gathered the dead limbs from the scraggly bushes the workers had cleared away until they had a great fire.

It was dusk, and they trudged back toward their village.

They never spoke of the caverns. When the families of the workers asked after them, the alderman claimed a foreign prince had paid them to join his army. They augmented their tale with gold, and it was believed. Soon their gold had its effect. They built houses, repaired walls, built a cathedral. People moved to Hamelin. All was well for years. Some village gossips suggested that the town's leaders had sold the workers, but how could such things be said of such pious men? They went to Mass every Sunday; they gave to the monks and the poor. And in time they died off. They died young but uneventfully with one exception: when the mayor died, his house was overrun with rats. They even defiled his corpse.

Years passed. There was a new mayor, and new aldermen. The city prospered. One summer people began complaining of bites. Flea bites. Everyone itched; most children scratched themselves bloody. Some broke into a terrible fever where big black sores broke out on the skin. Doctors gave out sachets of useless herbs, priests prayed. Even the local witch tried her hand at stopping the fever. The rat population increased. Rats bit babies and the elderly. Rats ate grain and flour. Rats scurried across the dinner table. Rats reared their ugly heads on the cathedral's altar. Rats stole the body of Christ from the priest's hands.

People were leaving. Everyone was complaining. The mayor offered a thousand guilders to anyone who could get rid of the rat problem. Then two thousand guilders.

One day, the shortest adult anyone had seen came to town. He wore a fool's motley. He came into town riding a large brown dog that growled fiercely when anyone drew near. And he let it be known that he was expert in dealing with rats. In spite of his tiny stature, he was perfectly formed. It was as though the finest sculptor had made the little man from white marble. The mayor summoned him at once.

"I want twice my weight in gold," announced the dwarf.

No one made a jest. A previous mayor had told them that a very ugly little person might show up some day claiming gold. He should be paid. But surely this handsome young man was not the imp of legend. They viewed beauty and ugliness as surface things.

"How will you deal with the rats?"

"That is my business."

His exorbitant price was agreed to. The dwarf pulled a syrinx from his pack and began to play the most unearthly melody. Rats ran up from the sewers, rats ran out of the spaces between the walls. Rats came from the banks of the Weser. Rats poured out of holes in the cemetery. The dwarf paused to call his dog. He mounted the strange steed, and the dog began trotting off through the woods. The huge, smelly, chittering pack of rats followed him. The mayor and the aldermen followed. The dwarf rode to the west to Klüt Hill. The region was said to be haunted. When the dwarf arrived he began playing with fiendish energy. The rats screamed and began to pour into a large stone door cut into the side of the hill. It took several minutes for the living tide to go through the half-opened door. The dwarf dismounted and kicked the door. It swung shut with a huge crash.

The dwarf stopped his piping.

"I am ready for my gold," he said.

The mayor replied that it would take a few days to assemble the gold, but that he would put the dwarf up in his own home. He spared no expense. He brought women and wine and the finest foods that the town could manage. The town council met at midnight.

The mayor told them that if they paid the dwarf his fee the town would be bankrupt. It was agreed then. The mayor would kill the dwarf while he slept. It was a sad thing, but it ensured their jobs and the city's welfare. The mayor set off to his home.

The next day the dwarf rode his dog to the town hall. The mayor was nowhere to be seen. The dwarf announced that he would collect his fee in three days. The aldermen demurred, saying they could not pay the amount requested. He rode off to the west.

For three days the town attempted to gather as much gold as it could. Truth be told, a good deal of gold was hidden around the town in the fine homes of the aldermen who had dealt so badly with another dwarf a hundred years ago. These families loved their gold and kept most of it. The little man would have to be satisfied. The dwarf rode into town. The small pile was offered to him.

"This is too little, this is too late!" He made no move to gather the gold, but rode away again. The walls were sealed that night and all the good citizens locked their doors. An hour after sunset the piping began. It came from everywhere or nowhere. It echoed round the bones. People tried to block their ears, but unlike Odysseus' sailors, the mad piping came through. The children began to dance. Parents tried to stop them. One father even broke his son's leg, but they danced. After an hour of dancing and piping the children went out of doors. If their parents restrained them, they fought. They battered walls with their heads, bit their parents' arms, screamed in an unknown tongue. So they were let out of their homes. After they had screamed at the town gate it was opened.

In the moonlight stood the pied piper and his dog. He set off for Klüt Hill. Some brave souls followed, but most ran back in their homes and barricaded the doors. The dwarf played madly. All the children save for the lad with the recently broken leg entered through the gate into the hill. The dwarf walked in behind them. The great gate slammed shut. The lame boy beat against the door until his fists were bloody. For three days he listened to the screams and the music.

Then the townspeople came and covered the door with stones and dirt. Europe forgot as a new disease began spreading—the Black Death the rats brought. Who in the face of such horror can remember a fairy tale?

Hamelin became a city with four great forts. A watch was kept on Klüt Hill for nearly seven hundred years. Only once in the twentieth century was anything untoward seen there. A short man, but by no means a dwarf, was said to be seen digging himself free from the earth. He later rose to power, but being denounced by a woodsman who believed in fairy tales did not stop his career. Some did think the man had a rodentlike cast to his face, but such remarks were dangerous to utter.

Since then all has been quiet on Klüt Hill. The tales are forgotten, and no one believes in the Pied Piper.

(For Richard Lupoff)

A Game of Nine Pins

Nathan Pedersen was at a great place. He was three-quarters of the way done with his thesis. He would finish two months ahead of time. His father had only received a GED, his mom had dropped out of high school to have him, his granny had two semesters at a junior college. Everybody was so proud, and then he met the nutcase. All that happened to Nathan can be blamed on the fact that was ahead of schedule; if deadlines were looming, he would have never gone on the trip that weekend. If you learn anything from this fable, kids, it's this: put off your schoolwork to the last minute.

Nathan had chosen English because his mom and dad both had suffered with English at Sam Houston High School in Doublesign, Texas. Nathan had an amazing academic life considering that none of his people had made it through college. He was valedictorian at Sam Houston High, he got a full scholarship to Rice University in Houston, he graduated with honors and went on to Yale. All his schools didn't know what to do with him as a data entry—he was brown and spoke Spanish like his mom, Juanita Pedersen, but his surname made him an Anglo. His mom and dad lived in a two-bedroom house with warped wooden floors and cracked stucco. Neither of them had ever read a book for pleasure, neither of them had any clue about why Nathan was so smart, neither of them could be any prouder of their son. Everyone in the Doublesign Pentecostal church had seen Juanita's photos. Every drinker in the Shamrock Bar had heard Rolf's sagas about his son. His teachers at the high school still sent him Christmas cards jokingly warning him about New Haven's winters. Nathan worked hard, had high self-esteem, and had never been really frightened of anyone or anything in his life.

The nutcase was a different story. He would have dropped out of school because of a drug problem, and he knew more about fear than most humans ever should.

Nathan was writing about Washington Irving's source material. He sought out folklore, fakelore, and contemporary writings. He felt he had uncovered almost all Irving's sources, certainly every source that could be uncovered. Dr. Winslow Tyler, his thesis advisor, foresaw a great teaching career for Nathan, as well as the possibility of reworking his thesis into a popular book. Dr. Tyler urged Nathan to practice reaching out to a literate audience. So, with the backing of the English department, Nathan arranged a Halloween reading of "The Legend of Sleepy Hollow" followed by a mini-lecture about Washington Irving. He impressed the crowd by telling them how Washington Irving had read young Edgar Allan Poe's "The Fall of the House of Usher" in manuscript and helped Poe revise it. He recounted Irving's suggestion to Francis Scott Key, "Francis, you set your poem 'The Defense of Fort McHenry' to music, it could catch on. Why not call it 'The Star-Spangled Banner'?"

"You know, folks, growing up in Texas I always thought that song was about my cousin—you know, José, can you see?"

The audience loved it—undergraduates, graduate students, even some townies. What could be more American—a young brown from Texas, talking about one of the people that gave birth to American literature on Halloween, the most American of all holidays?

A slightly fat, gray-and-black-haired man came up to him after the applause. The guy looked to be in his forties, didn't look crazy, and you'd never have guessed that he had had electroshock therapy. He had congenital blue eyes and scars on his lower lip like two knife cuts.

"Dr. Pedersen," he began.

"Not 'doctor' yet," Nathan countered.

"OK, Mr. Pedersen, I loved your talk. I may have something for you. My late father was an amateur Irving scholar. I've still got his papers, I tried to give them to Yale a few years ago, but since Dad never finished his doctorate, they weren't interested. I know Dad would really have loved it if somebody could make use of them. I mean, I don't know if they're groundbreaking scholarship. I run a coffee shop, but I would love it if he could be mentioned in a footnote somewhere."

"I would love to look his stuff over."

"Thank you. I could drop them off to you, or if you come by Brewed Awakening I'd treat you to coffee and danish and my dad's story."

"That's in North Haven, right? I loved the pun."

"We're on the 300 block on Washington. I know the street is named after the general, but for Dad's sake, pretend it's named after Washington Irving. Drop by any afternoon. This would be a big deal to Dad—being part of real scholarship. You know he was the first in his family to go to college; he didn't get to finish, the recession, so it would have meant so much."

Thus works fate.

Nathan stopped by Brewed Awakening next Tuesday afternoon. It had been an especially cold fall, snow mixed with fallen leaves, and the black squirrels of the Yale campus had gone into hibernation. Nathan had a strong oversized mocha and a diamond shaped piece of Brewed Awakenings' "Choclava." Max Bowen handed him a large brown envelope of yellowed typescript.

"These were before the era of the personal computer. I remember how proud Dad was of his Selectric II. I remember watching him type and that little typeball thing spin and make the letters."

"So you father was in Yale or UConn?" asked Nathan.

"He was a Yalie. It was his senior project. He had tracked down some Indian legend, a Lenape legend of the 'Sleepers,' which Irving had heard during his time in the Catskills. He later used the story in 'Rip Van Winkle.'"

"Wow. I have been looking at Irving's sources for a couple of years and I had never heard of it; that is exactly what I am doing my dissertation on. If I can follow your father's research he'll be more than a footnote. I can't think you enough—if it pans out, I mean. But I have to level with you, there are pretty strong links showing that Irving took his story from the German folktale of Peter Klaus or the Christian legend of the Sleepers of Ephesus."

"Oh, it will pan out. Dad was methodical. He left no stone un-turned."

"So economics made him leave school?"

"There was a downturn in the early seventies. Dad's family used to own a restaurant just a couple of blocks from here—Tom's Grinders. It went out of business, Granddad had a stroke, Dad started working as a short-order cook."

"If it's not personal, what happened to him?"

"Lung cancer. Dad could never wean himself from the cancer sticks."

"I'm sorry. What was your father's name?"

"Just like me, Max Bowen."

The packet contained the beginning of a research paper, a spiral notebook that seemed to have served as Bowen's journal, and four or five Xeroxed articles or excerpts from books.

The first article was about Lenape legends. It was from the 1923 *American Indian Culture and Research Journal,* "The Concept of 'Real People' in Unmai Folk-Stories" by Clifford Johnstone. Dr. Johnstone had collected verbal folklore from a "southern" Lenape (or, as the English had called them, a "Delaware"). He had asked his informant if the term "Leni Lenape" or "Real People" expressed anything more than xenophobia. The informant claimed that there were nonhuman races living in the hollow hills of the Lenapehoking. These dwarfs—Johnstone had used the unfortunate term "Leprechauns"—were to be avoided. One bought them off by leaving dressed deer carcasses in the spring and the "Three Sisters"—corn, squash, and beans—in the fall. These creatures had the ability to steal human souls and use them for prolonged periods in some sort of sorcerous endeavor. Their victims lay in a deathlike sleep for decades and were often buried alive. They were given the name Pagwadjinini, which Dr. Johnstone translated as "Sleepers." Apparently these guys were not exactly human in shape, but could pass for humans if spotted at a great enough distance.

The second Xerox was from *Of Evill Sorceries Done in New-England of Daemons in No Humane Shape,* some sort of Puritan Satan-scare book by one Rev. Ward Phillips. This lesser Cotton Mather devoted a few lines to an unfortunate Edward Phillips, who traded with the Dutch settlers in New York. Apparently Mr. Phillips had the bad luck of visiting the community of Indian Head in the heart of the "Kaatskille" Mountains. Traveling through the woods on St. Bridget's Day, he heard several strange sounds like unto thunder, despite the clearness of the day. He tied his horse to a tree and set off on foot to seek after this mystery. He came into a shallow depression where a group of little men or imps were playing some sort of game in and around a stone circle. Thinking that he had encountered a hitherto undiscovered tribe of Indians and having an eye to exclusive trading with this group, he ran back to his horse and gathered a sack of trade goods—beads and other gimcracks that were alluring to the native eye. He hailed the small men, whom he noticed were exceedingly pale of skin and possessed of full beards. These savages expressed great wonder at meeting a white man; they had not heard of the coming of the white race to their land. They offered to introduce him to their "Satan," who lived inside the hill. Phillips declined this offer. One of their women, somewhat taller than the little men, came out of the earth and proceeded to milk herself from one of her breasts. The milk, which looked like wine, was gathered into a hollowed deer horn and offered to Phillips. Revolted by what he had seen, he ran away, much to the merriment of the imps. As his horse galloped away, he again heard thunder and believed the very ground to shake.

Nathan was beside himself. If these sources checked out, he would earn an entire chapter in Irving studies. The next article proved disturbing because it removed these ideas from legend and folklore and put them in the context of lunatic tabloid journalism. It was from the *National Enquirer,* December 12, 1966:

A REAL LIFE RIP VAN WINKLE??

Albany, N.Y.—Twenty-five years ago Mr. Stanislaw Kandinsky left his Indian Head, N.Y., home to spend a weekend in the forest. Mr. Kandinsky was due to report for induction in the U.S. Army. He told his friends that he wanted to spend a weekend in prayer and getting right with God before going to fight Nazis. But he was never seen again. He showed up at the door of his old family home this week claiming to have been taken to

Heaven by strange light-skinned aliens. They had saved him from certain death in Europe and had only returned him recently. He is being held for observation at the medical school of the State University of New York. So far he has issued no statements about the saucer that had abducted him, nor the location of "Heaven." We will watch this story carefully.

Max Bowen may have been caught up in the pseudo-scholarship of the early seventies. Erich Van Däniken and Carlos Castañeda were making mint by rehashing old legends of one sort or another with enough pseudo-anthropology thrown in to appeal to a gullible public. Bowen couldn't have meant to include the *Enquirer* snippet unless ironically. Nathan was tired and went to bed.

Nathan worked as a TA in the morning helping freshmen attack English 101. He turned to the notebook that afternoon. Something had clearly fried Max Bowen's brain, but 1969 was a year that young American brains were fried as often as Kentucky chicken.

Jan 15

Dropped six hundred mikes with Connie. There was an older dude at her place, I thought he might have been an archaeologist. His trip was time. Connie and Tom were talking about time in dreams. Dream time seems really long some nights, like time dilates on some trips. This guy said that more primeval people understood this better than we do. There were ways to experience years in a night. I thought he meant drumming because I have been reading about shamanic drumming as part of the Rip Van Winkle story. What if someone had some kind of trippy experience with the Delawares and told Irving? He said sound was a big part of it, but I couldn't follow much of his story. Then Tom turned on the TV and we all sat around watching the war, and we kind of forgot about this guy. Later I remembered, but he was gone.

Jan 17

Ran into Connie. I am almost over the fact that she doesn't love me. I asked her about the guy at her house. She doesn't know him well. Turns out he is an archaeologist, who had done digs in the Caatskills. He had helped chart some colonial Dutch farmhouses and some Delaware/Lenape stuff too. She had met him at a poetry reading at the Blue Moon Room. They had snuck out back and shared a joint in December at the "Reading you were too busy to go to." I apologized for that like the thirtieth time. I asked if I could meet the guy. Which was the **wrong** thing to say, because I got lectured again about how overly interested I am in my own projects and nothing else.

Jan 20
Got some good stuff on Lenape legends. Now if I can just find anything that suggested that Irving might have heard any of them. I can make a pretty good circumstantial case, but Dr. Evans warns me that is not quite scholarship. I ran into the archaeologist on campus; he says that he is familiar with the Lenape "Little People." He wanted to know how serious I was and could I handle "really heavy shit." I indicated that I was as serious as I could be. In reality, unless I can tie the Lenape stuff directly to Irving, I can't use any more stuff on the Indian side of the equation. We got Nixon today. Goodbye, LBJ, how many kids did you kill today?

Jan 28
I am freaking out about the oil spill near Santa Barbara. Shit, we've got to wise up about this planet. I spent a long time talking with Dr. Perault. The man is either a really important scholar or bugfuck crazy. He claims that the Little People are real, and that he has encountered their "remains" in a dig. He said he gave the "evidence" to Yale and that it was hushed up by the government. I asked him if they were an American Pygmy, and he said that he doubted they were genus homo. So I called him out on it—if you had found anything like that you would be calling a press conference, not making a gift to Yale. He got really mad and told me to meet him later. He came by Dad's place. Dad gave him coffee thinking that he was one of my professors. He had this tiny hatchet with him, an "artifact." It was really small, but it could have been a child's toy. I asked how did he know this wasn't a toy, and was his specialty American Indians anyhow. He said I should go home and think about how serious I was, because he could lay proof on me, heavy proof, but that I would leave my life behind. I called Connie to talk to her, to try and find out anything about Dr. Perault, but she was out and Tom was tripping. Tom began talking about UFOs. He asked me what would I do if one landed right in front of me and asked me if I wanted to go with them. Would I go? Just go like that? I've been thinking about that. For a long time I was thrilled to be the first Bowen to finish school, and not any school but YALE! But after I broke up with Connie all I do is watch the news every night. I see guys my age being blown up in Vietnam. Yet the next day I see professors playing campus politics with a straight face as if

what they were doing were real. What kind of shit is that? And everyday Dad makes grinders for the Yalies who laugh at him, and every night he curses them while rubbing his aching hands, and his biggest revenge on them is that his only-begotten son IS one of them. And I look at how the blacks are treated and Kennedy. I think I would say yes to the little green men. I think that I would fly away. I think I'll see whatever "heavy shit" Dr. Perault can lay on me.

Jan 29

I asked around at school. Perault was on the faculty until 1963. He flaked out after the Kennedy assassination, claimed to have found some earth-shaking revelation, but wound up screwing his TA. His male TA. I don't know if this guy just wants to get into my pants or really knows something and can't get any attention because he's a faggot. I am still game, but I am going to be stone cold sober.

Jan 30

I can't believe it—the Beatles did a free live concert on the roof of Apple Records! The fuzz busted it, of course. This will be something people will talk about for years. Can you imagine, you're walking down the street and there are the Beatles. The Russians have one rocket ship in orbit now and it is believed that they will launch another one soon to dock with the first. The Beatles and the moon race! Dr. Perault told me that the heavy shit was about this quickening of human history, too. Do you think the world could change any faster? But Perault says that's a side effect of this stuff the Indians were exchanging with. He laughed and said that it was all about how to tell time. "How to tell Time to serve you!" he said. He told me to meet him in front of the library at six-thirty tomorrow morning. We are going to the dig site where he found the little tomahawk. He said that he had found the ruins of their ball game. I guess it is midget-sized. He probably did find something amazing like a race of American pygmies and then went crazy. His find seems full of cosmic significance as if he's on a permanent LSD trip. But I figure I am grounded enough to take advantage of his find. I might be a big man in American letters. Not just the first Bowen to go to college, but someone that rewrote the book on Amerindian studies. It will be cool, but not as cool as the Beatles.

After reading the journal Nathan called Max Jr. It was after ten at night. Max answered. He had clearly already gone to bed, his voice was all dreamy.

"So what happened?"

"What happened is that Dad never came back."

"So where are you in this story? I don't see any notes about 'my baby son, Max'?"

"Little Max was conveniently with Grandpa. I was a senior year of high school mistake. Nothing could screw with Big Max's college career."

"So what do you feel now?"

"For a long time I was angry. I didn't get to go to college, I busted my butt, slinging hash. Then in my thirties, I got scared. I dreamed of him with little not-quite-men. I know it's stupid. I wanted you to tell me it's stupid."

"What do you want now?"

"I want you to go with me to the dig site on February 1. St. Bridget's Day."

"You know that's a stupid date. It wouldn't be a Delaware holiday."

"I know the whole thing is stupid. But it's what I want."

Nathan thought about the good place he was in. Eight weeks from now. At worst it would be a story. At best an adventure, more of an adventure even than leaving central Texas and coming to Yale. Besides, unlike a drugged-out undergraduate in 1969, he had nothing to lose by going. He was twenty-seven and the world was his oyster.

"Sure, I'll go. I mean, what the fuck?"

It was a four-and-half-hour drive mainly up 90 and 91. Billboards suggested the many tourist traps of the Catskills like the Shawangunk Wine Trail. There was no real country in New England compared to Texas. As Nathan rode in Max's van, there was never a moment that you didn't see another car. The roads were covered in gray and black slush; the van smelled of grinders. After they had left New Haven, there had been little to say for the next two hours. Heck, you can drive from Doublesign to Dallas in two hours.

"How did you locate the dig?"

"Perault published. It was small and dry and preliminary and only suggested an unknown tribal group that might have lingered on until colonial times. I am not real smart, and shit, I hired a graduate student in anthropology to track it down."

"You been there?"

"Once in midsummer. There's some standing stones. Nine of them. But I don't think it was Washington Irving's nine pins."

"You know I played that as a kid. A lot of Germans settled in central Texas; there are some really old nine-pin bowling halls near Doubleisgn and Flapjack."

"There's really a town called Flapjack?"

"Honest Injun."

"We're getting close. I've got to watch the road. This isn't exactly GPS-supported."

Less than mile later Max pulled the van off onto some snow-covered gravel. "We walk now."

"Aren't we supposed to bring them some deer?" asked Nathan. Max just stared at him. It was two o'clock. It was three degrees above freezing and the sky was pile of dirty gray blankets. The air smelled of smoke and ammonia and tar. The leafless trees seemed to have never had leaves at all. Nathan could not believe this could ever be a place of scenic beauty. He regretted coming. What could he do—make some pictures of rocks with his phone? Max just headed off into the woods. Well, with his phone he couldn't get lost. Just cold and wet. He trudged after Max, the shallow snow chilling his loafers. Nathan could barely make out a trail through the woods. It twisted and turned and sometimes he found himself bumping against a tree as though the logic of the trail was non-human. Maybe deer used this. Max stayed ahead of him because the trail was narrow. Nathan began to feel a little scared; for some reason he wanted to see Max's face. After only a few twists into the forest, Nathan noticed how different New England woods were from the Lost Pines forest near his hometown in Texas. They exuded silence. He couldn't hear the road at all, even though they must be within fifty yards or so. No birds chirped, but he attributed that to the coldness of the spring. Nathan could tell the general path led downward.

"Don't worry," said Max. "Soon we can walk two abreast after we pass beyond the ridge." They walked over a small black berm of gneiss that stood like a black iceberg in the snow. On the other side Nathan could easily tell they were entering a valley. Max's face glowed with sweat. Looking at his fleece-lined denim jacket, Nathan realized that it bulged at the right shoulder. Max was carrying a handgun. Nathan wondered if Max meant to shoot him. They had not encountered barbed wire yet; these woods were not like Texas.

"Is this public land?" asked Nathan.

Max answered, "You probably won't believe me, but this section simply doesn't show up on maps. I had the devil of a time finding it the first time."

"What did you do the first time?"

"I looked at the rocks. I spent the night. I don't know, I was hoping Dad's ghost would show up."

Max walked faster. Nathan tried to find his cool voice, the neutral tone he used as TA. "So what do you think happened to your father?"

"You know. He slept. That which is not dead . . . he dreamed."

"'What dreams may come,' eh?" asked Nathan. He didn't know what to say; he had never spent any time with a *bona fide* crazy person.

"Just like Dr. Perualt said. Dreams in which time is accelerated. The sleeper spends a few years in sleep in regard to the outside world, but lives tens, hundreds of years."

Nathan stared at the trees, the black ridges of stone. He had no place to run to. Max unbuttoned his jacket as he walked. The trees were larger, thicker, older.

Then a loud scraping/striking sound echoed through the silence. "What the fuck?" asked Nathan.

Max said calmly, "They've started the game." He nonchalantly took the pistol from his shoulder holster. "You've figured it out by now. You're the deer."

"You're going to kill me?"

"Only if you were so stupid as to run. Of course I wanted to run; I didn't know I was being dragged to Heaven. You sure won't think it's Heaven for the first few hundred years, though.' Max laughed, then continued, "I am paying my way into another dream-round. You will dream for them. Once you have you'll do what I'm doing, unless the world ends while you sleep."

Max started to say something about waking up, but the scraping sound boomed again. The gray clouds seemed to darken.

"This is for real," said Nathan.

"This is for real," agreed Max.

"How old are you, really?"

"I'm sixty-five. You don't age much while you sleep. I look as bad as I do because of how they treated me at the Capital District Psychiatric Center in Albany. They get an aphasic like me every ten years or so—always found on the same stretch of highway in the Catskills. They shock us until we start talking, then flood us with anti-psychotics. Then when we're all human and shit let us go."

"Is this some cult thing?"

"It's me escaping to Witch Mountain. I am buying back in. My body will die under the Sleep this time. I'm lucky, most of them stay locked up. My dad still ran his diner, I convinced him I was a long-lost nephew."

"I suppose if I gave you the 'You don't have to do this' speech, it wouldn't work?"

Max just gestured with the pistol. Nathan had a flash that he was not the first deer, just the one that might be curious enough and chicken-shit enough *not* to run.

Max said, "I'll need you to step in front of me now. The last couple of hundred yards is steep. Watch your footing, we'll be going down into the pit. There's loose gravel, mixed with snow. I fell a lot the first time."

Max's words proved true. They were descending shortly into a vast amphitheater of basalt maybe a hundred yards in diameter. It seemed to hold night in its center, as though darkness were a liquid. Nathan could see a score of pale gray figures dancing among tall stones. He couldn't study the scene except by short glances; mainly he watched his footing. Max prodded his back with a drawn gun from time to time.

Max asked, "Can you imagine my life? The day Perault led me down here, the biggest thing in my life was the fucking Beatles. I dreamed down here for thirty years. Poor young Max missed Woodstock—just a few months later and twenty-five miles away. When I awoke it was 1999. I couldn't talk for months. I stumbled out of here when I figured out what I had to do. A truck picked me up on the highway. I had seen such things, couldn't relate to my fellow humans for two fucking years. When I tried to tell them, they gave me electroshock. So I forgot enough that I just became human again—and I learned to shut up. Remember that you'll need to. You will have seen such things that you won't be able to talk."

"What did you dream of?"

"I lived. It wasn't a fucking dream; they sent my psyche elsewhere. They throw us into worlds and things like worlds—and they eat something we make—or maybe the stones do. I've seen polychromatic waterfalls of flame on worlds far from any sun. I've heard debates between philosophers with three mouths and no eyes about the worms that eat time. I've eaten thick music in a decade-long orgy under the sub-crypt of a temple built on a comet. Hundreds of scenes there are no words for. I'm not a poet; I don't have the words. Fear? Ecstasy? Shit, man, what you will have will make those words sound lukewarm and mildly chilly."

Then two of the stones struck each other, throwing sparks at least twelve feet on either side. It was so loud that Nathan was deafened. For minutes all he could hear was an aching whistle in his ears. Nathan didn't realize that Max was still talking until Max poked with him with the gun barrel again. Nathan looked back at him. Max was probably shouting, overcome by the need to share his experience with another human. Nathan stumbled—sliding ten, maybe fifteen feet before falling onto the loose gravel. He half crawled, half fell on into the valley. The rocks cut his hands. He was very aware of the smell of his blood as well as the smell of sparks. His coat was wet and dirty. As he managed to stand and look up at Max, he could make out some of the words of the shouter in the darkness.

" . . . more dreamers . . . in those days only one or two humans at a time . . . humans better . . . semi-rotten nourishment . . . speeds up human history for the One . . . nightmare wine . . . blood dance in the court of the Thousand Moons . . . I saw Him who . . . the Mao games

. . . the labyrinth of laughter . . . the things in the rings of the twelfth planet . . ."

Nathan looked at the stones. Tall, thin, and sickly yellow—they looked like coral. Maybe they were life forms. They would suddenly move to smash one of the tiny dancers between them, illuminating the amphitheater with sparks. The dancers stood less than three feet tall; vaguely insectlike, they danced on their hind legs. Some held jugs in their middle legs. Where their heads should be were masses of white feelers that could have been mistaken for long white beards. Some of them bore triple rows of nipples from which dribbled a wine-colored sap that was gathered into jugs. Some naked humans, male and female, danced among them. Max struck his face with the gun, then kicked him on the back of his legs, forcing him to kneel. The dancers swarmed over to him very quickly. Their insect motion and blinding speed made him feel nauseous, and their *smell* . . . The swarmed up him. Their tiny pincers grabbed his hair; others grabbed and pinched his lips and pulled them downward.

They forced his mouth open. The drink was thick, sweet, and metallic. They poured maybe two ounces in him. Nathan tried to throw up, to no avail. Their pincers cut into his neck; he could feel his hot blood running down his spine, though it felt good compared to the cold New York air. He thought of his mother and father and Texas sunsets.

Two rock columns smashed together a few feet from him, and regrettably he saw the faces of the dancers underneath their feelers. Before he could scream the drug knocked him out.

And for what he saw then, there are no words. He was not a poet.

(For Simon Strantzas)

Powers of Air and Darkness

Being a waiter on R 418 *Balmoral* was Ernest MacVeigh's dream job. As a young boy in Kansas he was captivated by the Phantom Airship stories. For two years humans all over the globe reported encounters with mysterious airships. Like many young men and women, he dreamed that he too would be taken on a ride with the strange airmen. The stories had inspired dime novels, stage plays, and finally the invention of real airships. The skies were filled with Mr. Wells's invention— great silvery cylinders that challenged the blue skies or cast wonderful shadows against the full moon. Ernest's older brother was a captain of the R 118 *Empress Victoria* that had gone down in Benares. It had been the last of the hydrogen ships. There was great irony in its holocaust— its flaming debris raining down on the vast open-air crematoria that fill the holy city of Benares. Brother John's ashes mixed with the stink of the city and the sacred water of the Ganges.

John had been the smart one. Top in his class at the University of Kansas. He had excelled in mathematics and astronomy. He believed the airships were mankind's first step toward leaving the Earth. Ernest was the dreamer. Instead of doing well at school, he had pored over the romance of Mr. Poe, the "scientific" tales of Mr. Twain, and Charles Dickens's *Eben Mizer on the Moon*. When his brother wrote one of the first serious studies of Roentgen's X-rays, Ernest was reading the uncritical accounts of how X-rays could do anything from curing blindness to reanimating the dead. The day brother John submitted his patent for an improved sextant, Ernest had joined the Hermetic Brotherhood of Luxor—a mail-order occult group. John was tall, blond, and well built. Ernest had dark brown hair and brown eyes set too far apart. John attracted ladies, Ernest attracted fellow fanatics and enthusiasts. John had been drawn to commercial air travel because he wanted to be part of the modernizing of the world. Ernest wanted to be nearer to air elementals. John believed the world was ruled by reason; Ernest believed the world was ruled a vast conspiracy run either by Jews, communists, or demons (assuming these *were* different groups).

The *Balmoral* flew around the world every two weeks. Paris, Chicago, Victoria, Tokyo, Peking, Moscow, Paris. A heady mix for a young man from Overland Park. Ernest had spent time in each of these cities. He had hoped for love and for adventure. Only at the very end did he receive the latter.

The letters from John had reached him in Victoria, British Columbia. With some irony they had been chasing him around the globe for nearly two years, and the five envelopes were almost black with grime. The first three letters were commonplace. John described Rome, Tehran, Benares, Barcelona, Mexico City, Honolulu. He told of romance and fine dining. The last two letters were of a different sort. Ernest wondered if they had been meant as a joke, but John was not really the joking sort. He genuinely cared for younger brother, as much as he sometimes taunted him for uncritical thinking.

John MacVeigh
Royal Victiora
British Air Mail Service
September 18, 1894

Dear Ernest,

My brother, I had never supposed that I would write you about such matters. Do you remember as a child when we first heard of airships? You were a true believer. You thought the story of the Dallas airship that kidnapped a steer from a rancher's field was gospel truth. Remember how you couldn't sleep for weeks? I have come to wonder if there might be something to those stories. Months ago in Cairo, I spent an evening with a renowned Egyptologist, Wallis Budge, who told me that during certain dynasties Egyptians believed that they were dealing with beings that lived in the clouds. These creatures were not gods or demons *per se,* although they were in league with the darker gods of their pantheon, Set and Nyarlathotep. "Hotep" is an EgyptiAn word meaning "satisfied" and "Nyarla" means "dark churning." The name itself means "He Who Is

Pleased by Stirring Up the Dark"—or perhaps "the Silence." It was an interesting discussion, and I wished you had been there as mythology is more your hobby-horse than my own. But at the end of the evening Mr. Budge mentioned that the cloud beings were invisible unless viewed with certain special lenses. Now Mr. Budge had no way of knowing this (and I am *risking my job* telling you), but all the British Dirigible Company's dirigibles carry a special optical device that can only be taken from its special case by very high-ranking company officials, even I lack the clearance to use these glasses. The rumor has been that the German or Russian dirigibles have been treated with a special paint that renders them invisible—and that this news is being kept from the general public to avoid mass hysteria. The special glasses unpolarize the light and reveal the ships.

I did not rush to correlate these facts, but I found that I could not stop thinking about the glasses. They rest in a small chest in the captain's office, I'm sure the *Balmoral* has a pair. I am writing to you so that you may have a record of my discoveries and (in the event something should happen to me) let the world know. Making a long story short, I arranged to buy some lock-picking tools from a criminal in Barcelona. He was a jewel thief who plied his trade on the *Victoria*. The ship's detective was never able to catch him, and I had invited him to the captain's table several times because I admired his incorrigible nature. He explained the use of the tools. Since I had the opportunity to spend several hours alone with the case, opening it proved no problem. The glasses were simple goggle-looking affairs in no way remarkable. I took to wearing them anytime I could be unobserved. I saw nothing of interest for nearly nine weeks. Then while passing over the Himalayas I spotted several *flying* creatures one night entering a saucer-shaped platform. I will not describe the nightmare city, save to say that I have come to believe that there are certain *shapes* and *colors* that humans cannot look upon without damaging their neural tissues. I nearly screamed in fear and pain. I removed the special glasses. The creatures, which resembled a sort of flying crayfish, were not invisible, but their platform could only be seen with the glasses. I realize that the Royal Air Force is not hiding the truth about Germany or Russia, but about the state of the world. I replaced the glasses in their case. I wrote a letter to Mr. Budge asking about the sources of the cloud-people legend—wondering if that was the remotest of coincidences or if perhaps this planet has been occupied for thousands of years. I remember your quoting of Fort that humans are property. I do not fear for my life; I doubt the powers that be would be able to keep this secret much longer—and how could they (whoever "they" would be) know that I happened upon this secret? I wonder if the Russians or Germans know. I wonder what these creatures are and what they want.

Dearest brother, it seems that you are right about many of the aspects of this world. I hope this validation of your beliefs impels you toward health and happiness rather than shocks you toward morbidity. Perhaps letting that secret society you are a member of know about this would be the correct first step. How would mankind deal with this knowledge?

Sincerely,

John

The effect of this letter upon Ernest was galvanizing. The Hermetic Brotherhood of Luxor taught that humans were under the influence of another species, a sort of galactic overlord that helped steer human evolution. The Brotherhood claimed to be in contact with these Beings, who were said to live in the Himalayas. Ernest was thrilled; he began drafting letters. What if astral communication wasn't the most efficient way of contacting these space brothers? What if airships could simply dock at their cloud cities? His brother would be seen as a hero, and that secret role of leadership that the Brotherhood always claimed to have held would become something manifest rather than secret. What if he profited by this news and didn't have to scrounge for tips by complimenting overweight matrons and vain business tycoons? By the time he read the second letter, he was already naming colleges after himself.

Dear Ernest,

I suspect this letter will find you after some accident has found me. Budge wrote me confessing that he has known for years that all four national dirigible companies know and are in league with the "Fungal Fliers." It seems that in exchange for a certain number of human lives a year, the Fliers give out technology. The difference engine, the X-ray, pneumatic limbs, dirigibles, cure of cancers, wireless lighting, machine guns, have all been exchanges. But Budge says that these items are designed to make great wars possible. He says weapons far worse than these have been given to the great powers, and that Nyarlathotep is playing a game. Each of the four great powers has been given a different sort of weapon harsh enough to end life as we know it. He thinks the British have a terrible bomb, the French have some airborne plague, and the Russians have the ability to summon horrible creatures from the past. He does not know what the Germans have, although he suspects it could be a fairy tale sort of horror—an army of trolls or werewolves. Nyarlemheb, another of the god's names, means "Churning Darkness Is in Jubilation." The creature lives off of chaos and misery. His servants have less abstract needs. They need metals from Earth, and He won't stir up the final battle until their needs are met. Each of the great powers knows this, yet each believes that their own weapon will cause them to win the final battle. Budge says the god's needs are not the simple bloody sacrifices, but the pent-up desires, fears, and hatreds. He points to the killing of the Sioux by Custer's airborne and the germ-driven Herero and Namaqua genocide of the early 1890s as trial runs. He says similar but unreported incidents have happened in the Khirgiz region of central Asia. He hopes that the truth will filter out into the world. He warns against occult groups that claim to be in contact with hidden masters such as Blavatsky's mahatmas or the Vril Society. These groups are actually putting in place the equivalent of feeding stations to tap into the coming despair of all humanity.

He says that the huge investments the great powers made in Egyptology after the Napoleonic wars was a scramble to find devices that could be used to contact the floating cities. The fungal fliers are nearly finished mining the earth, and they intend to pass it off to their Master. Budge thinks perhaps a few men in each country could avert the madness of mutually assured destruction. I have my doubts. Part of me wishes simply to run and spend my last years in a grass shack in Hawaii with a simple brown maiden who speaks no English, but part of me wishes to be in the fight. You must make your own decision as to fleeing or fighting. I leave it to you to seek after the special glasses aboard the dirigible you work in. Go see. Decide. Tell others or hide away. Knowing what I know, I have been unable to avoid the temptation of telling you, and I know that I have given you a burden that you did not deserve. Had I not looked upon the floating city, I would not have believed it. Ironically, this cancer of my psyche feeds the very entity I wish to fight.

Written in love and fear,

John

This could not be so. All the things John had written about were signs of progress. They were real discoveries of human ingenuity. Everyone knew that the golden age of man was about to begin. John had been duped. Some paranoid man in Cairo had shared his fears. The lightning that struck the *Empress Victoria* was an unfortunate accident. He would forget all this. He would burn the letters.

But he couldn't burn the letters. Every night as he brought rich desserts to richer humans in the *Balmoral* he heard how a new invention had turned up here, a new sort of engine there. The turn of the century was approaching, and everyone spoke of a New World Order or a New Age.

Then the dreams started. He dreamed of British dirigibles dropping bombs on Rome, Berlin, Moscow. He dreamed of Russian airships deploying a living light that mesmerized the enemy, who would simply and happily watch its rainbow flickers while dying of thirst and starvation. He dreamed of the French spreading a powder in the air that called up the Black Death in New York and San Francisco. He spoke less. He got fewer tips. His skin color grew pallid. He wrote his superiors in the Hermetic Brotherhood of Luxor and asked them how they knew the aliens they sought to contact were benign.

His Praemonstrator in the Brotherhood wrote him back and suggested that he was developing male hysteria, and that he should seek a job on the ground. No doubt the rarefied air, plus the gravitational stress of flying in the opposite direction from the Earth's rotation, was affecting him badly.

Ernest resolved to search the captain's quarters. He began by exercising more and eating better. He told his superiors in the Brotherhood that his doubts had passed. He became charming. He started stealing desserts from the kitchen to give to the cleaning crew that took care of the captain's quarters. Ernest found out that the captain did have a small safe in his room. He never opened it. The captain had even told his orderly that the safe contained "papers" that could only be inspected by a vice president of the company.

Ernest began to suggest that the small safe contained gold or diamonds or something else small and very valuable. Surely it would be easy enough to open it when the captain was not around—perhaps the day before they were due to dock in Paris. There were *places* to sell things in Paris. The theft could happen and the captain would never

know. He didn't open the small safe anyway. At first the orderly disbe-
lieved. Why should there be something very valuable that the captain
had no access to? But Ernest asked the opposing question—why so
much security for "papers"? Surely the item was something the captain
could use in an emergency to buy the ship's freedom. It was a big and
bold lie, but Ernest had read adventure novels all his life. He raised the
threat of the Yellow Peril—what would happen if they crashed in China? How could safety be bought for the rich men and women on
board from a Chinese warlord? This could be believed. The orderly
knew no money would be spared to save him, but vast money would
be moved to save the rich from inscrutable Oriental torture.

Ernest came up with a perfect plan. The orderly would simply act
as guard one night when the captain was away. Ernest would open the
safe by removing it from the wall with a saw. He would open the back
of the safe with a diamond drill borrowed from the machine shop. He
would take the valuables out and then replace the safe. Unless the captain inspected the safe closely, it would go undetected for weeks. They
could sell the diamonds or rubies or platinum to a French fence and be
on their way to the good life before anyone was the wiser.

The night came. The captain had taken an interest in a beautiful
blonde American and was visiting her in her quarters. The orderly kept
watch. The tiny hand-held saw, made from one of the new metals discovered last year, cut through the aluminum wall that held the safe like
a hot knife through butter. Ernest MacVeigh lifted the safe out and
applied the drill to the back. It seemed to take forever; each moment
he was expecting the captain to show up. Who knows? Maybe the captain would be intrigued enough by the tale at least to find out what was
in the safe. How could he live with such a grueling mystery? In the objective world it took less than twenty minutes to make a hole large
enough to draw the goggles from the safe. My God, John was right.
Ernest put the safe back into the wall. Only the smallest of cracks
showed that the safe was no longer a permanent fixture. He slipped the
goggles into his pocket and began the second half of his scheme. He
walked out of the captain's quarters and told the orderly that the safe
had been empty. The orderly immediately suspected that Ernest was

cheating him. Ernest challenged him to search him. The orderly did so. He found the goggles in Ernest's pants pocket, but goggles are clearly not an item of life-changing value. Ernest repocketed them. The orderly began cursing and pummeling Ernest. As expected, the noise attracted other workers. The crazed orderly was quickly subdued. He couldn't very well say that he had been part of a plot to steal from the captain. In less than twelve hours the orderly was fired and left in Paris.

Ernest wore the goggles every chance he could. For months he saw nothing. Perhaps John had been crazy; perhaps reading about John's madness had merely infected his brain. Hysteria could be catching, according to alienists. Then one moonlit night as the *Balmoral* sailed over New York, he saw a floating city. Ernest watched through the thick quartz of an observation porthole in the lower decks. John had wisely not tried to describe the floating madness. The city bristled with waving spires of living metal in a thousand colors of gray and a dozen colors that Ernest could not name. Parts of the fliers, themselves a horrible mixture of lobster, beetle, and slimy fungus, were welded into some of the walls. The city had angular mouths with triple rows of obsidian teeth that bit at the fliers. It had exposed wiring and gears and vents that released steam, and mechanical eyes and organic eyes. It had gutters running with pulsing green fluid that bore tiny red flowers. It had living, slow-moving statues of creatures untouched by the sane symmetries of Earth. It had glaring searchlights that flashed unknown messages to the cosmos. Human parts had been welded into the living walls as well, and Ernest knew this had something to do with the myth of the twelve men and women sacrificed to the minotaur in his labyrinth—and he knew if he understood exactly he would go painfully mad. The shape of the city was a Symbol, a Hieroglyph. It would make any true sentient creature have certain thoughts, and Ernest realized that the divided brain of humans, the brain of yes and no, was NOT a brain of a truly sentient creature. Ada Lovelace's difference engine was a sort of joke on humans—a bad binary brain to simulate bad binary consciousness. The human brain with its Evil/Good, Love/Hate, Right/Left was bad mock-up of the real brains of the crustacean Outer Ones: it was a useful device for making fear and anxiety—and his last clear thought before he tore the goggles from his face was that if humans ever became thinking creatures and correlated the contents of their mind, the pains of hell would not be myth.

Ernest fell against the observation porthole. John must have managed because he was smarter. He had always been the stronger one. Mother's favorite. Simple truths like the latter can keep intact minds that look upon things not meant for humans. They found him in the hallway as the *Balmoral* floated above the stockyards of Chicago. Ernest kept saying, "It's all stockyards. Everything is stockyards." They put him off the ship, and the kindly officials of the city of big shoulders put him in an asylum.

For the first years he could not talk. He kept a pair of unusual goggles with him all the time; finally an official from the British Dirigible Company came and retrieved the glasses. When 1900 came and the great war had not come, Ernest began talking about hysteria and anxiety and the shape of human brains. When the Russians put a man on the moon in 1901, he predicted the end of the world—but everyone was making that prediction. By 1903 so many people had a paralyzing madness because of the rate of change of life and warfare capacities that Ernest wasn't considered special enough to be kept in an asylum. There were now seven great powers instead of four—China, Turkey, and America had joined the club with the power to end organic life on this planet. Each of them had their own terror weapon. There were skirmishes. French germ warfare versus Chinese mechanical men in Vietnam. German trolls overran Greenland and renamed it Mhu Thulan.

He took up his old job of being a waiter at a rundown cafe near Hull House. He visited mom in Kansas and his uncles in Texas. He got used to the killing summer and the sharp winds off Lake Michigan in winter. He tried to write down some of the revelations that crowded his brain when he had looked upon the floating city of the fungal fliers—and with an irony he was sane enough to appreciate, he crafted them into pulp stories. He could spot, here and there, others who knew. It didn't matter; these fragments of truth made for more fear as well. Everything he could do served the Churning Darkness, everything anyone could do served this Force. Millions of years of breeding made the fake brains that humans have; he couldn't change that. Laws of society and the rules of civilization laid down in the dark dynasties of shadowy Khem made humans the cattle of the gods.

In his last year, 1913, when the British placed a military base on Venus, Ernest took to spending all his free moments in the stockyards. He would talk freely to his fellow cattle. He sang to them often— especially William Blake's hymn "Jerusalem." He thought for a long time that the fliers would kill him, but he had not been a threat like John. The world was far too rotten with nervousness and hysteria to note yet another fool blaming it on the powers of air and darkness. Just another cow walking up the chute to the slaughter . . .

(For T. E. Grau)

Casting Call

Night Gallery, originally to be called Rod Serling's Wax Museum, ran on NBC from 1970 until 1973. Serling as host would introduce the segments with reference to one of Tom Wright's paintings of macabre or surreal subjects. Wright had to produce almost a hundred paintings. In the first season he worked with oil on canvas; the later years he resorted to faster-drying acrylic on particleboard. Here's a fact you won't find elsewhere, my little cryptlings: several artists would show up at the studio each week with their own paintings (not understanding that NBC commissioned Tom Wright for each painting to match an existing script). Their horrific art, they felt, could have inspired the writers for the glass teat. Some of it, I recall, was pretty dang horrific.

—Tycho Johansen, *I Was Rod Serling's Bodyguard*
(North Hollywood Books, 1983)

Felix Ramirez's first thought when he saw it was horrible. Not bad-taste/bad-art horrible. It might have been that. The colors were perhaps a little garish. The graveyard mold a little bit too much on the slate-blue side. The ghoul's doglike face seemed (to Felix) to be a little too elongated. Felix tried to think of the painter who did that, but Amedeo Modigliani's name eluded him despite Art History 102 two years ago. But he certainly thought of Goya's *Saturn Devouring One of His Sons*. The ghoul's wide-staring eyes, his gore-smeared mouth clamped down on the naked figure's thigh, seems to have a leering grin. Felix watched Rod and the big dumb Dane look at the painting. Felix thought Rod would love it. Partially because the ghoul's staring eyes looked more than a little like Richard Nixon's, and Rod, the "angry young man of Hollywood," wanted to punish Nixon for the war. Felix wanted to walk over to Rod, wanted to introduce himself, but you didn't just walk up to studio execs in NBC. Felix was waiting with other cattle for a screen test. But he clearly heard Serling say something about "Pickman's Model" and express some regret. The great man's elevator came and Rod and his bodyguard boarded.

It was 1971 and big things were happening. Eighteen-year-olds could now vote as well as die for their country. We went to the moon twice. The World Trade Center was opened a few weeks ago and they've started building the Superdome in New Orleans. And Felix Ramirez had a plan. He is ready to be one of the first Chicano actors to make it big. Everything points to go. They've got that new show *All in the Family*. They axed *Hee-Haw, Green Acres, Mayberry R.F.D.*, and *The Beverly Hillbillies. The Lawrence Welk Show* was replaced by *The Sonny and Cher Comedy Hour*. What did you not see? Mexicans. Felix knew that at some point Mexicans were going to be interesting. So he had a plan: monsters, then villains, then heroes of his people, then finally the serious actor. He would do it for Momma. Momma had died the same week as Kennedy, so it wasn't a big deal, not even to the nuns at school. Probably that November he had begun to hate the world.

His cousin Guillermo had called him from Mexico City and told him to try out for *Night Gallery*. He figured it out; nobody will care if a monster eats enchiladas in its off-time. Then it is a clear step to villains, and then when Mexicans become commercial—there he would be.

The trouble for the grand scheme was that Felix was not drawn to the macabre, unlike Guillermo. He tried watching Karloff stumbling along in *Frankenstein*. He tried his best Romanian accent imitating Lugosi. He just wasn't scary. But the painting leaning on the guard's desk: *that* was scary.

Felix had a "call back"—he was being considered for a ghoul. He would get the paintng as a model. He almost ran to the guard's desk. A bored African American guard reading a comic book, *The Forever People*. The painting was gone.

"Excuse me, sir," said Felix.

"Yeah."

"There was a painting here."

"Sure was."

"Do you know what happened to it?"

The guard looked up. Felix saw that one of the superheroes was black; the other ones looked like hippies. It was a sign. We were in a new age.

The guard said, "The artist came and got it. At least she told me she was the artist. Why?"

He sounded a little worried; maybe he realized that he should have asked the "artist" for some ID. But on the other hand, who would want that monstrosity behind their couch?

"I thought it looked really scary. I wanted to study it. For my next role."

"Oh, you're an actor. Well, I will agree with you on the scary part. That thing gave me the willies. It had been against my desk for a week. At night I would turn it against the wall." He gestured. "A lot of people leave stuff here. They think that Serling buys art for his show. The first season we wouldn't let them leave it. He looks the stuff over now. I think he does that to annoy the network artist. He can be a dick sometimes."

"He ever buy any of it?"

"He doesn't even run the show. Laird runs it. Serling got tired of doing everything over at CBS."

"So what's he looking for?"

"He does his thing. I do my thing." The guard began to pick up the comic book.

Felix persisted. "I really want to meet that artist. Maybe she can help me out with makeup tips."

The guard reached into a trashcan. "I had just filed her phone number."

He handed Felix half of a torn envelope.

She was Mexican. She was a maid. And one of her weirdo clients had the biggest collection of science fiction and horror shit in all the world. His home was in the fashionable Los Feliz section of Hollywood. Her name was Carlotta Rotos, and the first time Felix met her was on a driveway with a sign that said, "Horrorwood, Karloffornia." Carlotta spoke to Felix rapidly in Spanish. She had invited him here because she didn't want to meet him first at her tiny home. Her boss had encouraged her to try and get the painting on the show. He was a little weird.

She was dark and very pretty and in an actual maid's outfit.

A super-energetic man introduced himself as Forrest J Ackerman. He asked Felix what he was interested in, and Carlotta said, "Lovecraft." Felix had no idea who Lovecraft was. Ackerman was ushering him into the house, the "Ackermansion." At the doorway he pointed further up Los Feliz There appeared be to be a Mayan temple. "Frank Lloyd Wright's 'Maya House'—it was the exterior for *House on Haunted Hill.* That starred Vincent Price; some people think I look like him. Lovecraft, eh? I've got a postcard from him."

Ackerman ran to an overstuffed desk. He couldn't find it. Then he handed Felix a copy of *Dracula.* "Signed first. But that's not so rare; there are five of those. Look at the next page."

It was covered with signatures from Bela Lugosi to Christopher Lee. Everyone who had been the Count.

For the next two hours there were props from TV and movies and books, books, books. And magazines. And more magazines. At one point Ackerman had shown him a copy of *Weird Tales.* "This was my first magazine. I kept buying them. My mother actually told me that if I was not careful, by the time I was an adult I would have a hundred of them." The crazy laugh that followed would have done any mad scientist proud. The Unique Magazine showed an Egyptian scene; a brown man and boy were coming over an outcropping toward a crude sphinx with pyramids in the background. "Imprisoned with the Pharaohs" by HOUDINI. Thrills! Mystery! Adventure!

Felix was a little dizzy when he walked out into the Los Feliz twilight. Ackerman hadn't been able to find the postcard. "Things walk out of here all the time." He had explained to Felix that "Pickman's Model" was a short story by Lovecraft. When he had heard that NBC was filming it, he suggested Carlotta try and submit the painting. "I've got a few items that Lovecraft used to own." Carlotta looked very guilty when he said that. He showed off Lovecraft's annotated copy of *The King in Yellow.* Felix could tell that he was supposed to be impressed, so he acted impressed. He was, after all, an actor. At the end of the tour, Ackerman pointed to the Maya House again. "That little number is pretty Frank Belknap Long itself. Bad angles. Bring bad things. Frank Lloyd Wright had been putting the finishing touches on it when his houseboy went berserk at Taliesin and killed seven people. It was said the house was cursed. He built it for a shoe magnate, and the man lost everything in the Depression. The next owner's wife jumped off the parapet. Tindalos hounds, Chihuahua style if you ask me. I've got a book on that too somewhere. The Mexicans knew. Six owners in forty-four years."

Carlotta looked as if she were going to cry. When she walked him to his car, she gave him her East LA address.

It was brown stucco, had four floors, and was on a different planet than the Ackermansion. But it was the planet that Felix had grown up on. Planet Barrio. There was a cop car parked in front of the liquor store on the corner. It was Tuesday, the smog index was high, and it was hot. He buzzed her box, she buzzed him in. Her room was on the third floor. It had horrible and fantastic studies of ghouls hung on its tiny walls. Some were scenes from Egypt or Rome, others were modern—on the easel was a mainly finished study of a human male being initiated into ghoul society at Forest Lawn. Two ghouls were painting his naked body with a blue-green liquid. A female ghoul with rows of small breasts like a dog reclined on a tombstone holding a broken human skull. Gore ran down her lips and she stared lewdly at the human. Her face was Carlotta's.

"I am not sick, Mr. Felix," she said. "I used to paint normal things."

She pointed to two small canvases up in the corner of the room. One was a reproduction of Van Gogh's *Sunflowers*. The other was a somewhat insipid seascape.

"It was because of my brother and the book."

And she told Felix Juan's story.

Carlotta's mom was a maid, her father a Zoot-suiter. A pachuco. Mom worked for Hollywood go-getters. Dad was in and out of jail. Sometimes Dad was Juan's hero, hater of the Anglo culture machine. Sometimes Dad was Carlotta's villain—drunk, womanizer, shit-disturber. Momma was Thanksgiving; Papa was *Cinco de Mayo*. Papa got a knife in the side, Momma got to dust an Oscar. Momma was the real world, working hard every day. Papa was Juan's world.

As a teenager he was in gangs. He tried to find common cause with the blacks. Six years ago he had been in the Watts Riots. Then Juan changed. He buckled down. He went to school.

Juan Rotos wanted what every American wants: gold and knowledge. You go to school to learn stuff and get a good job, *comprende?* All good Americans want Faust's deal. A Peruvian named Carlos Castañeda had found it. Carlos was an Angelino. Just a couple of years ago he had published *The Teachings of Don Juan: A Yaqui Way of Knowledge.* Don Juan was a "Nagual," which comes from the Nahuatl word *nahualli,* one who could turn himself into an evil animal-like being for the purposes of evil sorcery. He made a bundle off the books. In Aztec mythology the God Tezcatlipoca was the protector of nagualism, since he governed the distribution of wealth and the powers of black magic. Juan discovered that shortly after the Conquest, a certain "Black Friar," Thomas de Castro, had written an account of the magic involved. *Dioses Malvados del Laberintho.* The book had litanies for invoking Tezcatlipoca in his forms as Cetl, the Night Axe; Huemac, the Double; Eihort, the Demon of the Labyrinth; Nyarlotothep-Metzli, the Messenger of the Moon. The book then explained how certain drugs could be smeared on the body in cemeteries, how teeth could be pulled, and how certain sex magic rituals could make one into a Nagual or *Brujo Negro.*

Juan had decided de Castro's book could be his meal ticket. Anglos would love the drugs and sex—and dominant cultures always fascinate on the magic systems of the people they conquer. It was making millions for Castañeda and it would make millions for him. Now it seemed that the bad priest's book had vanished, so Juan was forging one. Then he spotted a little article on the books that inspired a horror writer named H. P. Lovecraft. It mentioned de Castro's book *Dioses Malvados del Laberintho.* There was a copy in LA in the Ackermansion.

Juan asked Carlotta to steal it. Borrow it at least until Juan made a copy.

Sure, what was the harm? Juan might make his millions. She picked up the book; she could return it after a copy was made. Juan wouldn't be a jailbird like Papa; he could make good money for Momma's retirement. Mr. Ackerman wouldn't even miss it.

Then Juan decided that it was for *real*.

The hexes, the spells, the visions, the power. Juan wasn't going to return the book. Juan was going to become one of Them. The shape-shifters. The flesh-eaters. The ghouls Mr. Lovecraft wrote about. It could be the vanguard of the Revolution. Juan found E. Duran Ayers's report of the Zoot Suit Riots. The guy that the LAPD had as an expert witness against Papa and the other pachucos. He taped it to his mirror:

> Mexican Americans are essentially Indians and therefore Orientals or Asians. Throughout history the Orientals have shown less regard for human life than have the Europeans. Further, Mexican Americans had inherited their 'naturally violent' tendencies from the 'bloodthirsty Aztecs' of Mexico, who were said to have practiced human sacrifice centuries ago.

Juan got a tattoo over his heart: ¡Yo soy un Azteca sanguinario! I am a bloodthirsty Aztec. He also had a white football-looking sigil added, the sign of Eihort. His momma decided that he was going to hell. She died a few weeks afterward.

Juan began reciting the litanies, buying the herbs. He got a few of his friends to break into a vault at Forest Lawn. Carlotta broke into tears at this point.

"One night he came here, very late. His face was all black. He had pulled his teeth and put black glass. Obsidian chips. He gave me the book. I don't know if he was crazy, or not really human anymore. I never saw him again. But I have these."

She went into her tiny kitchen and pulled open a drawer. She had a handful of newspaper clippings. Graveyard vandalism. Disappearing children. Bodies stolen from morgues. A criminal gang in Halloween drag.

"So I read this horrible little book. At least the parts in Spanish."

She handed Felix the small volume. A reprint from 1863 Mexico City. *Biblioteca de la Luz Oscura*.

The black and white illustrations were crude but effective. Ghouls among Aztec ruins. Ghouls eating corpses. Orgies on the roof of the National Cathedral. There were a few notes in Lovecraft's handwriting; Felix recognized it from the other book. God names were underlined. One section had been labeled "Changelings." One of the most horrible illustrations had the underlined note: "Drawn from LIFE." The last section was in Latin, "Ordo Novo Astrorum." It was full of dates, and latitude and longitude tables and astrological symbols. Again Lovecraft's note: "De Castro says when the stars are RIGHT check alignments monuments of Tullan." There were a few strange sketches of buildings; one did look like Wright's Maya House. Another, perhaps a giant door, was labeled Paseo de Ya-R'lyeh.

Carlotta had broken down. Rivers of mascara ran down her brown face. For the first time Felix realized how young she was. She was his age (or just a few years older). And how sad. And what nice breasts. She lunged on to him, and he stared at demonic lustful Carlotta in the painting. Her tears fell hot on his chest, and there were black stains on his light blue cotton shirt. He knew that if he understood why she had to keep painting the thing she feared, he would understand fear. He would be the next Karloff, the next Lugosi. He held her. He patted her. He hoped she couldn't feel his hard-on.

When the storms of emotion passed he took her to Chabelita's. Tacos. Burritos. Hamburgers. Mexican food. He had a burger and coffee and asked if he could borrow the book.

After the litanies and the offerings the book was a makeup guide and acting manual. To become a ghoul, you had to cover yourself with a blue-black mixture. It was partially graveyard dirt (to make yourself pleasing to the Lord of Worms), ground Seer's Sage (pipiltzintzintli), "magic" mushrooms, soot, and turkey fat. There were useful suggestions on how to make the jawline appear more doglike, how to make the hair ropy. The book really suggested replacing teeth with obsidian chips and making an incision at the base of the spine for the tail to grow. There were a few notes on the language—"meeping" Lovecraft had glossed.

The ghoul not only ate the flesh but the memories of the deceased. Wizards and priests were highly prized. It had limited powers of invisibility. It was immortal, although de Castro was unclear about this. It faded from the world of the "tonally"—the everyday world made from parts of the sun. The ghoul lived in a dream-world untouched by the healthy sun of earth.

No wonder Juan went crazy. De Castro's informants had been drug-crazed Otomi shamans plotting to throw the Spanish out. Their post-Conquest oppression had been great; if bullets couldn't be had, magic could.

Felix had a week. He began with regular makeup products. He painted his teeth black, thinking the obsidian would be overkill. He even scared himself in the mirror.

He didn't call Carlotta during his preparation time. He knew he could fall in love with her, and she would be scared shitless that he was using the little book at all. He had sort of, kind of, suggested that he would just drop it into Mr. Ackerman's mailbox. Besides, she was probably crazy too. She had had to rationalize Juan's actions. She must at least partially believe that he had become a ghoul. Felix wondered if she worried about her momma's dead body; one of the clippings had been about a Mexican graveyard . . .

Anyway, it bothered him how hot he got thinking of the naked many-breasted Carlotta in the painting. He wanted to be scratched by the long gore-stained nails, rub his tongue down the rows of canine teats.

Three days before *Night Gallery* would be casting the ghoul for "Pickman's Model" Felix had a breakthrough. He had an honest-to-god gimmick. He could claim to have Aztec sorcery on his side! Man, how cool is that?

The magic-using personality can always find omens of confirmation. That night's "Late Late Show" was *The Time Travellers,* in which Forrest J Ackerman played a bit role. The gods were in favor.

Getting the Seer's Sage or the "magic" mushrooms wasn't easy; he used Crisco for turkey fat, but he did scoop some real live cemetery dirt. He had to add some more routine pigments to make his blend. Then he called the NBC studios in "beautiful downtown Burbank" and asked if he could be allowed to do his Aztec ritual before the casting call. This was California, so the "yes" was a foregone conclusion.

He decided it would be better to say the incantation in English, so he translated the chant 93:

> Lowly Father of Worms, whose moon face is disfigured with rotting death,
>
> I am you and you are I. Behold, I wear the dead skins like my uncles the Priests. Behold, my teeth are the stones of Tezcatlipoca like my uncles the Priests.
>
> You taught that to walk, which should not walk.
>
> You have fatted me on the bodies of wizards!
>
> You are Eihort. I feast with Thee! You are Nyarlatothep-Metzli! I mock with Thee!
>
> You make liquid my flesh! You make dead my mind! You make long my bones!
>
> Yr Ngg Eihort Ebloth Yetl! Yetl! Shinn-ngaa!
>
> I am you and you are I! I am your flute. I am your teeth!

Felix practiced the chant, trying to make it look American Indian—that is to say, like every cowboy movie he had ever seen. He fell asleep at three in the morning. He awoke with a terrible hangover. The door of his apartment was open and there was blood on his lips, but Felix Ramirez was not an imaginative man.

On the big day it seemed that everything that could go wrong did. Someone had locked the studio and the key couldn't be found. Then they couldn't get the air turned on. Then Mr. Serling had to go to another set, and they had to wait. Some of the wannabe fiends left. The audition was supposed to happen at three. At six-thirty they got to their dressing room. Felix had tried to tell everyone about his new-found religion. The black security guard listened with the "I've heard it all" look. The white receptionist seemed interested in the sex magic part. Two of the ghouls-to-be had joined a new religion that month also. One was about UFOs, the other had to do with screaming.

There was another delay. The goop on his face had made it numb; now it was making him a little dizzy. Felix didn't know what "Seer's Sage" was—but it came across as pot from hell. It defiantly gave him the munchies. Weird thoughts kept creeping into his mind. *You know, if I was high on this shit I could pull my teeth out. That would feel real good, like coming. I wonder if Chinese people taste like Chinese food? I bet I could jump really high. There's probably not much human left in Juan Rotos; I bet worms pooped in that graveyard dirt. I am probably wearing dead people. I want to say to Rod Serling, "I submit you for Eihort's approval!" I am really hungry. I shouldn't have thrown away that pizza; the mold might make it taste better, who knows? I want to bite that white girl receptionist.*

Felix got up and paced. This was getting too weird. Juan had probably got a bunch of his angry young Mexicans to try this, and then do a little graveyard vandalism in some rich white cemetery. Probably Forest Lawn—what an emblem of what's wrong with white America! That would have set them way over the edge! He took a deep breath. He would sit down and focus on the chant. The room was a little too bright, a little too hot. The eight other guys done up as ghouls were beginning to bug him. He wanted to meep at them.

Two more ghouls left. Felix saw through the open doors that the moon had come up. The Otomi said the moon was once the equal of the sun. Then the sun threw a rabbit in its face. All the craters astronauts visited were an insult to the moon. The moon gave his flesh to worms, which became people. It was people's job to revenge the moon's insult. The messenger of the moon mocked other gods. It was people's job to get with the program. Felix closed his eyes. The moon called to him. Revenge me! Make red!

Mr. Serling strolled in with his big Dane bodyguard. Felix jumped up and said he was going to do his chant now.

"What's that clown doing?" asked Serling.

The words were coming out all wrong. It had started in English, but it became something else. The bodyguard pushed Serling backward. "If this is a publicity stunt it is stupid."

Felix felt his arms growing/lengthening. He should have made the cut for the tail. That was going to hurt. The security guard had dropped his comic book. One of the ghouls was yelling about the space brothers.

The smells! The room was full of the revolting smells of living things, all hot and shiny smelling like the sun. Like Tonatiuh! The insulting sun, enemy of the thousand-faced moon. Felix grabbed the arm of the space-brother worshipper. He yanked hard. It didn't come off the first time, but tore free the second. Make red. He squeezed the forearm as if he would have squeezed a toothpaste tube. He loved the taste as it squirted into his mouth. But his teeth were wrong. They were white like the sun. Something hot burned into his chest. The guard was shooting him. Serling was screaming as the big blonde pushed him into an elevator. Felix yelled, "I submit you for Eihort's approval! You are entering a place between substance and shadow, things and ideas! I am filing you under 'S' for snack!"

Then Felix could see it. A big crack in the world. He could see it, the place between substance and shadow, things and ideas. He could see the nagual, the dreamlands. He could see a long stairway of onyx or obsidian hanging off the crack, which both was and was not in space. The guard threw his gun at Felix. What did the fucker think was going on? That this was *Dragnet!*

Felix knew he had to re-establish order. These people weren't focused. He yelled out, "Ninoyoalitoatzin inic nehuatl inic chicnauhtopa! Nimoquequeloatzin Niehort! Yo es Nyarlatothep-Metzli! I am the Father of Worms!"

No one bowed. They were supposed to bow. The Mocker Moquequelaotzin had made worms walk to make fun of the gods. Religion was the black joke. He charged at the screaming receptionist. He grabbed her fat little cheeks like tamales. He stuffed them in his mouth. Her screams were laughter.

He could see into the earth now as though the floor, the ground were purest crystal. He could see Eihort. It was a bloated white football resting on tiny legs. The ghouls were feeding on bodies. When it moved it made the countless little earthquakes LA suffered. The entire Pacific Rim shook when it shook. Eyes formed in its jello and they looked at Felix with love he hadn't felt since Momma died.

Police were running in the door. The moon looked about twenty times as big. Moonlight sounded so sweet. He loped toward the door. The cops were shooting, and then they were running. Out in the parking lot was a big white van. It was open.

Inside was Carlotta, her sixteen tiny breasts displayed. There was a ghoul driver. Juan, no doubt. She meeped and barked, but she clearly meant, "¡Vámonos!" Felix ran to his mate. The van careened out of "beautiful downtown Burbank."

The night the press called "Attack of the Ghouls" was one of the closest calls I had with the boss. He had been having fits filming "Cool Air" and was on set for many extra hours. There was an audition for the ghouls for "Pickman's Model"—and like always with NBC the message to call off the audition was lost in the main switchboard. The boss decided to go over. He felt sorry that the poor actors had been waiting for so long. As soon as we walked in, one of them—clearly some kind of hophead—began mumbling some weird stuff. I tried to push the boss away, but he was all irate as usual. Then another one of the ghouls runs up to the first one. The hophead pulls the other ghoul's arm off. We all thought it was a publicity gag. Then the security started shooting. I got the boss out of there. NBC put a big hush on the story. They decided that people would think it was a really stupid ad campaign. Of course, some of the story did leak out in the town of "It bleeds, It leads." Some reporter tried to connect the incident with some graveyard vandalism, but I tell you it was just another snapshot of how people act in Hollyweird.
—Tycho Johansen, *I Was Rod Serling's Bodyguard*
(North Hollywood Books, 1983)

(This is my thank-you note to the late Forrest J Ackerman for many things, including the tour.)

Acknowledgments

"The Man Who Scared Lovecraft," first published in *Postscripts* Nos. 22/23 (2010).

"The Megalith Plague," first published in *Black Wings III: New Tales of Lovecraftian Horror,* edited by S. T. Joshi (PS Publishing, 2014).

"Lavina's Lament," first published in *Deathrealm* No. 23 (Spring 1995).

"The Gold of the Vulgar," first published in *High Fantastic,* edited by Steve Rasnic Tem (Ocean View Press, 1995).

"Wilbur's Song," first published in *Deathrealm* No. 23 (Spring 1995).

"Sanctuary," first published in *Cthulhu's Reign,* edited by Darrell Schweitzer (DAW, 2010).

"Wilbur's Brother," first published in *Deathrealm* No. 23 (Spring 1995).

"Platinum Hearts," first published in *The Stake* No. 5 (1994).

"Plush Cthulhu," first published in *Dead But Dreaming II,* edited by Kevin Ross (Miskatonic River Press, 2011).

"Emily's Rose Window," first published in *Cyaegha* No. 4 (Spring 2011).

"Looking Glass," first published in *Pot Boiler* 1, No. 10 (Spring/Summer 1985).

"To Mars and Providence," first published in *War of the Worlds: Global Dispatches,* edited by Kevin J. Anderson (Bantum Spectra, 1996).

"Powers of Air and Darkness," first published in Lovecraft E-zine (online).

"Doc Corman's Haunted Palace One Fourth of July," first published in *Horror for the Holidays,* edited by Scott David Aniolowski (Miskatonic River Press, 2012).

"Casting Call," first published in *Black Wings II: New Tales of Lovecraftian Horror,* edited by S. T. Joshi (PS Publishing, 2012).

All other works in this collection are previously unpublished.

www.ingramcontent.com/pod-product-compliance
Lightning Source LLC
Chambersburg PA
CBHW061430030726
47503CB00005B/1357